To
from Symon
Summer 2021 :)

THE "SPC"

Symon Vegro

A (relatively) boring page, but necessary

Published by New Generation Publishing in 2020

Copyright © Symon Vegro 2020

First Edition

The author asserts the moral right under the Copyright, Designs and Patents Act 1988 to be identified as the author of this work.

All rights reserved. No part of this publication may be reproduced, stored in a retrieval system, or transmitted, in any form or by any means, without the prior consent of the author, nor be otherwise circulated in any form of binding or cover other than that in which it is published and without a similar condition being imposed on the subsequent purchaser.

ISBN: 978-1-80031-883-0

www.newgeneration-publishing.com

"Lawyers, I suppose, were children once"

(from 'To Kill a Mockingbird' by Harper Lee)

For the author's views on the Law refer to the case of Jarndyce v Jarndyce

(from 'Bleak House' by Charles Dickens)

That's enough Legal blurb.

New Generation Publishing

About the author

He was born in a vineyard in southern France and, abandoned at birth, was raised first by wolves and then in a Convent. A musical and mathematical prodigy, he wrote his first opera at age six and solved Fermat's Last Theorem at age seven but remained anonymous to protect the privacy of the Nuns. He became a Chess Grand Master at age nine. Leaving the Convent, he travelled the world for many years in the sole company of a French language teacher and double-jointed gymnast, Alice, ten years his elder, for whom he retains a lasting affection. He studied English Literature at Cambridge, then Music, Philosophy and Classics at the Sorbonne, and completed his formal education at Princeton where at age twenty three he became Professor of Mathematics. He summers in Provence, autumns in New England, winters on an atoll in the Indian Ocean, and springs between his apartments in Prague, Florence, Madrid, St. Petersburg, Rome, Havana, and Paris. He was the first amateur cyclist to have been invited to ride the Tour de France solo without a team affiliation (2014). Turning down the lead role in the film adaptation of "Fifty Shades of Grey", instead he chose to take up the invitation of countertenor in King's College Choir. He has written 151 books, including acclaimed biographies of John Keats, Albert Einstein, Gandhi, Bach and Shakespeare, as well as the first translation into High Elvish of 'Don Quixote'. A natural calligrapher, he can reproduce exactly the signature of Pafutny, founder and hegumen in the fourteenth century of the Avraamy Monastery on the Volga. He can also draw, unaided, a perfect circle. He is the only person in history to win the Nobel Prize in three separate disciplines: Literature (for 'Gender'), Physics – twice (first (2009) for finally reconciling quantum theory with gravity, and second (2077) for discovering the Chronological Constant as a precursor to stable worm-holes which led to the first working Time Machine), and Peace (for reconciling the supreme conflict between his head and his heart). In 2013 he climbed Mount Everest alone and for recovery swam the Bering Strait naked. He took up a position of Principal Conductor at La Scala in May 2014. He is the only Michelin Starred Chef who cooks only vegetarian food and who is unwilling to tie himself down to a particular establishment, preferring to "guest" at restaurants in Barcelona, Hong Kong and occasionally New York. He dislikes raisins, golf, and right-wing politicians, loves Dostoyevsky's use of the word "even", and is an expert on the sexual behaviour of axolotls.

Also by the author
or
"Look on my Works, ye Mighty, and despair"

All That You Touch

Gender

Stories of Increasing Length

Stories of Decreasing Length

A (relatively) interesting page, unnecessary (but important to the author)

Dedication

KD, who taught me to cool a hot bath down by adding cold water

Thank you

Lise Lotte Lystrup for reading it first, as always
Jayne Maitland for her corrections and insightful comments
Luke Mazur for his corrections and feedback
Dan Topping for his marvellous generosity and friendship

History of this book

It started life as a short story, destined to be included in 'Stories of Decreasing Length', but it was so much fun to write that it took on a life of its own, and turned into the novel that you are about to read and, I hope, enjoy

The entire book – all **88,000** or so words - was typed on a phone, and subsequently edited on a desktop computer. Having Parkinson's, I find this an easy way to write (although I do get some strange looks from people who think I'm sending incredibly long messages)

Background reading

Mention is made of Isaac Asimov's 'Foundation' series, and his famous Laws of Robotics are alluded to. There is no need to have read these in advance, although they are brilliant – in my (and many other people's) view the greatest science fiction books ever written

Eligibility

For the record, if the SPC existed, I would be eligible

Note: the following text was found on an encrypted memory stick in a taxi in Desborough, a small town between Kettering and Market Harborough. It is here reproduced in its entirety, unaltered, including where the author, presumably to preserve his (for reasons that will become apparent we know the author is male) anonymity, replaced some words and numbers with x and n sequences respectively.

At first, we thought that some sections were missing, due to the numbering sequence. Close examination of the chronology of events, however, suggested that this was not the case, a conclusion confirmed when we realised the numbering was the Fibonacci sequence. At the time of printing we do not know why this sequence was used.

There has been considerable speculation – and much disagreement – on the significance of "SPC". Some believe it is an acronym, some believe it is a cipher, some believe it is completely unrelated to the actual organisation – if indeed it really exists – and is designed to throw the reader off the scent, perhaps again to preserve anonymity.

Finally, there is serious disagreement on whether it is a work of pure fiction or autobiographical. Certainly, there are events described that, as far as we can determine, did not happen, and others that we do not believe could have happened, (these will be obvious). That said, certain passages reveal an honesty and a degree of openness suggesting they were based on (if not strictly a scientific description of) reality. Whose reality (i.e. who xxxxx was) we have so far been unable to identify.

SEGMENT 0

If you think I'm having a pop at the Masons, I swear I'm not, they just serve as a useful introduction. Far from slagging them off, in the generalised sense and to a considerable degree I find them laughable. Those funny handshakes and wearing one trouser leg rolled up and being forced to wear cheap black suits and learn uninteresting long-winded quotes (when they could be learning 'Hamlet') and giving themselves very silly titles ... it's all rather amusing from the outside.

Of course, there's a sinister side to it too. The exclusion of women, for example, (although why the fairer sex wouldn't want to hang out with a bunch of misogynistic weirdos who like dressing up in weird clothes and who take themselves too seriously should need no explanation). Then the fact that they all look after one another - senior police officers, Tory politicians, judges, criminals etc. - is a clear and present danger to the correct functioning of our judicial process, to name but one problem; (the next time you see a drunk driver get a suspended sentence, 2 penalty points and a £150 fine for mowing down three kids on a zebra crossing, check out what Lodge the driver, the prosecutor and the judge all belong to).

I digress. They are a secret society (and not, as a Mason I know, and who is, admittedly, a bit of a twat, once told me, a "society of secrets") and that's what we have in common with them, (we being the SPC and them being the Masons). There are differences however, as you might expect.

In the SPC:
    I.   No-one eligible is excluded, ever
    II.   Everyone eligible is, in fact, already a member - even if they don't know that they are (see if you can top that for secrecy, Most Worshipful Sovereign Grand Master)
    III.   No-one eligible would not want to be a member
    IV.   Once you know you're a member - formally, that is - it is incumbent upon you to seek out new members (see point 1)

Then there are the 4 Laws, which are sacrosanct:
    I.   A member may not harm a fellow member or, through inaction, allow a fellow member to come to harm
    II.   A member must obey orders from a more senior member except where such orders would conflict with the First Law

III. A member must protect his own existence, as long as such protection does not conflict with the First or Second Laws
IV. A member must never reveal or allow through action or inaction to be revealed the existence of the SPC or any of its members to anyone who isn't a member without the express permission of a senior member with the appropriate clearance and unless non-disclosure conflicts with the First, Second or Third Laws (note: I have a special dispensation permitting me to write this brief narrative)

It is this Third Law that signals the only obvious similarity (other than secrecy) with the Masons - that use of the word "his" ... for we are exclusively male. Not, however, because we're misogynistic weirdos who like dressing up, but for what I might call *evolutionary* reasons.

It's worth saying at the outset that, referring to the 4 points above, I) I knew I was eligible long before I knew there was a society I was eligible for; II) therefore I was indeed already a member *ipso facto*: III) I most definitely want to be a member; and IV) I am on a mission to find new members, and this is where my part in this narrative begins.

I was at a quiz night with a group of friends. Our team, "Thinner than the Winners" (so named as we were always beaten into second place by a team of rather large schoolteachers who always took the table next to us) was arguing about the picture round. We couldn't agree on who all the Prime Ministers were.

'I'm sure that's Gladstone.' somebody said.

'No, it's Disraeli.' said somebody else on the team.

I had no idea who it was, so I decided to go to the toilet. One of the rather large schoolteachers was peeing into the adjacent urinal, and he nodded at me as I began to pee.

As we were washing our hands in adjacent sinks he turned to me.

'Gladstone was SPC, you know.'

'SPC?' I said.

'That's right. And Walpole. And William Pitt. The younger, that is.' He lowered his voice almost to a whisper. 'It's ok. They're all dead. It's only the living ones we can't reveal. Right now we have two members of the Cabinet, three members of the Shadow Cabinet, a smattering in the Welsh and Scottish Assemblies, a Law Lord, and ...' at which point he leant very close to me and lowered his voice even further '... a prominent Royal. And I mean *very* prominent.' And I do believe he winked at me at this point.

'Sorry. I must have missed something. What were, are all these people? What's SPC?'

He beamed at me as he went back to his table. 'You'll see.'

When I got back to the table they were still arguing about whether it was Gladstone or Disraeli. Someone asked me. 'Has to be Gladstone, surely.' I said.

'I thought you said you didn't know any of them?' I was asked.

'I don't. It's intuition.'

The team wrote down Disraeli. When the quiz was over we swapped our answer sheet with that of "Thinner than the Winners". I'd only contributed a small number of answers, as usual, and was more interested in checking whether I'd got any right than in the team's overall performance. When it came to the Prime Ministers, the correct answer was Gladstone. I tried not to gloat.

'We were doing really well up to now.' said someone.

We ended up losing by one point. Before we threw our paper in the bin someone stopped us.

 'Look. They've written something next to the photo of Gladstone. Looks like ...' he strained his eyes '5PC'.

'Here, let me see.' I said. 'That's an S not a 5. It's SPC.' I thought back to the conversation in the toilet. A little later I found myself at the bar next to the schoolteacher.

'Congratulations. You win again. By one point.' I smiled.

'Why didn't you put Gladstone?'

'I was outvoted. Fair enough, really, I'm usually wrong.' My drinks arrived. Before I went back upstairs I asked him 'So what's SPC? You wrote it on our answer sheet.'

He bent down and whispered something to me. I almost dropped my tray of drinks.

'How ...'

He interrupted me. 'Not here. I'll explain all when we meet. Can you come round tomorrow afternoon, say 2ish?' He gave me his address, which was a short walk from my house.

Other events distracted me during the following morning, so it wasn't until about 1 o'clock in the afternoon that I thought any more about the SPC. With an hour or so to go I had a shave and a shower, and got ready to go. The question at the forefront of my mind concerned what I later termed my eligibility - how could he possibly have known? I was soon to find out.

His house was one of the big new ones on the outskirts of the village. I'd often wondered who could afford to live in a place like this, and now I knew. Perhaps he wasn't a schoolteacher after all, although I'm sure that's what "Thinner had the Winners" had told us they all did a while back. I knocked at the door, expecting the unexpected. I wasn't disappointed.

'Hi!' said the guy who opened the door. I didn't know his name but had seen him in my local a few times. 'Come on in. We're all waiting to welcome you.'

All? I thought, but before I had time to think about it too much I was led into a large room where about twenty guys were sitting chatting. Rather embarrassingly, and somewhat unexpectedly, they gave me a round of applause. I knew I was blushing quite badly. The large guy from the quiz night who'd invited me came straight over and shook my hand warmly.

'Welcome, welcome.' he said. 'This is the first day of the rest of your life. Make yourself comfortable. Want a drink? Tea, coffee, or something stronger?'

'Is beer an option?' I said.

'Sure is. Come and have a look, I've got a few different beers in the back.'

He led me through a fantastic looking kitchen full of wonderful devices and utensils, most of which I didn't recognise, into what I can only describe as a "Beer Heaven": a room with floor to ceiling shelving on all sides, with two of the walls completely refrigerated, every shelf full of an astonishing array of different beers.

'What's your poison?' he asked with a smile.

'Got any Bud, King of Beers?' I asked. He looked horrified. 'Only kidding.' I said quickly. 'I like pilsners. German, Czech. Have you got one of those?'

He showed me to his "pilsner shelves", where he had about thirty varieties. I chose a rare (and quite strong, 7%) Slovakian beer that he recommended, and went back into the main room where he introduced me to everyone, and where I learned his name was Peter. I forgot most of the other names almost immediately.

After a little while I grabbed a seat and it gradually all went quiet. Peter spoke.

'Well here we all are to welcome our new member.' Smiles all round. He now addressed me directly. 'I know how you must be feeling. We all do. We've all sat in that chair, once upon a time. You must have so many questions, and we will answer them all, in time, I promise. Before that, though, for reasons that I hope are obvious, you must undergo the validation. It's not an unpleasant experience. Meet Olga.'

In walked who I presumed to be Olga, a woman, whom I hadn't noticed before. She was *hot*. She shook my hand.

'Before Olga validates you, there's one question that's probably top of your list which I'm able to answer now, namely, how did we know. Or more specifically, how did *I* know. There are various roles within the membership. Management, of course, legal, finance, fund-raising, HR, events and hospitality, IT, procurement, security, and so on. My particular specialism is what we call "recognition". You've probably heard about the

Israeli counter terrorism unit's ability to spot suicide bombers? They use pragmatic observation skills and psychological insights to derive a list of behavioural indicators that strongly suggest imminent terrorist activity. Exactly the same approach works for us, except the insights and indicators are clearly different. We have seven things to look for on the list, and you exhibit all seven very strongly. We've had our eyes on you for a while.' He paused. 'I've never been wrong. Now Olga, if you'll take things from here please?'.

'Of course,' she said, taking my hand. 'Come with me.'

'You'll enjoy this!' said one of the guys, I think his name was Josh, as I passed him. And he wasn't wrong.

As validations go, (and I hadn't had too many, in fact, *any*), this was one of the best imaginable. After the formal part of the validation, which only took a few minutes, Olga proceeded directly to what she called the "informal phase" which was most pleasant. Decorum - and confidentiality - prohibits me from explaining exactly what she did ... suffice to say that she didn't spill a drop.

Olga told me immediately that I'd passed the validation, and went off to tell Peter. I waited a few minutes to calm down before going back into the room. This time everyone stood up and cheered, and sang 'For he's a jolly good fellow.' Josh handed me another Slovakian pilsner, and the atmosphere turned positively party-like.

After a while Peter asked everyone to be quiet again and said a few more words.

'Ok guys, that's today's business concluded. I'm not in a rush to kick you all out, but I have a plane to catch at 5am tomorrow from Heathrow and I've got quite a lot to get through tonight. Shall we say, out of here by 4 at the latest? Now,' (looking at me) 'Would you come into my office for a few minutes please?'

As soon as we were alone he congratulated me again, and poured me a glass of champagne.

'Vintage stuff. From Napoleon's private cellar, which we got our hands on a few years back. We always open a bottle for new members.' He proceeded to tell me that the SPC's overarching mission was to 'enhance the lives, the happiness, the fulfillment, the available choices, and the financial security' through 'all available means' of its membership.

He demonstrated the society's handshake - very subtle but unmistakable when you knew - to recognise other members (if you haven't got the recognition skills). He gave me a security pass giving me access to SPC Offices around the country.

'Leeds, Manchester, Birmingham, Edinburgh, Cardiff, Belfast, Newcastle upon Tyne and of course Head Office in London. We have three floors of the Shard.' He took me through the stuff on eligibility and the 4 Laws (as outlined earlier). He explained the branch structure: 'There's a branch in every major town or city and several larger villages, like ours. We have a very flat structure, no bloated hierarchy or anything like that and certainly no silly titles - we model it on the "First Speaker" principle in Asimov's "Foundation" books. Have you read them?'. I told him that I had. 'Good. Then you know how we operate. I'm First Speaker in this branch, and Vice Chair of the National Recognition Committee. You can be as active, or as passive, as you want. Some of our members we never see. Others get heavily involved. It's up to you, no pressure at all. All I'll say is that, like everything in life, the more you put in, the more you get out.' He handed me a folder. 'Here's your welcome pack. Should tell you everything you need to know, but ask me if you have any questions. There's a few forms to fill in. I'd prioritise the one from IT as it gives you enhanced secure email and access to our private layer of the internet, as well as a few other goodies. Once you've got a login you can access the member's site and enter your bank details.'

'Bank details?'

'All members receive a stipend, and if you take on extra roles it goes up. Another reason to get involved.'

'But who pays for all this? It seems ... incredible.'

'We've been in existence for centuries, and over those centuries have amassed *vast* wealth. We discovered the whereabouts of the Templar's hidden treasure, and that of the Cathars, the Mayans, the Incas, the Aztecs, the Romans, the Egyptians, and the Persians, to name but a few. We are very well connected, globally, in banking. We also found Marie Antoinette's jewellery - which was fun - and, lest I forget, the Holy Grail. And Shakespeare's original manuscripts, including the prequel to 'Hamlet', as well as the official autopsy report for John Keats. In addition to this historic wealth, we have some extremely wealthy member donors including ten heads of state and one Russian multi-trillionaire. At the last count we had roughly a thousand times more ready cash and assets than Apple, the Catholic Church, the New York Stock Exchange, and the Middle East's oil industries combined. The interest alone covers our global running costs without ever touching the capital.'

By this time I'd worked up the courage to ask about the stipend.

'You'll start on the minimum, but it's index-linked and like I said increases as you take on new responsibilities. For a new member it's £5,000 a month, tax free, courtesy of some friends in HMRC. And then there's the car allowance of course.'

SEGMENT 1

"Man is the measure of all things: of the things that are, that they are, of the things that are not, that they are not." So wrote Protagoras, five centuries before Christ. According to my new SPC Handbook, Protagoras was a possible Founder of the society, although other evidence suggests it was Pythagoras. Either way, his name began with a P and ended with an -agoras, and it's been in existence for over two thousand years. And why not, I thought to myself? I flicked through several pages. "If you read Shakespeare's 'Tempest' you'll find many references, particularly concerning Caliban. Shakespeare was SPC, although of course it wasn't called that at the time."

Curious, I dug out my 'Complete Works of Shakespeare' and found 'The Tempest', which incidentally was one of my favourites. 'For I am all the subjects that you have' and 'As wicked dew as e'er my mother brush'd with raven's feather from unwholesome fen...' and 'Thou dost me yet but little hurt; thou wilt anon, I know it by thy trembling'.

None the wiser, I turned back to the handbook and flicked through more pages until I came to the following passage: "... although for policy reasons no written records were kept, there now seems very little doubt that Leonardo da Vinci, Isaac Newton, Albert Einstein and Ernest Hemingway were all First Speakers. Moreover, when we look at the continuing isolation of North Korea ..."

My reading was interrupted by a knock at the door. I'd been reminded on several occasions not to leave any SPC material lying around, so I hid the handbook in my desk before answering the door. It was a delivery driver. 'Deliveries for you.' he said. I wasn't expecting anything. 'Please sign here.'

I signed, and he went to his van and brought back four boxes. One contained several bottles of the finest wines available to humanity, the second contained a Fabergé egg (thought lost), and the third several punnets of peeled grapes wrapped in rainbow-coloured edible champagne and ginger tissue along with the note: 'Welcome to the SPC. Yuri (avoiding the truly awful awkwardness of non-peeled grapes).' I'd heard about Yuri in the three weeks since my validation. He was the Russian multi-trillionaire and major SPC donor, who sent welcome gifts to all new members.

That left the fourth box, which was very small. It contained the key to an Aston Martin DB7 Vantage which was "now available to collect from Mayfair Motors of Nantwich. Ask for Ivan."

Fucking hell. I don't swear all that much, except at Tory MPs on Question Time (which is not only understandable but obligatory) but *Fucking Hell.* I lay back on the sofa - still holding the car key - and thought about the last three weeks. And smiled. Properly smiled, without a hint of melancholy. For the first time in about fifteen years. It felt ... good. Eligibility for SPC was one thing, but the benefits were quite another. And in that moment of bliss I realised what my vocation was. To find new members. To help others, who were eligible, to experience what I had recently experienced, and to realise that eligibility could actually be a *good* thing. I leapt off the sofa and rang Peter.

'I have to find new members' I told him. 'I have to let people know that being eligible is a good thing. Or can be, anyway. This is all just fabulous.'

Peter was pleased, and said that there were various ways I could help. He reminded me that all members have an obligation to recruit new eligible members, of course, but that more proactive avenues were available, including his own area, "Recognition". I pressed him.

'The first thing to say is that "Recognition" isn't to be undertaken lightly. Some of the more obvious indicators are easily assimilated, including the obvious one. But to be a fully trained recognition expert takes months of dedicated onsite training. Unless you have a very understanding employer and/or work for John Lewis, it's a full-time role. For which, naturally, you get paid.'

'So, I'd have to resign from my job?'

'Not necessarily. You might be able to take a sabbatical. Or some unpaid leave.'

'How long is the initial training for?'

'Well, first you go on a one month programme at our specialist facility near Perth. Then you're examined, and it's tough. There's only a 20 percent pass rate. If you get through that, you spend a further two months with the Israeli military on the West Bank. That's the end of the formal training, but then you'd get a field placement.'

'Serious stuff then!' I said.

'It's a serious business.'

'And the month in Scotland. Do I ..."

'It's Perth in western Australia.' he interrupted. 'Not Scotland. And if you're serious there's a new programme starting in about three weeks. I can get you the details. After that the next one is three months away.'

'When do I have to decide by?'

'Well, by the end of next week, really, at the latest, so we can get everything organised, flights and so on. Fancy popping into the London Office tomorrow to have a chat about it? I have some free time in the afternoon.'

'I was going to get the train to Nantwich tomorrow to pick up the Aston Martin.'

'Oh, is that what Yuri decided in the end? We swapped emails about it last week. I said I thought you were more of an E-type kind of chap myself, but what do I know, eh? Well if you can't come into London tomorrow, how about a quick pint on Friday night in the 'Rat and Rat Catcher'?

In the morning, I was woken up by the doorbell before 9 o'clock. It was a Royal Mail Special Delivery. I opened it up. An insurance certificate for the DB7, AA Gold Membership, a Fuel Card valid anywhere in Europe, and a packet of Mint Imperials. Is there anything these guys don't think of, I thought, with a big smile on my face? I'd already checked out how to get to Nantwich by train - into London, Euston to Crewe, Crewe to Nantwich. I ordered a taxi for 10 o'clock and jumped in the shower.

The train journey into London was uneventful, but made notable as it was on time. I had a veggie burger with a banana and peanut butter milkshake at Ed's Diner outside Euston Station before boarding the train. I got a window seat with a table, plugged in my phone as it kept going flat, and started reading the copy of 'Private Eye' I'd picked up earlier.

'Mind if I sit opposite you?' I heard a woman's voice, and looked up. And nearly passed out. I'd read about - and I think once seen a video clip of - the very first moment that someone blind from birth sees something after surgery. Although I couldn't empathise totally, not being blind from birth, *technically*, I realised that, in effect, I *had* been, to all intents and purposes, sort of, until then!

'Of course. Sit down.' I managed somehow to spit out these words, and moved my bag so she could settle in properly directly opposite me.

I pretended to look out of the window, but I was constantly looking across the table at her, catching micro-glimpses of her extraordinary beauty. Once settled in she took out of her bag 'The Adventures of Tom Sawyer', which was the moment when I started believing in God.

'Great book.' I said with a subtle and very poorly practiced nonchalant smile.

'Yes, it is' she said, and this time I noticed that she spoke with what I took to be an Eastern European accent. I thanked the God I now believed in.

'Do you think it's the great American novel?'

'Isn't that supposed to be 'The Great Gatsby', although I never really understood why?'

'I'm with you on that. For me it's ...'

'Let me guess' she said, looking me up and down. After a while she said: 'You look to me like a 'Catcher in the Rye' man.'' And smiled.

'How would you know that?' I smiled back. She was right, too. I didn't even have to pretend.

'I use pragmatic observation skills and psychological insights to derive a list of behavioural indicators, that strongly suggest you empathise deeply with Holden Caulfield.'

'Doesn't every man?' I said.

'Maybe I've just met the wrong men?' she said. 'Until now, that is.' She reached out her hand to shake mine.

'My name's Emily. What's yours?'

    (The first part of the next line had been replaced with xxxxx followed by) 'I like Emily. It's a nice name.'

'Thank you. My father named me after the song by Pink Floyd.'

This must be what falling in love felt like. It had never happened to me before. 'I can't place your accent' I said. 'But I'm guessing it's east of here.'

'Guess.' she said.

'Poland?' Shake of the head. 'Latvia?' another shake. 'Russia?' another. 'I give up.'

'I'm Hungarian' she said, 'and my mother is Romanian. From Transylvania. And before you say it, no I'm not a vampire. Although my mother was the daughter of a Count.'

'So what brings you here?'

'Literature. I studied English and Russian Literature at the Sorbonne, and am now doing my PhD at Cambridge.'

'What's the topic?'

'The female characters in Dostoyevsky's works.'

'Really? Who's your favourite? Mine's Natasia Filipovna from 'The Idiot' '

'Do you mean favourite as in who I like the most, or who is the best character, which may be different?'

'Either. Both.' I added hurriedly.

'Natasia is my favourite too, in both categories.' And she said it in a tone of such seriousness that we both burst out laughing.

'Drinks. Hot and cold. Sandwiches. Snacks.' The man pushing the trolley had reached our table.

'Can I have a coffee please?' she asked. 'Black. No sugar, thank you.'

'I'll have the same' I said. 'Let me treat you.' I added.

She looked at me with a delightful little frown. 'So ... that means that I'll have to take your number so I can return the favour sometime.'

'Does it?' Well, I wasn't going to contradict her.

'Yes, well, of course I'm not buying you this coffee so you buy me one back. I'm buying it because I want to. Giving is more pleasant than receiving.' Corny as Hell, but I was on a roll.

'Receiving can be pleasant too!' She said with an unreadable smile. At least it was a smile.

I gave her my number. 'Can I have yours?' I asked, trying to keep the pleading out of my voice.

'You'll get it when I send you a message.' she said coyly. 'Where are you going to, anyway?'

'Nantwich. Changing at Crewe. How about you?'

'Chester. Spending a few days with some of my friends.'

Was there any chance, at all, I wondered, that she wasn't going out with a Cambridge Rowing Blue with 3% body fat and a degree in astrophysics, or even worse, French Literature? I tried to find out in my usual subtle way.

'Do you have a boyfriend?'

'Not yet!' with a smile to rival the Mona Lisa's.

Our coffees were handed to us, she thanked me, took a sip, and opened her book. I took this to mean she didn't want to talk anymore, so I dug out my headphones and pressed PLAY on the latest "Reasons to be cheerful" podcast from Ed Miliband. I kept looking at her, though, surreptitiously, and watched how the sunlight through the window fell across her face and how her extraordinary eyelashes flickered and how she gave occasional little frowns and smiles and how kissable her lips were. Indeed, I had never wanted to kiss anyone as much. I even almost asked her, but I chickened out.

We were a few minutes from Crewe. I put my headphones away, packed up my bits, and reached for my jacket which was in the overhead shelf. She looked up and smiled.

'Nice to meet you. Have fun in Nantwich.'

'Nice to meet you too. Have fun in Chester. And don't forget you owe me a coffee.'

'I won't' she said.

'Promise?'

'And hope to die.'

I got off the train - still thinking about kissing her and wondering if I'd ever hear from her again - very mindful of the immortal words of whoever said them, that "it is more important that heaven exists than that we should be able to get there" and waited for the connecting train to Nantwich.

I got to Mayfair Motors and asked for Ivan, who, incidentally, gave me the SPC handshake, and who, with the minimum of fuss, took me to my Aston Martin which was parked round the back. It was the second most beautiful thing I'd seen that day, and the first that let me inside.

After the briefest of chats Ivan said he had to go, so I shut the door and prepared to drive off. Boy, was I going to enjoy this. Just as I started the engine a text message came through. It was from Emily and read:

REALLY NICE TO MEET YOU. SEE YOU SOON I HOPE :)
EMILY
X

I smiled and put my foot on the DB7's accelerator.

SEGMENT 1

My boss took my resignation well, considering I'd dropped him in the shit. When I'd told him I wanted to travel the world, he understood. 'These opportunities don't come around very often' he said, and I agreed.

Everything was arranged for my trip to Perth, which was now only a week off, except that I hadn't been able to see Emily. And, if I saw her, and we hit it off, I'd have to tell her I was going away for a month, and obviously couldn't tell her the truth.

We'd spoken several times though, and eventually managed to agree a date and time to meet. I drove to Cambridge and met her in a pub in the City Centre. She was already there when I arrived, and if possible looked even more gorgeous than when I first met her.

'Hi' I said casually.

'Hi' she said. And we both laughed the laugh of imminent lovers.

Later that night, in bed, I told her I was off to Australia for about a month, in about a week. She didn't say anything at first, she just gave me one of her little frowns. We looked at one another for a long time without speaking. Then I said: 'Would you come with me?'

'But we've only just met.'

'I know' I said.

We looked at one another for a long time without speaking. And then she kissed me again.

A few days before we were due to leave, I visited Peter in the London Office for a briefing. He didn't say much, just explained the format of the programme, reiterated the low pass rate and how hard I'd have to work, and wished me luck.

I told him that I was taking Emily, and he said that was a great idea, as long as she didn't distract me too much and of course that she didn't find out what I was really being trained for. He asked me what my cover story was. I told him that I'd said to her that my work was classified and that I couldn't tell her, and he said that was perfect if I could get away with it. As I left he gave me a printout of an article from 'The Intercept' on how to spot a terrorist, according to the TSA, as background reading. There are, apparently, 17 "stress factors", each worth 1 point, 15 "fear factors", each worth 2 points, and 6 "deception factors", each worth 3. If a traveller scores 4 or more points they should be referred for selective screening, according to the instructions.

The 17 stress factors are:
- Arrives late for flight
- Avoids eye contact with security personnel
- Exaggerated yawning as the individual approaches the screening process
- Excessive fidgeting, clock watching, head-turning, shuffling feet, leg shaking
- Excessive perspiration inconsistent with the environment
- Face pale from recent shaving of beard
- Facial flushing while undergoing screening
- Faster eye blink rate when individual requested to submit to screening procedures
- Increased breathing rate, panting
- Obvious "Adam's Apple" jump when requested to submit to screening procedures
- Protruding or beating neck arteries
- Repetitive touching of face
- Rubbing or wringing of hands
- Strong body odour
- Sweaty palms
- Trembling
- Whistling as the individual approaches the screening process

The 15 fear factors are:
- Bag appears to be heavier than expected or does not suit the individual's appearance
- Bulges in clothing
- Cold penetrating stare
- Constantly looking at other travellers or associates
- Exaggerated emotions or inappropriate behaviour such as crying, excessive laughter or chatter
- Exaggerated, repetitive grooming gestures
- Hesitation/indecision on entering checkpoint
- Individuals who are seemingly unrelated but display identical dress or luggage
- Powerful grip of a bag or hand inside the bag
- Rigid posture, minimal body movements with arms close to side
- Scans area, appearing to look for security personnel
- Shows unusual interest in security officers and their work routine
- Displays arrogance and verbally expresses contempt for the screening process

- Wearing improper attire for location
- Widely open staring eyes

The 6 deception factors are:
- Appears to be confused or disoriented
- Appears to be in disguise
- Asks security-related questions
- Does not respond to authoritative commands
- Maintains covert ties with others
- Repeatedly pats upper body with hands

I thought these were interesting, and wondered how like these the SPC's recognition factors were, and, not for the first time, how any such factors could possibly reveal someone's eligibility.

The night before I was due to leave I popped into the 'Rat and Rat Catcher' for a cheeky beer or two with my friend Sam, nicknamed "French Gooner" as he hates the French and is a Spurs fan. We hadn't had a proper catch up in weeks, and there was lots to tell him, not least how I could afford to buy an Aston Martin and take off to Australia when I'd just resigned from my job. And he wanted to know all about Emily, of course.

'I didn't even know I had an aunt until I got the letter. My Mum told me she didn't know she had a step-sister until she was in her fifties, and between them they agreed not to tell me or Sally. Not sure why.' I took another sip of my beer.

'Well, as surprises go, this has to be one of the better ones.' said Sam. 'So, I guess she didn't have any children of her own.'

'That's right. And never married, either. A proper old spinster. She lived all alone in a cottage in the Cotswolds with half a dozen cats and half a million books, apparently.'

'Don't tell me you've inherited that as well?'

'No.' I took another sip of beer. 'That's been left to a local cat's rescue centre.'

'Blimey' said Sam. 'The perfect spec for an old spinster eh? I wonder if she solved murder mysteries as well. Fancy another one? And who's this Emily then?'

I half wished that my cat-loving spinster aunt was real, but of course if she was then she'd have died. Can you mourn a fictitious or fictional character, I wondered? I guess you could, as I mourned for Little Nell when she died in 'The Old Curiosity Shop'. Sam came back with two more pints.

'Come on then. Emily. Tell me all about her.'

'We met on a train. She's ...' I paused, not knowing what to tell him.

'Hungarian. And gorgeous. And sex mad!'

'What does she do?'

'She's still studying. Doing a PhD at Cambridge.'

'Wow. Sex mad and clever too. What the fuck does she see in you?'

I gave Sam the number of the mobile the SPC had given me for the Australian trip, and told him that I'd send him some photos when I'd settled in.

'So, will you get to travel around a bit? Sydney, the Barrier Reef, Ayers Rock?'

'Not sure. We're going to start in Perth and play it by ear.'

'Well, have a good trip. Send me a postcard.'

An SPC driver picked me up at 10 o'clock the following morning. Emily was going to meet me at Terminal 5. They were going to get me a First-Class ticket, but I persuaded them to pay for Emily and me in cattle class, which was in fact cheaper.

She was waiting for me in 'Giraffe', as agreed, and had already ordered us a couple of beers.

'I still can't believe this is really happening.' she said. 'Am I dreaming?'

'Is all that we see or seem but a dream within a dream?' I smiled.

'Edgar Allan Poe, no less.' She smiled her beautiful smile.

'I still can't believe someone as beautiful as you can even exist!' I replied. She blushed her beautiful blush.

Not much to report about the flight, except when we got to the gate we were upgraded to First Class anyway.

'Do you have a Fairy Godmother?' asked Emily. I told her I did.

We quickly settled into a routine in Perth. She had contacted the University of Western Australia, and as luck would have it she could continue her research there, and even do some teaching. I was "trained" all day every Monday and Tuesday. Wednesdays were dedicated to sports and other activities. I got heavily into surfing and joined the Chess Club. Thursday was more training, and Fridays were set aside for a variety of research projects which I'm not at liberty to discuss. We had the weekends to ourselves. Emily made some very nice friends at the University who we met up with a few times. On one such occasion one of them asked me what I did.

'That's classified.' said Emily. 'He can't tell you.'

'Really? Classified? Wow. Must be military or something?'

'Emily's right. I can't tell you. But I can promise you it's in a good cause.'

'A good cause in the Machiavellian sense, in that the end justifies the means?' another friend asked in a snide sort of a way. I thought he was a bit up himself, and didn't like the way he kept looking at Emily's boobs.

'Like I said, I can't tell you.' I said, and stared him down.

Later that night, as we climbed into bed, Emily asked me if she could ever know what I did. I said I didn't think so.

She said: 'Not even if we were married?'

'Is that a proposal?' I asked, running my hand up her thigh.

'Touch me like that and it might turn into one!'

It got me thinking though (after we'd finished, I hasten to add). What was the policy about wives and girlfriends? There had to be one, surely? And although the SPC was all male, what about Olga, and presumably others like her? And come to think of it we had some female staff, too. The next day I asked the local First Speaker.

'Let me remind you of the 4th Law' he said. '"A member must never reveal or allow through action or inaction to be revealed the existence of the SPC or any of its members to anyone who isn't a member without the express permission of a senior member with the appropriate clearance". That's pretty clear. And completely unrealistic, of course. We can't really expect members not to discuss such things with their partners, who after all, and let's be pragmatic here, must know about the SPC anyway, even if they don't know that they know, if that makes sense. There are aspects of membership that it's quite reasonable to want to discuss with non-members, especially partners. On top of that there's the possibility - and it happens all the time - of papers being left around, or conversations being overheard, stuff like that. And occasionally it can be quite difficult to explain away our meetings, or how we get given Aston Martins, for example.' He smiled.

'So, to cut to the chase, can I tell Emily?'

'Do you trust her?'

'Yes.'

'Then tell her. And ask her to keep it secret.'

'And if she doesn't? Or if we split up or something? What then?'

'Simple. We'll kill her.' He said it with a straight face before bursting out laughing. 'Listen. We've survived, and prospered, as a secret society for thousands of years. Of course, people know about us, some of whom we wish didn't. But we always get by!' He smiled again. 'Tell her, and when you get a chance let me know how it goes.'

'You're joking, right?' Emily said that night after we'd made love.

'No. I'm serious.' I replied. We lay on our sides, arms entwined, looking at one another.

'What are you thinking about?' I asked.

'I'm thinking what a ... I don't know what to say ... crazy thing it is you've told me. It's barely believable. The scale of it. And the importance you attach to it. It's ... it's...' She hesitated.

'It's what?' I asked, smiling.

'It's so silly!' she said, smiling.

Over breakfast I explained what it was I being trained on, and how I was getting on.

'So, you can really tell, what's your expression, "eligibility", by observing people? It seems far-fetched.' Emily asked.

'The use of pragmatic observation skills and psychological insights to derive a list of behavioural indicators, remember? That's how you knew about 'The Catcher in the Rye' isn't it?'

'Hmm. Seriously, though, how can you tell?' She sipped her coffee. 'What am I even saying? The thing is ...' she frowned her beautiful frown, 'This question of eligibility. It's such a, I mean, I still can't believe it.'

'But it's true. It's all true.' Just for a second my face dropped. She came over and hugged me.

'You're just tilting at windmills, you know that?'

'My other favourite book,' I said as I got my jacket on. 'Still want to marry me?'

A week before the programme was due to finish the lead facilitator gave all the candidates a nice surprise. 'We always do this' he said, 'Keep a few days in the bank. Your training is over. Take a few days off. Enjoy yourselves. Be back here for dinner on Sunday evening ready for two days of interviews and tests Monday and Tuesday. Results on Wednesday, fly back Thursday. Marie in Travel can sort out any trips you might want to make.'

Emily and I flew to Sydney, and I proposed to her on the famous harbour bridge. She cried - I hope with joy - as she said yes. To celebrate we had dinner at 'Sepia', and then went back to our hotel, took some champagne into the bath ... and both fell asleep. The cold water woke us up about 3 in the morning, and we both ran into the bedroom and snuggled up under the duvet to get warm. Magical night, and without getting out of bed we had a magical morning too.

Back in Perth on the Sunday evening Emily went out with some of her University friends while I had an early night in preparation for the following day's tests.

Monday started out with an interview, then a written test, then a lunch break, followed by a role play, and to finish an observed group exercise. We stayed on site that night, and wisely I restricted myself to two beers from the free bar. Tuesday began with a gruelling 3-hour panel interview, and then in the afternoon an actual recognition test - using all the observational skills we'd acquired to test real people for their eligibility. We weren't told the results, of course, they would come later. The last part of the day was a brief chat with the First Speaker, thanking me for my commitment and explaining that my results would be given to me in a one-to-one session tomorrow at 4 o'clock. He then told me about the big end of programme dinner at Perth's trendiest restaurant, to which partners were invited.

I was completely drained when I got back to Emily, and just wanted a quiet evening and an early night. She asked me how I thought I'd done.

'It was tough. Really tough.' I said. 'I honestly don't know. There's lots of talk about whether there's any significance in the timing of tomorrow's one-to-one. Some people think if you're on in the morning you've passed. Some people think it's the other way around. Mine's at 4 o'clock. I guess I'll find out then. Anyway, forget all that for now, what's done is done. What about the big dinner tomorrow night?'

'The restaurant looks fabulous,' said Emily. 'And a band. And there's dancing too?'

'Ever seen me dance?' I said.

'I bet you're as good at dancing as you are at everything else!' Emily smiled her beautiful smile.

'Flattery will get you everywhere.' I said.

I had nothing to do all the next day until my one-to-one, so did a bit of packing as our flight home was the next morning, and a bit of surfing. Nothing could take my mind off worrying if I'd passed or not, though, not even seeing Emily model her dress for the evening, or helping her out of it.

At 4 o'clock I sat in the waiting area looking at the door through which I'd soon be invited in. There was nothing on the table I wanted to read. I got up to get myself a drink of water, and the door opened. I saw a guy called Mark come out looking very miserable. He just nodded at me and walked off quickly. Shit, I thought, it was right what they said about the afternoon sessions. I was called in. I took a deep breath, and walked into the room.

'Sit down.' said a guy with glasses who I hadn't seen before. He was looking at various papers on the desk in front of him. Once or twice he looked up at me, showing no emotion, and carried on reading. After what seemed like ages he looked up at me again and said 'You've achieved the highest marks ever scored, including 100% in your recognition exercise. That's never been done before.' He held out his hand. 'Congratulations. You've not only passed, you've won a scholarship.'

SEGMENT 2

So began the happiest days of my life. The repercussions of winning a recognition scholarship were way beyond anything I could have anticipated, even given the extraordinary standards of the SPC. It turns out that only three people had previously achieved it since 1973, when scholarships were introduced. I entered a whirlwind period of meetings, seminars, workshops, forums, dinners etc. at all of which I was feted like some sort of superstar. It was embarrassing at first, but I soon got used to it and realised just what wonderful news it was.

I was even asked to mentor some new members, informally, and was sounded out over working full time at the Perth facility. But the best moment of all came when I was out for a drink in Cambridge with some of Emily's friends, and actually spotted a new member using my new-found expertise ... and introduced him to the organisation. He was delighted, and it felt like one small step for man but one giant leap for mankind.

My relationship with Emily went from strength to strength, and it really felt perfect. Every morning when I woke up next to her I couldn't believe my luck. The only thing that matched her external beauty was her internal beauty. I had never met anyone so kind, thoughtful, sensitive, fun, bright, witty, amusing, gentle (although thankfully not always), and just all round brilliant. And amazingly she was happy with me! No wonder I'd started to believe in God. As her great love Dostoyevsky did indeed say, "To love someone means to see them as God intended them."

The time came to meet her parents. We flew to Budapest on a Friday night, they were going to collect us the following morning and drive us to their place in the country. As we got off the plane I saw a couple of emails, one asking for details so my Israel trip could be arranged, and the other saying that my stipend had been increased to £11,000 a month tax free, with immediate effect, and that I'd been awarded a special award of £75,000, as usual tax free.

I was really trying not to take all this for granted, but it was hard. The extraordinary was becoming ordinary. The amazing was becoming commonplace. It felt, finally, as if I was one of the people who had won the glittering prizes. And that wasn't even counting Emily.

We were having breakfast in the hotel when her parents arrived. I could see where Emily got her looks from, they were both very good looking. After lots of hugs between them her mother gave me kisses on both cheeks before her father shook my hand ... at which point there was a fraction of a second of mutual astonishment as we simultaneously realised that the other had the handshake. Just as my definition of innocence was that period in one's life when you thought James Hurley might have killed Laura Palmer, that moment became my definition of serendipity.

We spent a fabulous few days at their "place in the country", which I likened to a medium-sized castle. They even had a butler. I think they approved of me - I certainly tried my hardest to make the right impression. I drank very little, so little in fact that Emily asked if I was ill and her mother encouraged me to "get a little drank" (that's how she said it). They were very old fashioned. Even though we were engaged, we were in separate bedrooms. I did wonder if I should sneak into her room at night, but mentioned I was afraid her mother might turn me into a bat. She punched me in the stomach, and not all that gently either.

On the afternoon of our last day there she went shopping with her mother, leaving me alone with her father. He and I were served tea and panettone in the library, which was a beautiful room. Each wall was lined with ancient-looking books, floor to ceiling, and the view from the window was what I can only describe as a perfect feast for the eyes - it was almost too wonderful to really exist. There was a leather chair in the window recess, and I thought this would be the spot where someone could write a masterpiece.

'This is where I wrote my masterpiece.' said Emily's father.

'What was it?' I asked politely.

'A treatise on the true authorship of Shakespeare's plays. In Latin.'

'You don't think Shakespeare wrote them then?'

'You'll have to read it. I'll give you a copy.'

'I'm afraid my Latin isn't up to much. In fact, anything. I went to a Comprehensive School.'

'Ah. The English education system. So ... wasteful of talent. So narrow.'

'I know, I know. Still, worse things happen at sea.' I couldn't think of anything else to say. He looked at me for a few moments.

'Your results in Perth. Most impressive.'

I didn't think I'd ever heard anyone say that apart from Darth Vader.

'I'd heard about the results, of course, but I never made the connection it was you. Very well done.'

'Thank you. I'm delighted. Things are going well.'

'So, what next for you? In the SPC?'

'Israel for further training. Then I'll look at my options. Perth want me full time, but I'm not sure I want that. And of course, Emily must be happy. It's my mission in life.'

'She's very much in love with you, you know. Her mother and I are delighted.'

'Well, I do try. I'm very much in love with her too.'

'I can see that. I can see that you'll look after her. And we intend to look after you too.'

'Thank you. I intend to make her the happiest human being that ever walked the earth.'

'A bold objective!' he said. 'But I approve. Of course. Now let me give you something.' He pulled an envelope out of his pocket. 'This is for both of you. On the day of your wedding we'll give you the address.' He handed me the envelope. 'You can open it.'

'Thank you.' I opened the envelope. In it were a bunch of keys.

'We've bought you a house in Hampstead. A wedding gift. We hope you'll be very happy there.' He paused. 'But you don't get it until you're married. You obviously wouldn't ever stay overnight in the same place until then, would you? With my daughter?'

I blushed in what can't have been a very delightful way, and stammered a little. 'Of course not. That's very, very kind of you. Thank you.'

'So. Enough of the formalities. Drink wine with me?'

Who was I to refuse, especially when the butler brought in a bottle of (the said butler informed me) the best wine ever produced by humanity? Resisting the urge to ask him how it compared with the best wine ever not produced by humanity, I accepted a glass with good grace. Wow. I'd had some very nice things in my mouth before, but nothing quite like this.

On the flight home Emily told me her parents liked me. 'Really?' I said. 'They're hard to read.'

'Father in particular. Which is unusual, as he never liked anyone I ever took home.'

'You mean you took people home before you met me? I thought I was the first!'

She punched me again. 'Compared with you, no I didn't.'

A few weeks later she submitted her thesis, after which we celebrated by flying off to Santorini, leaving our phones behind.

'Let's just remember what it was like in the good old days, before social media. I want to be off the grid for a while and properly relax.' she said.

I was all up for that.

On our third night, over dinner in a gorgeous little restaurant in Oia, Emily looked tired, and asked for water instead of wine.

'Feeling ok love?' I asked. 'Tired?'

'Never felt better.' she said, and gave me the strangest look.

'Are you sure? Don't you like the wine?'

'I love the wine. I just don't feel like it, that's all.' I saw tears run slowly down her cheeks, but she was smiling. She held out both her hands and I took them in mine.

'You mean ...?'

'Yes.' she said. 'Twelve weeks.'

I thought about saying 'I thought you were looking a bit fat' or 'your father will fucking kill me!' but I opted for 'I love you so much' ... at which point she might have seen tears run slowly down my cheeks.

When we climbed into bed I asked if we could still make love, whether it was, you know, ok.

'If you don't make love to me right now I'll hide your book!' (I was re-reading 'Don Quixote').

'Fair enough,' I said. 'I'm really enjoying it.'

She punched me again, before spoiling me quite a lot to make up for it.

Not that it matters all that much these days, as about 18 in 20 babies are born out of wedlock, but we wanted to get married before the baby was due. Some conversations with her parents later, and a date was fixed about 4 months hence. I wondered at first whether that gave us enough time to organise everything, not least the venue, someone to do the honours and so on, but I'd reckoned without the power and influence of the SPC and the tenacity and sheer bloody-mindedness of Emily's mother (hereafter Angelika, as that's her name).

The agreed location was a tiny Caribbean island, owned by the Russian multi-trillionaire, on which was (amongst other things) a beautiful church from a village near Carcassonne which had been moved across the ocean and then painstakingly rebuilt stone by stone (remember that ever since meeting Emily I'd started believing), and a 7-star luxury private hotel which was impossible to book - you had to be invited to stay there.

All the guests - some 300 or so - would be flown by private jet from Miami, and all travel, accommodation, food and, above all, drinks, costs would be met by the SPC, including getting to and back home from Miami. Sam would be my best man and Emily - who was an only child - chose four of her friends from Cambridge to be her bridesmaids.

The date now being fixed, Sam could go ahead and organise the Stag Do - he chose Blackpool from a shortlist including Amsterdam, Prague, Berlin, Cape Town and Rio de Janeiro - and I could fix my two-month stint in Israel with the country's counter-terrorism unit. Emily wouldn't be able to join me for that - two whole months apart - so she agreed to stay with her parents and "get ready". She would, however, be able to join me for a couple of days at the end of the programme.

Everything now being organised, and with three more weeks to go before Israel, Emily and I decided to relax and have masses of sex. I distinctly remember the last night before my trip. We'd already had sex three times that afternoon and if I'm perfectly honest I was feeling a bit sore, so when she did that thing she did to get us both going, for a fraction of a second I was unresponsive. Only for a fraction of a second, mind, as a fraction of a second later she did something I swear no sentient sexual being had ever had the imagination to do before. Afterwards I lay there panting, unable to move and barely able to breathe, while she wiped the walls and ceiling. 'Thank you, God' I smiled to myself, (and thought of that funny moment near the end of 'Animal House'), but can't deny there was a part of me that felt slight relief that I'd get a bit of a respite. I knew it wouldn't last though. "Note to self, must remember to pack my three odd socks".

I left very early the next morning and didn't wake her. She'd asked me to, but a) she looked zonked, b) I felt she could do with the rest, c) I didn't want to see her cry (or her to see me cry) and d) I was worried she might want sex again.

Anyway, she didn't know, but it wouldn't really be two months before we met again. Although I'd told her that sadly I wouldn't be able to make it, I'd got a dispensation to miss two days and nights of the training so I could attend her PhD graduation ceremony.

'So, you're the guy with the big dick and the big grades from Perth'. was how the Colonel in the Israeli Army welcomed me to the West Bank. He looked at me with utter disdain, as if I was a cockroach he couldn't even be bothered to squash. I wasn't sure whether to reply or not, so I didn't. 'Hmm. Mute as well eh? The standard of recruits just keeps on dropping. Tell me, do you know what I think about Perth?'

'No, sorry.'

'No Sir to you, sonny. Got that?'

'Yes. Sir' I added hastily.

He swivelled a blackboard round on which was written PERTH IS FOR PUSSIES. 'Don't get me wrong. It's impressive enough, what they teach you, for what it is. But do you want to know the big difference though. The big fucking difference?'

I nodded.

'If they miss someone, the result is, nothing. If we miss someone, then twenty-five people get blown up, including eight kids, and if you're lucky you only lose both legs, the sight in one eye, and the ability to eat solid food. Got it?'

I nodded again.

'All those behavioural fucking indicators. Good for a Lee Child novel but shit in the field. Let me demonstrate what we'll teach you. Say cheese.' I wondered if he was going to take a photo.

'Cheese' I said.

'Your favourite cheese is grilled halloumi, which you like almost burnt. You're also very fond of comté, provolone and manchego. You're quite partial to cheddar, especially if it's strong. You often eat it grilled on toast with English mustard and raw tomato. When you ate spaghetti last week you declined the offer of parmesan. The last Greek Salad you ate didn't have the right proportions of feta, red onion and tomato, and the accompanying bread was a bit stale. You're trying to remember if you packed your electric toothbrush and extra tissues. When you got out of bed this morning you bashed your shin against a table. The first Beatles song you ever heard was 'The Ballad of John and Yoko'. The book you're reading is 'Don Quixote' but you're not yet enjoying it as much as you did the first time round, which is worrying you. And you have a drip of sweat running slowly down your back, which is making you really wish that this room had air conditioning and that you'd worn shorts instead of those chinos. I could go on.'

'You got all that from me saying cheese?'

'No. From your personnel records. Of *course* I did. But it's the *way* you said it that's important, the word itself is just the primer. Imagine what we can do with a whole sentence.'

'Jesus. That's impressive. I had no idea.'

'Of course you didn't. That's the process. We've taken the deciphering of body language and the spoken word to a whole new and previously unimaginable level.'

'But all the indicators. Don't they help? Sweating, avoiding eye contact, cold penetrating stares, all that jazz?'

'It's part of the process, sure, and can be helpful, but it's now considered fairly rudimentary. The bad guys know them all anyway now, so the more able ones know what behaviours to avoid. Like shaving their beards, for example.'

'I see.'

'By the end of this programme you'll be able to tell what time train someone caught, where they sat, and what drink they ordered three weeks ago, from the way they've tied their shoelaces.'

'And eligibility for SPC?'

'Piece of piss. With the primitive techniques you already know, added to ours, you'll be able to detect eligibility in the dark and in complete silence.' He paused. 'Good for catching the bad guys too.'

And so, my enhanced training had begun, and it was truly relentless. I'm not at liberty to reveal what I learned, or how I learned it, but it was out of this world. Not literally, but you know what I mean.

It was also exhausting, so quite apart from the joy of seeing Emily again it was something of a relief to be on a flight back to the UK knowing I could have a lie-in in the morning. Her ceremony wasn't until the following evening, so I'd have the whole day to relax and mooch around a bit. She had no idea I was going to be there, and she wouldn't find out until she got up on stage. I had a front row seat.

We had been in constant contact though, talking about the wedding preparations, where we wanted to go on our honeymoon, what we'd been up to (I couldn't really give her any detail) and of course how much we missed one another. Late one night we even sneaked in a dirty phone call, which we'd never done before.

Nothing much happened on the flight. I watched a couple of forgettable movies and listened to some music, and dozed for a bit. When I landed an SPC limo was waiting to drive me straight to my hotel in Cambridge, where I went straight to sleep without setting my alarm.

I didn't need to get to Emily's College until just before 7, so after a nice lie-in I broke with my usual routine and had a bath immediately after breakfast. There's something special about a morning bath isn't there? - like a midnight feast or afternoon sex, it feels somehow indulgent. I can't quite explain it. Afterwards I got a cab out to Grantchester Meadows, had a snack in the Rupert Brooke tea rooms (as I call them) and then in an unusual moment of spontaneity I hitched a lift in a punt back to the city with some Belgian tourists. We talked about Eddie Merckx, beer and chocolate.

I still had most of the afternoon left, so I walked around the city centre for a bit, bought some books, had a wet shave, and finally went back to my hotel to get ready. I had a bottle of champagne cooling on ice - surely Emily could have a sip - that was on the assumption that she'd come back to the hotel of course, since she didn't know I was coming.

I'd decided to go in disguise, so even if she looked at the front row when she went on stage she wouldn't recognise me, which got me thinking about the effectiveness of disguises generally, which we'd been studying intensively. On this occasion it worked a treat. The disguise was amateurish but fun - a black wig and moustache and glasses - and I was fairly sure that the untrained eye wouldn't know it was me. I sat right in the middle of the front row, and had to wait about an hour until Emily was called onto the stage. The bump was quite visible now. She looked gorgeous. I was so proud of her that I cried, and when she turned to the crowd and bowed I stood up and applauded. She looked a bit bemused, not knowing who I was, until I took off the wig and moustache and glasses ... at which point she held her hands to her cheeks, gave a little whoop of joy, and burst out crying too.

They had to get through several more people, so it was about another half an hour before we were in one another's arms. 'You said you couldn't get away!' she said, with tears streaming down her cheeks. 'You think anything could have kept me away?' I said. We didn't, wouldn't, couldn't stop hugging.

And it continued after we got into bed (after polishing off the champagne). You know how sometimes when you're trying to get to sleep with someone you just can't get comfortable whatever you do? You try spooning one way, then the other, but an arm or a leg keeps getting in the way and you keep fidgeting. That night was different. We lay face to face, locked in an embrace where the maximum amount of our bodies were touching. The joy of skin on skin was exquisite. I could feel her bump against my belly and I felt complete. Neither of us said anything, we just looked into one another's eyes. I'm not sure we could ever recreate the position we'd somehow managed to get into, but it was perfect, and we fell asleep with our lips still touching, as if enjoying an everlasting kiss.

I had an unusual dream. In it Emily and I visited a Fortune Teller and the giant from Twin Peaks kept shaking its head as if to warn us against doing it. It was exactly the same as it was during the Miss Twin Peaks competition at the end of the show's second series.

I wasn't being collected until 12.30, so after breakfast we had a wander around the city centre. On Parker's Piece there was a fayre, and I saw a Fortune Teller, and I wanted to go in.

'Don't,' said Emily. 'I don't like them. They're sinister.'

'Oh, come on,' I said. 'You know it's all bullshit. It's just that I'm curious, given what I've been learning over the last few months, what they can deduce from just looking at us. Can we?' Emily relented, and in we went.

I am a bit of a sceptic about these things. I mean, how can they possibly predict the future, but was it Thomas Hardy who wrote "Perhaps they know things that know not I?" about a moth? I can't quite remember. It matters not. We sat down and were told all sorts of incredible predictions like "I can see a life-changing event coming up" (Emily's tummy looked huge) and "There is a happy day on the horizon" (we weren't, of course, wearing wedding rings yet), and I was just on the point of switching off altogether when the whole mood changed. I can't explain how, but I felt an overwhelming sense of doom, and shivered.

The Fortune Teller looked Emily right in the eye and said 'I can see a wonderful future for you and your child. But you must not go on a long journey you have planned. You must not go.' She was quite scary.

'Come on,' I said. 'You're not supposed to frighten people. This is bullshit. What do you mean?'

The Fortune Teller looked at me. 'Do not let her go on a long journey you have planned. That's all I know. You must not let her.' We left with Emily in tears. I put my arm around her.

'They're not supposed to say things like that,' she sobbed. 'What did she mean?'

'It's utter bullshit,' I said. 'Forget about it. Let's have a quick sandwich or something before I get picked up.'

'I told you we shouldn't have gone.' she said. I looked back at the tent. Madame Gironde. I'd have cause to remember that name. I even took a photo of her tent on my phone.

We found a little café and ordered coffees and cheese sandwiches. 'Say cheese' I said. She did, and I predicted a life changing event and a happy day, and everlasting love. She smiled her beautiful smile again. It was time for me to go.

'Let me know when you get there.' she said.

'I will. Do you want a lift back to College?'

'No I fancy a walk.' We kissed and I watched her walk slowly away. The love of my life.

Back on the West Bank the training stepped up a notch, not least because of increased tensions between the Palestinians and the Israelis, exacerbated by Donald Trump foolishly sticking his nose in and behaving like the complete twat he is. I went on several live missions, and although several of them were tense, nothing bad happened.

The programme was nearly over, and I was relieved at the prospect of going home. The wedding was only a month or so away, and what a month it promised to be, including my Stag Do in lovely Blackpool. And here I was, at the airport, waiting for Emily to arrive and, as I always did at airports, welling up as I saw people reunited, reminiscent of the end of 'Love Actually'. It had taken time, I thought, but life was finally brilliant. "The future cannot fail me" I smiled to myself.

SEGMENT 3

It can be quite awkward having sex with a heavily pregnant woman, you certainly can't be too rough (and Emily did like rough). It's all about the angles. In the end, after quite a lot of giggling, Emily sort of squatted on me. It felt wonderful, and we both giggled when I finished. While I was still inside her she started to cry.

'What's wrong? Was I too quick?' I smiled.

'I just love you so much. Too much. You're perfect for me, you know that? Utterly and completely perfect. It's like the line from that song, I dreamt you into life.'

Tears were still running down her cheeks. Given the situation I found myself in it was difficult to fetch some tissues for her, so I wiped her tears away with my hands and then wiped them onto my own face. 'There,' I said, and then 'This isn't a dream. This is real life. Real love.' And I paused. 'I love you more than a hundred' (which was a little saying we had between us).

'Don't ever leave me. I couldn't function without you.'

'I'll never leave you. I promise.' I whispered.

She pulled herself off me, lay down next to me, and quickly fell asleep. I lay looking at her, gently stroking her hair, until I couldn't keep my eyes open any longer.

The following day we went to a market I'd been to a few times. I was dying for her to taste some freshly squeezed iced peach juice from a little stall I'd discovered the week before.

'This ...' she said as she took a sip '... is the nicest thing I've ever had in my mouth.'

'Really?' I said. 'The nicest thing?'

'By far!' she said and poked her tongue out at me.

We walked arm in arm around the market. I bought her a silk scarf in a delightful shade of blue. We saw someone selling multi-coloured bracelets.

'Oh, these are pretty' she said.

We agreed to buy each other one and put them on immediately to remind us of this trip. Hers was made of interwoven strips of leather and maybe linen or another cloth, and was pink and yellow and green and blue.

'I have a rainbow on my wrist.' she said and smiled her beautiful smile. Mine was black leather.

She started to feel tired, so we decided to catch a bus back. After all these weeks, I knew what bus to get and where to catch it. We got on. It was quite busy and there were no seats, but noticing Emily's bump a lady stood up and let her take her seat. We both thanked her. I remained standing. As more people got on at the next stop I was forced down the bus away from her.

'Two more stops!' I said to her.

At the next stop, some Israeli soldiers got on. I looked around to see if the mood on the bus altered in any way, but it didn't. Everyone seemed in a good mood. One of the soldiers gave a small Palestinian boy a lollipop, and although I couldn't hear what they were saying I could see him talking and smiling with the boy's mother. I couldn't see Emily now, there were too many people in the way. I hoped she'd remember we had to get off at the next stop. I turned away from the soldiers and looked out of the window. My eyes caught those of a man I hadn't noticed before.

Too late.

Screaming. Shouting. Sirens. Voices. Everything blurry. Everything slow. Something thick in my mouth, oozing down my chin. Hissing. Terrible hissing. Ears hurt. Eye hurts. Arm hurts. Back hurts. Leg hurts. Head hurts. Screaming. Shouting. Sirens. Voices. Everything hurts. Terrible hissing. Someone is standing over me. Indistinct. I think I feel them touch my arm. Put something on me. Eyes hurt. Silence now, apart from the hissing. I try to put my hands over my ears to stop it but I can't move them. Everything is slow, very slow. I try to speak but can't. Terrible hissing stops. Starts again. Something thick oozing out of my ears. Everything speeds up. Loud now. Shouting. Then I hear a voice, close up. Face looking at me. I feel myself lifted. I don't understand them.

'English' I whisper. Someone shouts again. 'Emily' I say. Hurts to talk. Mouth full of thick liquid. Choking. Coughing. The hissing won't stop. 'Emily.' I say again.

'Can you hear me?' I hear someone say. I can't focus.

'Where is Emily? What's happened?'

Indistinct voices. Feel people touching me. Still can't focus. Sirens again. More shouting. 'My ears are hurting.'

Then it's all clear. I'm on a stretcher being carried towards an Ambulance. I have a drip in my arm. I can't feel my legs. I'm scared to look down but I do. They're still there. I still have the hissing in my ears but I can see clearly now. There are police, soldiers, doctors, helpers, all around. Through the hissing I hear more shouting and, what's that, crying. Sobbing. My ears hurt.

'Where's Emily?' I whisper but no-one seems to hear me. It hurts to move my head but I turn over and look to the right. Bodies, everywhere. I see a doll on the floor covered with blood. I see a body covered up with a blood-soaked sheet. I see an arm, just an arm, not attached to anything, with a pink and yellow and green and blue bracelet still on it. I want to touch the hand but I can't reach. The ambulance door slams shut.

SEGMENT 5

I woke up with a start, and became aware that I was in a hospital and that it was probably night time. Over to my right the entire wall was a long series of windows and I could see a desk and nurses and doctors wandering around. To my left was what I presumed was the window to the outside world. I looked down. I had a drip into my left hand. I hated the thought of the syringe or whatever you called it being inserted horizontally into one of my veins, and that I couldn't move. My right arm was heavily bandaged, and I noticed that a sort of handle with a red button on it was strapped to my right hand. I guessed that pressing the red button was to attract someone's attention. I could feel various sensors and wires on my head and torso, all feeding into a bank of screens to the left of me. I looked at all the lines moving slowly across the screens, which showed I was still alive.

I still seemed to have all my limbs, which was a relief, but were any of them in working order? It's one thing having arms and legs, it's quite another being able to use them. I tried to move my feet. Nothing. My legs. Nothing. My arms. Nothing. I closed my eyes and told myself to 'get a grip', and with a great deal of effort pressed the red button. At least my right hand was still working.

After a while a nurse came in.

'How are you feeling today?' she asked.

'I don't know. I can't feel anything. Where am I and where's ...'

'Ssshhh' she said. 'Just relax. You've been in a bad accident but are on the mend.'

'How long have I been here?'

She straightened my pillow. 'Don't fuss. The Doctor will tell you everything. He'll call round to see you later. Now, are you hungry? Do you want anything to eat?'

'My mouth's dry. What are the chances of a nice cold beer?'

She smiled. 'I'll bring you a sandwich and a glass of water. Just relax and I'll be back soon.'

After my snack, I must have fallen asleep again, as the next thing I remember was hearing some familiar voices close to me. I opened my eyes. It was my parents and my sister Sally.

'Hi.' I said with an effort. 'Fancy seeing you here!'.

My Mum bent over and kissed my forehead gently. Sally looked like she'd been crying. Even my Dad looked a bit emotional. For him.

'Sorry I can't get up,' I said. 'They don't seem to want me to move.'

It was Sally's turn to kiss me. I don't think she'd done that in about 10 years.

'Things must be bad!' I said, forcing a smile.

A doctor came in. 'So. The patient is awake. How are you today?'

'The nurse asked me that. I don't know. I can't feel anything. What's wrong with me? Don't hold anything back.'

'All in good time. All in good time. You've suffered a series of injuries, including to your head. We're still assessing things but ...' he looked at my charts and glanced at the screens '... although it's early days, I think you're one of the luckiest men alive.'

'How long have I been here? And where is here?'

'This is your third week in a military hospital in Germany. We kept you in a coma for over two weeks and gradually brought you round. You've had a number of operations.'

I suppose it's understandable that I started to cry. 'My family?'

'They flew out as soon as they heard. They've been here all the time.'

I closed my eyes very tight and my tears felt as if they were burning my face. 'And Emily?'

I was in there for weeks. As soon as the Doctors said I was out of danger, my Dad and Sally flew home, leaving my Mum to worry and fret. She said I needed her there, and although I didn't think I did, in an unexpected way I quite liked her being around. She'd come in every morning and afternoon, and sit with me. Sometimes we chatted about the big things, mostly we chatted about trivia, and sometimes we'd sit there in silence both reading our books. I could hardly bear it, but I'd promised Emily I'd re-read 'The Idiot' after finishing 'Don Quixote', so I'd parked Cervantes for Dostoyevsky.

As I got better the Doctors started letting me eat what I wanted, and my Mum started bringing me in delicious fruit and biscuits, and she even managed to bring back some peach juice.

One day the main Doctor who'd been attending to me, an American called David, sat down on the end of my bed for a chat. My Mum was out shopping.

'Well, I hate to disappoint you,' he said with a smile, 'Since you clearly love being here, but I think we can discharge you in a few days. There's nothing more we can do. In fact, there's nothing more that needs to be done. You've made, more or less, a full recovery.' He looked at me seriously. 'You were incredibly lucky.'

'Hmm. Lucky? Yes, in one way I suppose I was. In another I wasn't.' I paused for a moment. 'So, when you say more or less... tell me about the less.'

'Well. Physically you're mostly ok. A few scars here and there. What we're not totally sure about is any other damage you might have suffered

- emotional scarring, PTSD maybe. Some of your readings are rather ... unusual. We're going to refer you to a specialist in Dallas, who may shed some light on things.'

'What do you mean by unusual?'

'Exactly that. It may not even be a problem, we just think some more tests would be advisable and we're not equipped to do them here. I can't really say too much more as it's not my field.'

In any event my Mum was delighted, and we made arrangements to fly back together. Peter at the SPC told me to take as long as I needed, and not to rush things. They'd keep the Perth option open for me, there were various other avenues I could explore, and I'd be getting a lump sum by way of compensation.

I checked out three days later, and travelled back to my SPC room, which was exactly as I'd left it that morning. Emily's stuff was still there. There was a knock at the door. It was the Colonel who'd first welcomed me, and a lady I hadn't seen before.

'I know it's upsetting, but we didn't want to move anything. We thought that was best, on balance.' I looked at her bedside table with some earrings she'd left on it, and her reading glasses. I picked them up and held them.

'Thank you,' I said. 'That was the right thing to do.'

'If there's anything you need. Anything at all. Call me.' She gave me her card. It said she was Karen Armstrong, Grief Counsellor.

'Thank you. I will.'

'And I can get someone to help you pack away her things. If you like?'

'I'll manage. But thank you. Really.' I must have looked very sad.

'Would you give us a minute please?' said the Colonel.

'Sure' she said and stepped outside.

He watched me play with her glasses for a few minutes before speaking. 'We'll help sort out the Memorial. Just say the word and it's done.' I could tell he was reluctant to say how little of her body they'd been able to piece together.

'Thank you.' I said. 'That'll be good. I'll check with her parents and we'll be in touch.'

'I thought you might like this.' He held out the red and yellow and pink and blue bracelet that she'd been wearing. The one on the arm.

'A rainbow on my wrist.' I whispered to myself. 'Here. Would you tie it on for me? It's difficult to tie it on.'

'Which wrist?' 'This one.' I said, holding out my left hand. 'Make it tight please. I'm never taking it off. Sir!'

He smiled as he did so. Then we shook hands. SPC handshake. 'Good luck.' he said.

'You bet!' I replied.

Mum and I flew back the next day. I spent a few days reacquainting myself with my flat, sorting out my post, and generally relaxing, before getting stuck into things. First up was getting pissed with Sam at the 'Rat and Rat Catcher'. And I mean properly pissed, I hadn't got into that state in months.

Next up was trying to find Madame Gironde the Fortune Teller. The fayre was no longer there, but I found the organisers online and got in touch.

'We've never had a Fortune Teller called Madame Gironde', they told me.

'You must be mistaken', I said. 'I visited her myself.' I even sent them the photo I took.

'Not here, you didn't', they were adamant.

I got impatient with them. 'Listen,' I said. 'I know who I visited. I've not made a mistake. You've made the mistake. Please re-check your records.' But they were unable or unwilling to look into it any further. I didn't leave it there, though. I instructed a top notch private investigator to find her for me.

It was high time to see Emily's parents. They said they were happy to come to the UK as I'd been through enough. It was heartbreaking, but they were, the words are hard to find, perfect about it. As perfect as it was possible to be, I mean. We agreed to locate her main public Memorial in the Non-Catholic Cemetery in Rome, near the grave of Keats, and a smaller private one, for family only, which I'm pleased to say included me, in the Tikhvin Cemetery in St. Petersburg, near the grave of her beloved Dostoyevsky. Both would take a few months to complete, even with the full support of the SPC's Special Projects Division (who were great at these sorts of things). Just before they flew back they gave me the address of the house in Hampstead.

'Be happy there. Emily would want that.'

Next up was the specialist in Dallas. I had a whole battery of tests of all kinds, several of which seemed to my untrained eyes to be way off the regular medical piste, so to speak. These were followed by about a week of interviews, many feeling more like interrogations. I finally found myself in a room with the specialist himself, who I'd not met until that point.

'I am The Specialist.' he told me modestly.

'Pleased to meet you at last.' I said. 'Tell me, what exactly are you a specialist in?'

'The unusual.' he said.

'So, is there anything unusual about me? The Doctor in Germany said that some of my results were unusual, but he didn't say what results.'

The Specialist held up his hand as if to indicate that he wasn't to be spoken to until he was ready. He turned over several pieces of paper, making notes, frequently frowning, and occasionally mumbling things to himself. I sat there patiently. Eventually he looked at me and told me his conclusion.

I laughed. 'You're joking, right? Tell me you're joking?'

'I am not joking,' he said. 'I never joke.' And looking at his face I believed him.

Later that day I was on the phone to Karen the Grief Counsellor. I was sobbing quietly.

'Nothing works,' I said. 'There is misery in everything around me. I can't feel anything. I can't taste anything.' I was struggling to breathe. 'I've lost my reason to live. The person that made it all worthwhile.'

She told me to take some deep breaths and focus on the positives. What positives, I asked her. She suggested I make a list. This is what I came up with:

1. The smell of newly mown grass
2. Putting on a new white cotton t-shirt that fits
3. Robert Frost's poetry
4. Hot baths/showers
5. Sunny days
6. Being in a lighthouse in a storm (I've never done that)
7. Terminal 5
8. Grilled halloumi
9. Chilled freshly squeezed peach juice
10. Paintings by Van Gogh
11. Beautiful music
12. Camden Market on a Sunday in summer
13. The view of the caldera from Imerovigli
14. The SPC

That's as far as I got. I must admit, it did help a bit. There are many reasons why life is worth living, many reasons to stay alive, but lately I'd been struggling to appreciate them.

Karen encouraged me to think about the emotional stages of grief, to understand it as a "process" that I'd need to work through: shock or disbelief, denial, bargaining, guilt, anger, depression, and acceptance/hope. I think I understood these stages, apart from the bargaining one - who would I bargain with, and about what? I doubted I'd ever get to acceptance/hope.

I got back to England and moved into the house in Hampstead. That felt good actually. I had all my stuff moved in and still had loads of space. One day I had an online frenzy and spent over £20,000 on stuff for the house. I shopped at Heals and the Conran Shop and Harrods, and in all sorts of little independent shops for bits and pieces. I bought hundreds of books and piled them up everywhere.

Another day I went for a long walk on Hampstead Heath, popped into a pub for a couple of pints of frothing ale and a steak sandwich, visited Keats House and bought a calendar, and then got back to the house, lay on my gorgeously comfortable bed with its clean white sheets and pillow cases and duvet, and thought about stuff.

Felix jumped onto the bed. I forgot to mention, I'd bought two kittens. A few doors down I'd seen a sign saying, "Good home wanted for kittens" and I'd gone in. They were only a few weeks old, and were so cute.

'How much are they?' I had asked.

'Free. All we ask is that you give a donation to the RSPCA'.

I was going to take one, but thought about loneliness so took two. I named them Felix and Hermione, and Hermione now jumped onto the bed too.

I must have fallen asleep, as the next thing I remember was the kittens nibbling my toes to wake me up. I fed them, made myself an omelette, and watched a documentary on TV about lizards.

When I woke up the next morning I decided that I ought to do something, go somewhere, basically, get off my arse. So, I decided to go to a Zen temple in China. It seemed fitting, I thought it would help. I read the 'Tao Te Ching'.

I spent the next few weeks organising the trip and sorting out my domestic arrangements. Sally would look after Felix and Hermione. Mum would pop round the house occasionally to check all was well, and oversee the installation of the swimming pool and the sauna/jacuzzi complex adjacent to the tennis court behind the apple orchard. I lent Sam the Aston Martin.

I visited Peter at the SPC's offices in the Shard. We talked about my offer from Perth, which was open-ended. He also mentioned that because of the Scholarship I could enroll in the First Speaker programme - this would be a bit like "an MBA on steroids" and take three years. It would involve immersing myself in several SPC disciplines, becoming in his words "an all rounder, a generalist with multiple specialisms". I'd spend time in Barcelona, Tokyo, Los Angeles, New York, Oslo, and Montreal, and become acquainted with the SPC research centre at CERN in Geneva and our archives in the Vatican City.

'Did you know, SPC researchers invented the printing press, the internet, the washing machine, the semi colon, and soft toilet paper, amongst numerous others? You'll find all the details in the archives.' he told me.

'Soft toilet paper, wow. Now *that's* an invention.' He could see I was preoccupied.

'Want to talk about it?' he asked.

I did and I didn't. I kept seeing the man's eyes on the bus. 'I should have done something. All that training, I couldn't save ...' I put my head in my hands and cried quietly.

Peter put his hand on my shoulder. 'It wasn't your fault. You had no time.'

When I finished crying I wiped my face and explained that I was off to a Zen temple in China for a while 'to find myself.'

'I didn't know you were lost.' he said.

I told him I'd think about the First Speaker programme and the offer from Perth while I was away.

'Like I said, no rush. They're non-expiry date offers. Take as long as you need.'

The day before my flight I called my investigator again about Madame Gironde. Still no news.

'It's very puzzling', he told me.

Too damned right, I thought. 'Well, stick with it', I told him.

SEGMENT 8

Karen told me, there may be a "process", and psychologists and people like that may write about and perhaps even understand emotions such as grief, but we all deal with it differently and in different timescales. Some people move through the "process" towards acceptance smoothly and quickly. I was not one of those people. I was stuck right at the start. Almost, before the start. With the expression in that man's eyes on the bus. I recognised his intentions immediately, of course, but he was already in the act of detonation. I had no time to act. His eyes revealed anger, hatred, fear, and, since his death was now not only inevitable but imminent, a certain sense of relief, perhaps even liberation. I looked at the rainbow on my wrist, as I did each day, and saw her arm again. I was already forgetting her beautiful smile, and her beautiful frown, and regretted once again the lack of photographs we'd taken.

There was nothing to soften my pain. Sure, Aston Martins and big houses in Hampstead and Felix and Hermione and getting pissed with Sam and spending large amounts of money on things I didn't need and my list of things that make life worth living helped, but they were no substitute. I mean, it wasn't fair on them, was it, to be considered a possible substitute?

Karen had suggested I keep a diary, not so much of events and stuff but how I felt. So, each day I wrote some numbers in a little Star Wars notebook a friend had bought me: on the scale of 0 to 10, a) how happy I felt, on average, by the end of the day; b) how optimistic I felt; c) how many times I cried; d) how many times I thought about my own death. That doesn't mean I was thinking about suicide, just about being dead. And the thing is, I did think about it, rather a lot. So, a typical entry might have been 4,4,2,2.

When I first read 'Zen and the Art of Motorcycle Maintenance' - which was *de rigueur* (I think the term is) when I was about 17 - I wanted to move into a stone hut or observatory a friend of mine had in his garden. I wanted to cast off the burden of materialism and eschew the unnecessary symbols of our decadent lifestyles, and live in harmony with nature eating only fruit and nuts and berries and drinking only fresh coconut milk. Of course, I needed a Hi-Fi to play my Wings albums on. The idea was impractical and I abandoned it - not least because my friend's Dad didn't want me living in it - but the seed of the idea lay dormant within me.

I mention this because the Zen temple in China was the real deal, and although I was a little nervous about its isolation I was excited about the prospect of getting away from it all, just as I had been at 17, and not just because of Emily.

For starters, there was no electricity or gas or anything of that nature, and apparently, the closest place you could pick up a mobile signal was a 3-day trek by yak. So, I decided not even to take a mobile phone. In that era of social media and round the clock connectivity this act alone was a big move. I would be properly disconnected, off the grid. There was no television or radio, or any contact with the outside world. That was the whole point, I figured. There were no shops or anything like that, for over fifty miles, and no mode of transport other than yaks and small boats. Food was collected by the monks twice a week from a village which took a day to get there and back from. It wasn't even connected by road, indeed, there was no road. When I landed at the airport I'd be collected and taken by car to the nearest town, which would take five days and would involve sleeping in tents. From this town, I'd be taken by boat to the start of the local yak trail - a day and a half - we'd sleep on the boat, apparently, and then I'd complete the journey by yak and on foot, a further two days.

Given the travel arrangements, and what would or rather wouldn't be there when I arrived, I decided to travel very light. In my trendy purple leather satchel, which served as hand luggage, was my Passport, tickets and documentation, the complete works of Shakespeare, some tissues, Murray Mints, a toothbrush and toothpaste, and a notebook and pencil in case I wanted to write anything down. My checked luggage was a waterproof rucksack containing a solar powered toothbrush with much more toothpaste and plenty of dental floss, a couple of changes of clothes (all the time in the Temple I'd be dressed as a monk, apparently, so all I needed to take was enough clothes to get me there and back in relative comfort), the complete poems and letters of John Keats, 'Crime and Punishment' by Dostoyevsky, and my wash bag (razor, shaving gel, cotton buds, flannels, shampoo, shower gel, nail clippers and scissors).

Given the lack of electricity, or shops, I took a cheap wind-up Timex watch, which I intended to take off when I got there.

My flight wasn't until 7pm, so in the morning I had time to have my hair cut. Given the fact that I was going to a Zen temple in China, I decided to have it very short. Not quite shaved, but like new recruits to the US military you see in movies, with crew cuts. It grew on me, so to speak.

Once I was through security at the airport I realised that I fancied a damned good novel to read on the very long flight, and not yet Dostoyevsky which I had to be in the mood for. So, I bought 'The Count of Monte Cristo' and 'A Tale of Two Cities, and, for good measure, 'The Master and Margarita' (I cannot prosper without the Russians).

It could get very boring describing the journey so I'll just stick to the highlights and lowlights. I decided, on the flight, that until the moment I landed back in the UK I wouldn't drink any alcohol, so I ordered one last beer as a sort of sign-off. I watched 'The Accountant' (4th time), 'Inception' (also 4th time I think) and 'Toy Story' (lost count). I also decided to become vegan, again until I got back, so I signed off with a chicken curry.

About 6 hours into the flight it dawned on me that I had no phone, no way of contacting anyone or being contacted, and moreover that there was no-one special to communicate with anyway (by special I meant Emily - I'd promised to call Mum from a pay-phone when I landed, just to stop her worrying, and send her a postcard once a week, although I had no idea if the monks had access to any postal system). It felt liberating, and once again I thought of my 17-year-old self.

The five-day car journey was uneventful. I slept very well each night. My flossing regime suffered, and I got a few insect bites. Something else dawned on me - what language would the monks speak? Mandarin? I hadn't even thought about that, didn't have a language dictionary or anything.

I was finally dropped off in the town, so-called, which was simply a chaotic mass of ramshackle wooden structures, mostly on stilts on the river. There were plenty of people selling all sorts of food though, and a market where I picked up some fresh clothes - cotton overall sort of things - and a small wooden box which I thought might come in handy later, although I wasn't sure why I thought that. I really felt like I'd arrived now.

I stayed there one night, in a hammock over the water, and early next day my new guide collected me and we set off in her boat. I now realised why this part of the journey would take a day and a half, as there was no engine, she paddled all the way. She wouldn't let me help, so I just sat there and admired the scenery. I took my watch off and put it in the small wooden box, having vowed to wind it up every day (which I forgot to do).

When it began to get dark she pulled the boat over and moored it (is that the term, when you tie a boat up to stop it drifting away?) to a tree, pulled out a blanket, and beckoned me towards her. We then lay down together and she pulled the blanket over us both and wrapped her arms around me.

'Warm' I think she said, the only English word she'd spoken.

She then closed her eyes and went to sleep. I lay there for a while, listening to the sounds of the river and the insects and the unseen animals, and thought how strange this was. Lying in a boat somewhere in a remote part of China wrapped in the arms of a woman I'd never seen before that morning, on my way to a Zen temple.

I could hear by her breathing she was asleep, but sleep wouldn't come for me. Despite the blanket, I started to feel cold, so I pulled it closer and pulled her closer until our lips were almost touching. I lay like that for what seemed like ages, until at last, I gently pressed my lips against hers. It wasn't really a kiss, I don't know what it was, but I promptly fell asleep with our lips still touching.

When we woke up we kept our lips touching for a while, although it still wasn't a kiss (or was it?), before she disentangled herself from me, unmoored (I'll stick with that terminology) the boat, and began paddling again. I didn't offer to help. The river got increasingly narrow, with trees creating a canopy over it. Through the occasional gap, I could see mountains in the distance. There was a thin white mist. It was staggeringly beautiful.

I was so deep in thought I hardly noticed that the boat had stopped in a small clearing. The river seemed very shallow at this point, full of rocks, and meandered (is that what rivers do?) over to our left, while it looked as if we were going to be getting out at this point and heading uphill to our right.

My guide sat in the boat with her eyes closed, as if she was in some form of trance. I didn't know what to do. I thought to myself, "sitting quietly doing nothing" is a Zen thing, so maybe I should try it. I emptied my mind of everything, or tried to. Emily. Eligibility for the SPC. My house in Hampstead. Mum. Dad. Sally. England. What "The Specialist" had told me. The sound of the river. The distant mountains. It lasted for hours, or seemed to, before I saw two men approach, with a yak, from the path on our right.

They looked uncommonly like Jedi Knights - think Obi-Wan Kenobi in the first ever Star Wars movie - in their mid-brown cassocks, except for their footwear. Come to think of it, I thought, I never remember seeing what Obi-Wan wore on his feet.

Very little was said between them and my guide before they put my rucksack on the yak and beckoned me to follow them. Before I did so I turned one final time to my guide, and saw her looking at me. It was odd, just as if we'd shared the most intimate of times the night before. Somehow *more* intimate *because* we hadn't had sex, or even properly kissed. She gave me *exactly* the same kind of look that Frodo gave Sam, Merry and Pippin before he boarded the elven ship at the end of 'The Return of the King' - even down to the faintest hint of a nod - before turning away, climbing into her boat, and paddling away without looking back. I don't really know why but I wanted to cry.

The monks - that's who I assumed they were anyway - never said a word to me until we settled down to eat and sleep that night in a cave, so I still wasn't sure that I would understand anything they said. They unloaded some rice cake things from the yak, which we ate along with some berries. We drank water from a still pool at the back of the cave, and then all lay down to sleep.

We walked all the next day, climbing slowly but surely. I don't know how far we walked, but I guess it was about 10 or maybe 15 miles. That doesn't seem too far, but it wasn't really a path at all, it was steep in places, and the yak slowed us down.

That night we slept in a sort of tree house. We ate more of the rice cake things, and what looked to me like twigs. We drank the tree sap from the palms of our hands. As I lay down to sleep in a sort of hammock made from branches and leaves, I reflected that Hampstead was quite another world.

The next morning, we set off just before dawn, and saw the most amazing sunrise. I was reminded of a poster I'd had on my wall when I was young, which I hadn't thought about in years. It read "Each Dawn Is A New Beginning". That day's walk was much steeper. Quite often we were scrambling up rocks and scree on all fours. Twice I slipped and nearly fell.

Eventually we turned a corner and I saw the temple in the distance. It immediately and very powerfully felt like a home, and I was reminded of the Robert Frost line "Home is the place where, when you have to go there, they have to take you in." I love that line.

It still took about another hour to reach it, the terrain was so difficult, but at last there came a moment when we stepped onto a grid of flat stones. We had arrived. Another monk came to greet us, and nodded but didn't say anything. Perhaps they didn't speak, I wondered. Perhaps they couldn't speak, or had taken a vow of silence between themselves or something.

My two companions left me, and the monk who had greeted us led me along several corridors, up and down flights of stairs, and through various courtyards, all made of stone, until we reached a doorway. He motioned for me to enter. It was a small room – which I came to call my cell - and was where I slept and passed much of my time during my stay. There was a window overlooking the valley. There was no door in the doorway. On the floor was a very thin futon with a blanket, and a wicker mat. There was also a small table which was quite low down - I kneeled on the floor when I wanted to use it. On the table was one of the brown cassocks.

The monk beckoned me to put my rucksack and satchel down, pick up my cassock, and follow him. He showed me where the toilets and sinks were, and then a scented room with steaming water rising from baths. I gathered from him that he wanted me to climb into one of the baths. I guess most of us have enjoyed the sensation of climbing into a hot bath at the end of the day, perhaps after a long walk or when it's cold outside. After all the days of travelling, this was the most exquisite sensation I could possibly have imagined. The water was exactly the right temperature, and although I stayed in there for quite a while it never got any colder. There was no obvious sign of what technology they were using to achieve this. When I got out I was completely refreshed. Hot towels were piled up in a corner - again I had no idea how they were kept hot - and the texture was perfectly rough, like the tongue of a kitten. Momentarily I thought of Felix and Hermione, and wondered if they were missing me.

Once dry I put on the cassock and was led back to my room to drop off my travelling clothes, before being led in the opposite direction until we reached the dining hall. There were rows and rows of stone tables with monks eating and drinking quietly. No-one was talking, not a word. There was an overwhelming sense of the purest serenity.

I was shown to a sort of self-service area where there were all manner of delicacies to eat and drink, and I was encouraged to help myself. I didn't know what most of them were, so I just piled various things into my bowl, poured some yellow liquid from a jug into a glass, and I nodded back and began to eat.

When I finished, I did what I'd seen the other monks do, and washed up my bowl and cutlery and jug in some sinks along the side of the hall, before having a wander alone to explore my new home. I didn't see a door in any doorway, obviously they weren't bothered about privacy.

After a while I felt tired, and after a few wrong turns managed to find my cell, where I lay down on my mattress to rest. Just as I closed my eyes I heard a voice.

'Sleep now. Tomorrow ... it begins.'

SEGMENT 13

I won't tell you everything about my time there. Not because of a *Catcher in the Rye* type of unwillingness (pretty soon after I arrived I wished I'd taken my most re-read book along) but because:

1. I was there very much longer (11 months 9 days) than planned (3 months max) and there'd simply be too much information …
2. … much of which would be boring for the reader (of course, no-one may ever read this - that's not why I'm writing it - but that's not the point). Descriptions of days spent "sitting quietly doing nothing" don't (I imagine) make interesting reading - even if the writer is as good as Dostoyevsky, which I'm not. (Neither am I aiming to be, but that's also not the point).
3. Some of it no-one would believe. I'm going to include some stuff that no-one will believe anyway, but not all of it. Everything I've included in this text is factual. Not, for the avoidance of ambiguity, "based on fact", but factual. As it actually happened. As I remember it.
4. Although confidentiality, as such, was never discussed, or even implied - indeed the very word (with its legal connotations) seems wholly incongruent even to mention in the context of the temple and what goes on there - I felt, and still feel, an extraordinary sense of - what's the right word? *obligation* to keep some things secret. I'm not coming at this from a reluctance to reveal secrets, or even from a "let's not cut up a flower to see how it works, let's just admire it growing in a meadow" (like my 17 year old self would have said), but rather a feeling that somehow the "magic" of the place would be diminished. I can't really explain what I mean. I don't even fully understand it myself.

So, the first thing I'm going to say - and this is one of those things you probably won't believe - is how we communicated. I mentioned that as I lay down on my first night I heard a voice. I did, too. But there was no-one there. At first, of course, I thought there was. I thought another monk was standing in my doorway (remember there weren't any doors). But I looked, and there wasn't. At the time, I was too tired to think about it, anyway, and went to sleep. But the following morning shortly after waking up (remember that I'd taken my watch off, so for the entirety of my stay I had no idea of the time. Rather, I came to see that "the time" as we usually see it, i.e. half past ten or whatever, was not exactly irrelevant or unhelpful, but simply *unnecessary* - at least in a place like that. We went to bed when we were tired, woke up when we were refreshed, ate and drank when we were hungry and thirsty, washed when we felt dirty, bathed when we wanted to, and so on). Anyway, I'd woken up, and could hear birds twittering outside my window, and I was lying there looking forward to my adventure and wondering what was in store for me when I heard the voice again.

'Good morning. When ready, please meet me beneath the white tree.'

I looked around. There was no-one there. I thought to myself, understandably, who was talking and where were they, and where was the white tree? And as if I had spoken aloud and as if someone had heard me I heard the voice again.

'I am one of your tutors. I am presently in the garden gathering berries. You will find the white tree in the third courtyard you saw yesterday.' And then, in answer to a question I hadn't even formulated yet, 'This is the way we can communicate, if we want to. Mind to mind. Spoken languages can be inadequate and clumsy, and can hide the true and intended meaning.'

I do want to say a few words about this. First off, it removed my concern about the potential language barrier. Second, I wouldn't describe it as telepathy, as such: it was as if thoughts were transferred even before they were words. Third, over time I learnt to control it much better than I did at first, and ensure that my thoughts went directly to the right monk(s), instead of to whoever happened to be in the vicinity. Fourth, it only worked in the temple and the grounds and buildings, which were extensive and covered several acres. Fifth - it's true. This is how we communicated. So henceforth if I write "I said" or "he asked" I'm just writing that to make "conversations" more readily accessible to you the reader: if I wrote something like *we cannot solve our problems in the same state of consciousness in which we created them* he transferred directly into my brain, you'll understand where I'm coming from.

'When would you like to meet?' I "said".

'When you are ready, and not before. Sleep more, rest, bathe, eat, reflect, if you wish. I will be ready when you are ready, and not before.' And before I thought of a response he "said" (I'll stop using those quotation marks now) 'There is no waiting. Waiting implies impatience. I am as the branch of the tree in the wind.'

When we met later he asked me why I was here, and I said to get over Emily.

'So you want to forget her?' he asked.

'No, I want to get over her death.'

'Death is a part of the cycle of life', he said.

'Ok, to get over her untimely death', I said.

He didn't say anything, in an "inviting further information" way.

'To get over her untimely, unnecessary and violent death', I said.

'What is that on your wrist?' he asked me.

'A rainbow. It was hers.'

'Walk with me.' he said.

We walked through the gardens. One of the monks walked up to me and gave me a seed to plant. I found a nice little spot and scooped some earth out with my hands and planted it.

'What sort of seed is it?' I asked.

'It is whatever sort of seed you want it to be' he told me.

'Should I water it?' I asked. It was a glorious sunny day.

The light changed, and huge and wonderful drops of rain began to fall. Within seconds there was a downpour. I took off my cassock and stood there naked, arms outstretched, feeling the rain run down my back. It was as far beyond exhilarating as a star is beyond a candle.

When the rain stopped, there was a fabulous rainbow, the biggest and most clear I had ever seen.

'There is no need for you to water your seed now' he told me.

That day I learned why I was there; how to enjoy rain properly (and appreciate it for the gift that it is); that plants don't always need to be watered; that you can reach the end of some rainbows (we did, as a matter of fact, and ate some fruit); and how to control the weather.

Over the following months, I spent time in the kitchen, and learned how to make delicious and healthy food from the simplest of ingredients. Gorgeous feasts solely from leaves and nuts. Wonderful drinks from rain water, tree sap, and yak's milk. I learned what the earth had to offer, which we regularly ignore. Basically, I learned how to prepare and enjoy food properly (and appreciate it for the gift that *it* is).

I spent time in the gardens, and watched my seed grow. I would sit by it for hours, doing nothing, embracing new life and smiling as its little leaves grew.

Some afternoons I would make new rainbows, and would sit at one end of one and read or sing or just look at the colours. Sometimes other monks would join me. Sometimes a yak would wander over.

I spoke to my tutors about Emily. A lot. And the SPC, somewhat less. And about what "The Specialist" told me, just the once.

I learned about true acceptance. I learned to be content "in whatsoever state I am". I learned to make music from the air, and from the wind.

One week I spent all my waking hours in a field of white flowers looking at clouds. I learned patience.

Once I went all the way back to the town with some other monks to collect fruit and some other things. I hoped our guide would be the woman I'd slept with on the boat on my original journey, but it wasn't.

And while thinking of sleeping with people, I hadn't had sex in months, but what's interesting is that I hadn't even thought about it. Hadn't masturbated or anything. I wondered if I'd become impotent, unable to get an erection. So that night I touched myself, and all seemed fine, except I didn't want to finish it off. In that place it just felt, I don't know, not wrong (like swearing in a church) but *inappropriate* (like doing it in your sister's bedroom or something). That's not quite the right word either, but it'll do. After all those months of communicating without using words perhaps my vocabulary had/has diminished.

You won't believe me so I won't go into any detail on these next points at all, but the monks also taught me alchemy, how to communicate with animals, how to alter the air around myself to appear invisible, and best of all how to fly. Without being told though I knew that I should use these skills sparingly.

I've just re-read this section. I don't want it to be a sort of 'The Piper At The Gates Of Dawn' section (different from all the other chapters of 'The Wind in the Willows') all mysterious and therefore considered otherworldly and possibly ignored. Not that I'm writing a novel, as previously mentioned, this is more of a diary - a sequence of reminiscences in chronological order.

One day I woke up and knew that my time there was done, and it was time to return home. In addition to controlling the weather, and learning how to enjoy rain (in fact, how to enjoy everything), and how to cook, and how to make beautiful music, and true acceptance, and patience, my little seed had grown into a little plant about a foot high. I gently touched its leaves with my fingers and it quivered as if it knew I was leaving. I mentioned this to one of my tutors, who said 'the sun shines and the trees grow' and that satisfied me.

Home. How that word, that *concept* resonated with me. I was reminded of the lines from 'Ode to a Nightingale':

"the very word is like a bell
To toll me back from thee to my sole self!"

(Ok, he wasn't talking about home but it's my text and this isn't a novel, or indeed a poem). I'd been in the temple for so long, and had learned so much, that I wasn't sure that I'd ever feel the same about home again. Hampstead, the Aston Martin, Mum, Dad, Sally, the London Underground, Harrods, Lords, traffic, noise, the sound of people talking, dentists, coffee, half past ten, politics, the Eiffel Tower, all seemed impossible, even unfeasible. Emily. Our child she was carrying. The SPC. Eligibility for the SPC.

On my last day, I sat under the white tree and talked to one of my tutors for the final time. He didn't ask me anything, he just listened as I talked about making rainbows. I couldn't think of anything else to talk about, I was very emotional.

He looked at the rainbow on my wrist and said, 'Existence and non-existence give birth one to the other; difficulty and ease produce the idea of the other; tall and short arise from the contrast of one with the other; musical notes become harmonious through the relation of one with another; being before and behind give the idea of one following another.'

They say that time heals. I'm not sure that's how it works. Time, or the passage of time, simply helps you forget: diminishes the *intensity*, but the pain remains. Thinking of time, when I went back to my cell I put my watch back on. It had stopped, and it felt odd. Even odder was taking off my cassock and putting on boxers and jeans and a t-shirt and packing up my rucksack and satchel. It would still be several days before I got to the airport, but already I felt different.

Two monks were going to escort me to the boat, although by now I knew the way. There was no grand farewell, or even a goodbye, there was just a nod. One thing though - just as I set off down the path one of my tutors handed me a piece of cloth with something tied up in it, and asked me not to open it until I'd spoken to Madame Gironde.

'My God', I whispered to myself, I hadn't thought about her in months and hadn't mentioned her to any of the monks. I thanked him and put it in my rucksack, took one last look, and was on my way.

SEGMENT 21

I don't know about anyone else, but I always find that when I return from a holiday it becomes a distant memory far too quickly. The day after I get back - historically, anyway - I'm still in a sort of post-holiday mode. Unpacking. Finding things in my suitcase I'd forgotten I'd bought. Doing the washing. Waiting for the Ocado food delivery, stuff like that. The day after that is what I used to call "Schrödinger Day" - after his cat - I'm half on holiday and half at work, (represented mathematically, both on holiday and *not* on holiday simultaneously). From the following day, it was if I was never on holiday at all.

So much for short holidays. After nearly a year away it was different this time. For starters, it hadn't been a holiday, of course. It had been what I'd come to call a "learning adventure". Although there's no way that does it justice. And thinking of learning, much of what I'd learned I seemed to have forgotten already. Not all of it, just the unimportant stuff like learning to fly and talking to animals.

Anyway, I'd been back almost a month and I still didn't really feel "connected". I'd called Mum and Dad. And Sally. And Sam. And Peter. But not seen any of them yet. I couldn't be bothered to collect the Aston Martin for the time being, not least because driving around London was a fucking nightmare.

Thinking of fucking - here's the thing - I wasn't thinking about it at all. I hadn't had sex in over a year. And here's another thing. Drinking. I hadn't had an alcoholic drink in about the same timeframe. And I wasn't sure I wanted to do either. I lay on my bed, with Felix and Hermione curled up next to me, wondering what to do next.

Luckily for me, I didn't have any money worries, so no spreadsheets or wanky micro-managers or targets or shit like that (sorry, must stop swearing!) which did get me thinking about the concept of "luck". "The harder I practise, the luckier I get" or so the saying goes. I hadn't needed to practise at all to get into the SPC, but I suppose I had practised hard in Perth and in Israel to perfect my recognition skills. There we go, Israel again - don't go there. Re-focus.

But was I lucky, truly? I guess it's all relative. I'm lucky compared to many. Unlucky compared to many. Lucky to be in the SPC? Unlucky to be eligible.

It was still only 8 o'clock in the evening. I decided to go to a pub, on my own, and have a couple of pints. Just to see what it was like, to see if I could do it again.

It was a beautiful summer evening. Warm, and the light was just so perfect. I hummed the drinking song from Verdi's 'La Traviata' to myself as I walked up the hill towards Hampstead Underground Station. I still hadn't got used to not wearing a cassock. I arrived in the pub, ordered a pint, and sat in a window seat and watched the world go by, inside and outside. Everyone I saw was with someone, talking and laughing, apart from one old woman I could see struggling up the hill pushing a shopping trolley bag thing. She looked poor. It made me well up.

I wondered if anyone was glancing at me, like I was glancing at them. Wondering who I was, why I was on my own, thinking I was attractive, or unattractive, or simply neutral and/or uninteresting.

I looked outside again but the old woman had vanished. The door of the pub opened and in skipped some ladies dressed in fairy costumes who handed out leaflets about a magical circus that was coming to the Heath next week. "NO ANIMALS" the leaflet boasted proudly but "Russian acrobats" and "Indonesian Fire Eaters" and "Bolivian Sword Masters" and "The One and Only *Madame Gironde*".

'Hello.' A man's voice said. 'Mind if I take this seat? The place is pretty full.'

'Not at all.' I said, and moved my chair slightly to accommodate him. One look and I knew he was eligible.

'My name's Tom.' he said, and shook my hand. The handshake. So, he was a member. 'As soon as I saw you I knew.' he said.

'You had me at "Hello"', I smiled. And then immediately worried that he might think I was gay. It was simply that this particular experience had never happened to me before. I'd recognised and even recruited people, but apart from that first time in the pub no-one had ever recognised *me*, or if they had they'd never said anything. We got chatting.

He was a professional musician, a violinist. A good one too, by all accounts, since he was in the London Symphony Orchestra. He asked me what I did.

'Resting' I said. 'No, seriously, between jobs. I resigned my job to go to Perth for recognition training ...'

'You've been to Perth?' he interrupted. 'Christ, you must be good.'

'And the West Bank.' I continued. 'I'm not sure "good" is quite the right word. I seem to have an aptitude for it, but the way I see it, no pun intended, is that I have an ability to spot certain colours. That's the way I usually describe it. Colours that others can't see. So, it's not really a talent, as such, it's just the way my eyes are wired to my brain. Just like an athlete with fast twitch muscles, or something, is going to have a physiological advantage when it comes to, say, track cycling.'

'You still have to work at it though. Not everyone with fast twitch muscles is going to win an Olympic Gold.'

We laughed, and he bought me a second pint. Half way through it I confessed I was starting to feel a little tipsy. 'This is the first time I've had a drink in nearly a year.' I told him.

'Any particular reason?'

'Yes,' I paused, 'But I don't want to talk about it now. Another time, maybe, but not now.'

I'd got so used to not having my phone on me that I didn't have it on me, which was unhelpful at the end of our conversation when we agreed to meet up again sometime. I remembered my number, though, so he forwarded me his details from his phone and to be on the safe side wrote his number on the leaflet that the ladies dressed as fairies had given me. If he hadn't done that, being as I was a bit tipsy, I might have forgotten all about Madame Gironde.

We left together but headed in different directions. I walked down the hill and he walked towards West Hampstead. It was still a beautiful evening. Cooler, but still warm. A perfect temperature. It wasn't quite dark yet, it was that delicious twilight time I love so much. I sat on a bench for a few minutes just to enjoy the moment. Some very drunk people stumbled towards me from another pub, and one of them fell over while another was sick. Two girls with them just laughed, and then kissed one another full on the lips.

I walked home slowly. When I got to Keats House I stood outside the gate looking at the House and recited one of his sonnets to myself:

> "Had I a man's fair form, then might my sighs
> Be echoed swiftly through that ivory shell
> Thine ear, and find thy gentle heart; so well
> Would passion arm me for the enterprize:
> But ah! I am no knight whose foeman dies;
> No cuirass glistens on my bosom's swell;
> I am no happy shepherd of the dell
> Whose lips have trembled with a maiden's eyes.
> Yet must I dote on thee,–call thee sweet,
> Sweeter by far than Hybla's honied roses
> When steep'd in dew rich to intoxication.
> Ah! I will taste that dew, for me 'tis meet,
> And when the moon her pallid face disclose,
> I'll gather some by spells, and incantation."

When I got home I went straight to sleep and dreamt about bombs.

I was quite busy for the next few days, by my standards anyway. First off, I decided to enroll into the First Speaker Programme. I called Peter to tell him - he thought it was the right decision - and (given the time difference) emailed the guys in Perth to tell them. Within an hour, I was sent an email from SPC's global head office (in Geneva) containing masses of information about the programme, including timescales. It would begin with a week-long "familiarisation workshop" in Barcelona, dates to be confirmed. I would also be assigned a remote mentor, details to follow.

I also visited my dentist. I hadn't been for over a year, and was a bit worried about what the hygienist would say, but I was delighted that she was so delighted with the state of my mouth.

'Don't you eat anything?' she asked me.

'I've been in a Zen temple in China for almost a year,' I said, 'eating only fruit and vegetables and the occasional leaf.'

She laughed and said it was good for oral hygiene, and would recommend it for all her customers. I liked it that she described them as customers and not as patients. I also liked the hygienist, whose name was Alice, and when I say, *I liked* I mean *I was attracted to*. I hadn't even thought about anyone else since Emily, and although I felt a bit guilty it did at least reassure me that I was still capable of desire.

When I got home I masturbated, partly to prove I still could but mainly because I wanted to. I thought about Alice. I'm pleased to say it worked out fine.

Being obsessed with oral hygiene, and mindful that I was now re-entering a world of shit food where everything is crammed full of sugar, I bought a fancy new "Intelligent Toothbrush System". My "ITS" was apparently capable of "learning" about my teeth and brushing/flossing regime, and therefore "maximising the HTI to propel the cleaning paradigm towards oral perfection." (I had to look up HTI in the 240-page user manual: it stood for Human Toothbrush Interface). Thinking about oral perfection also got me thinking about Alice and her snow-white teeth behind those slightly moist cherry red lips. One downside to my ITS though was that it was so high level I had to login to it before I could brush my teeth, and ever since I'd decided not to accept cookies it wasn't working properly.

I'd called Tom, and we'd arranged to meet up in Soho, grab a bite to eat, and then a couple of drinks. We ate in a really nice pizza place called "Princi" on Wardour Street, popped over the road afterwards for a swift rum in a place called "The Den", and then made our way to a pub called "The Admiral Duncan" on Old Compton Street.

We were on our second pint when I realised it was a gay pub. I'm not very good at noticing things like that, which is ironic given my training. Tom smiled and said he liked the vibe. I agreed it was nice.

I scanned the place for SPC eligibility, but didn't spot anyone. Just then though, a guy walked in who definitely didn't look as if he fitted in. He backed himself into a recess in the wall so he wasn't very noticeable, and I saw him drop a hold-all onto the floor and push it under a stool with his feet. We momentarily made eye contact and that was enough. I'd seen that look before.

I had to act quickly. I whispered to Tom to do exactly as I said, which was to walk with me immediately towards the guy as if we were leaving the pub and then grab both of the guy's arms to restrain him. We had no time to lose.

'Really?' Tom said.

I nodded. 'Now!'

We walked over and then grabbed the guy's arms and pressed him up against the wall. He struggled like a bastard and called us gay wankers.

'See that bag?' I shouted to someone else in the pub. 'Throw it outside, now, as far away from anyone as you can, and get the police in here. Do it NOW.'

The guy carried on struggling and someone else helped us restrain him. The bag was thrown outside, down a quiet alley I was told, and a 999 call was made. Two more guys piled in to help me and Tom, and the four of us managed to pin him down.

'What the fuck's going on?' the landlord shouted. I was almost out of breath.

'This guy brought a bomb in. He was going to detonate it.'

The police arrived quickly, arrested the guy, took him away in handcuffs, and then one of the officers spoke to me.

'Where's the bag?' he asked me. I told the guy who'd thrown it down the alley to show him where it was, and then sat down on the floor, exhausted.

About five minutes later I heard sirens, and a voice over a loudspeaker telling everyone outside to move away from the area. The police officer came back inside and over to me.

'You ok?' he asked. I nodded.

'The guy was carrying a nail bomb.' he said. 'Would have been carnage.' He paused. 'How did you know?'

'I've had military training. On the West Bank.' I said.

'We'll need a statement.'

'Sure'. I nodded.

Someone in army fatigues came in. 'Bomb diffused. It's safe.'

The landlord said that drinks were on the house all night, and said to me I'd never need to buy a drink in there again. I smiled.

'Thanks, but I was only doing my job.' I don't know why I said that.

'So, what is your job?'

'I'm not at liberty to discuss it with civilians,' I said. 'I'll have another pint though. And one for my mate Tom.'

We were kept in there for ages, making statements and stuff, and when we finally got outside there were TV cameras and reporters all over the place. Apparently, the incident had made national news. I'm not sure how coherent I was, being as I'd drunk three bottles of Peroni in "Princi", two large rums in "The Den", and (by this time) four pints in the pub, but according to my Mum who saw me interviewed on TV I made her so proud that she cried.

The next day I was woken up by someone ringing the doorbell before 9 o'clock. I had a stinking headache. I went downstairs in my dressing gown and opened the door. Two guys were there, who showed me their badges. One was from the Metropolitan Police Counter Terrorism Unit and the other from MI5.

'Mind if we come in?' they asked.

'Not at all. I'll get the kettle on.' Felix and Hermione were rubbing up against my feet while I was sorting out the drinks.

'Nice place you have here.' the MI5 guy said.

'Yes, thank you.' I said, and dropped the milk carton. 'Shit! That's all the milk I have.'

The cats were already lapping it off the floor.

'No worries', they told me, 'we'll take it black'.

We relocated to the sitting room. I sat on one sofa and they both sat on another opposite me.

'You did a good thing last night. Your swift action undoubtedly saved lives and prevented serious injuries. We'd like to know how you did it.'

'I explained all this last night,' I said, 'I've had specialist training. By the Israeli military.'

'Yes. You said that. The thing is, what sort of training, and why, and from who? We've checked your file. You're not and have never been in the armed forces or police. And there's no record of you being trained by the Israeli army, we checked that too. And you don't have a job. And you have over £100,000 in the bank. And you live in a place that must be worth well over a million quid. So, it's no surprise that we're a little curious.'

I took a long sip of my coffee, thinking to myself 'You did all that since last night?, and stroked Felix who'd jumped up onto the sofa next to me. 'Curious is fine. Curiosity is a *good* thing. Although it killed the cat!' I tickled Felix under the chin and he purred. 'But you're asking me personal questions that have nothing to do with last night's events, and are giving me the impression that I've done something wrong.'

'Like we said, we just want to know how you did it.'

'And like I said, I've had training. Or if you prefer I got lucky. I saw a stressed-out guy come into the pub who kicked a bag under someone else's stool. Anyone would have seen he was up to no good. I was just the only person to see him. Is that better?'

They looked at one another and got up to go. 'Tell me. Are you patriotic?' the MI5 guy asked.

'To the country as an entity, very much so. To our current government, not a bit. They are, if you excuse the expression, a bunch of fucking bastards.'

As they left they turned around. 'Thanks for your time. We'll be back.'

'Just make sure it's not before 9 o'clock' I said.

It was time to visit the magical circus and find Madame Gironde. I wandered over to the Heath and followed the signs. I found the Russian acrobats and the Indonesian Fire Eaters and the Bolivian Sword Masters but not "The One and Only Madame Gironde". I looked everywhere, and was just about to give up when I saw her little tent beneath a large oak tree. There was no queue, so I walked straight in.

'I've been expecting you.' she said.

'You're a hard woman to find.' I said.

'People find me when they're ready, and not before.'

I looked at her, unsure now what to say.

'I know what you're thinking', she said. 'How did I know?'

'Something along those lines.'

'I did warn you.'

'I know. But, but ...' I ran out of words.

'I have something for you. Here.' She reached down and handed me a small box. 'I think you have the key?'

'What's in it?' I asked.

She just looked at me.

'I'll be back later.' I said. I ran back home, it took about half an hour. I'm quite a fast runner. I knew exactly where the piece of cloth was that the monk had given me. I unwrapped it and sure enough there was a key that fitted the lock on the box. I opened it ... and almost staggered back in shock. It can't be. It's not possible! I dropped the box on the floor and ran back.

This time it only took twenty minutes. I was out of breath when I reached the oak tree. I rested my arms on my legs for about thirty seconds just to get my breath back. Then I walked towards her tent ... which was gone. Instead there was a Punch and Judy show with children laughing and clapping. I asked one of the parents watching in the background what had happened to Madame Gironde's tent, as I'd been here less than an hour ago.

'Don't know what you mean,' she said, 'We walked right past here an hour or so ago to check the time of the next show. There was no Madame Gironde. You must be mistaken love.'

I sank to my knees.

'Are you alright?' she asked me.

SEGMENT 34

I love Hampstead Heath. It strikes me as incredible that this much open countryside (nearly 800 acres, according to the internet) is in London, and even more incredible that Tory Councils haven't built on it or opened it up for fracking. It's full of lovely walks, and woods, and meadows, and has fantastic views over London. If you didn't know where you were, and didn't look over London, you would think you were somewhere in the country.

I've always loved walking there, long before I moved to the area, although now it's almost on my doorstep it's obviously a lot easier; being so accessible it still hasn't lost any of its charm for me.

My favourite time to walk there is late afternoon or early evening. To be there at twilight is magical, and I half expect to see spirits and sprites and fairies. (Note to self: add Spenser's 'The Faerie Queene' to my reading list).

At night, though, one hears of mysterious creatures and foul deeds. Witches. "Malicious, powerful, cunning demons" (Note to self: dig out my copy of 'Meditation I' by Descartes. Did I lend it to Sally?) Covens. Pentangles. Devil worship. Beheadings. Human sacrifices. That sort of thing. I avoid the place when it's dark. So you can imagine my dismay when I woke up in a little copse not far from where Madame Gironde's tent had, or, arguably, hadn't, been. I had no recollection of falling over or anything. The last thing I remember (Note to self: 'Hotel California' by the Eagles) was being told that Madame Gironde had never been there, even though I'd seen her there less than an hour before. Which brought back to me what was in the box that she gave me. I shuddered.

I got up and checked that my limbs were all there, and hadn't been cut off while I was asleep and fed to vampires or Tory Councillors (resentful that they hadn't made money from building on the Heath). Everything seemed intact. There was nothing for it but to walk home, en route pulling bits of twig and the odd leaf and thorn out of my hair and off my clothes. Just as I arrived at my front gate I noticed a tiny bright green caterpillar crawling up my arm. I very gently put it on a bush and went inside.

Having slept rough - if indeed it was sleep and not some enchantment (time will tell I suppose) I was desperate for a nice hot bubbly bath, accompanied as (almost) always by a plate of grilled halloumi, a pot of hummus, at least two satsuma oranges, some pretzels, and (historically) a large cold beer. I'd just climbed in and was thinking how nice it was when the doorbell sounded.

Shit! Bad timing, or what? Who the Hell could that be? Not MI5 again, surely? I got out of the bath, put on my Spider-Man dressing gown, went downstairs and opened the door. It wasn't MI5.

'Good morning. SPC Logistics, here to install your enhanced Comms package' one of two guys said more cheerfully than the time of day warranted. 'Hope you got the email.'

Bugger. I had, too, but I'd forgotten all about it. Something to do with the First Speaker thing, the home install of some kind of super advanced AI platform.

'Er, yes, come on in.' I said. 'How long will this take, exactly?'

'Should finish this afternoon' he said, 'Just depends on the Learning Protocols.'

'I see, well, I'll go and get dressed and ...'

'No need for that, boss. It's fully automated. We're just here to bring the equipment in and point things in the right direction. Go back to bed if you like.'

'Actually, I was in the bath.'

'Even better. You jump back in and we'll let you know if we need you.'

'Would you like a tea or coffee?' I asked.

'Brought our own, boss' he said. 'Don't like to impose, do we, eh?'

His colleague nodded.

So I jumped back in the bath and let them get on with it, although I wasn't exactly sure what "it" was. Nonetheless I had a very pleasant bath, for about an hour, got dressed, and went downstairs. The man who hadn't spoken was typing something into a tablet of some description. The man who had, was sitting at a stool in the kitchen drinking out of a thermos flask.

'How's it going?' I asked.

'Brilliantly.' he said. 'Like a dream. It's all plugged in and connected. Now it's learning. We're just doing some configuration work. Should be done in less than an hour.'

I looked around. Couldn't see anything, no wiring, nothing. 'What have you done, exactly?' 'I asked.

'Didn't you read the email, boss? State of the art stuff you have here. And you have the new AI chipset, the one the Chinese were working on. Didn't realise it was released yet. You're a lucky fella, if you don't mind me saying so.'

I hadn't read the email, or rather, I'd skim read it but not followed the links. I'd meant to do that before they came, of course.

'So, um, just remind me of the main features would you please?' I asked.

He took another sip of his drink before answering. 'Completely Localised Integrated Telecommunication Office and Residential Intelligence System, CLITORIS, for short.' (So Emily had been right all along, they *do* exist!). 'Links into everything. Knows pretty much everything, everything that's known, anyway. And learns exponentially. All you need to do, when we've finished configuring, is speak to it to activate its voice recognition systems, and you're good to go.'

'When you say links to everything ...' I began.

'That's right. The internet. Spotify. Netflix. Amazon. YouTube. Minecraft. Every movie or TV programme ever made, every piece of music ever recorded. Every known recorded fact. All your household appliances and systems. You'll see. How are we doing?' he looked across at his colleague who was still typing away.

'Almost ready' came the reply in a very thick eastern European accent.

'When you say household appliances ...'

'That's right boss. Central Heating. Fridge. Cooker. Lights. Alarm. TV. You name it.'

'But there's no wiring. How can it ...'

'Listen boss. This is state of the art, like I said, and I mean *state of the art*. Nanotechnology. Off-spectrum wireless. Quantum processing. Not your typical Apple shit.'

Cue a large DONG sound.

'Excellent,' said my man. 'We're ready. When I give you the signal say "Cheese" and the system will incorporate all of your voice patterns.'

'Is that all I need to say?'

'Sure is. Wait a sec.' He looked across at his colleague who after a few moments nodded, and then motioned me to speak.

'Cheese.' I said.

There was a slight pause, and then a very slow sexy voice said 'Hello xxxxx. I'm ready now and waiting. Your wish is my command.'

She sounded exactly like the computer in the movie 'Dark Star'.

'She sounds exactly like the computer in the movie 'Dark Star' - how is that possible?' I said.

'Isn't that what you wanted?' said my man, frowning.

'Yes, but, how did it know?'

'I told you. State of the art technology. There's a lot of information coded into the word "cheese" you know. All you need to do now is select your android. You can do that any time.'

'Android?'

'Sure. I mean, CLITORIS can do an awful lot, but it can't open cupboards and turn taps and pour drinks and open doors and put hot towels on radiators and stuff, obviously. That's why you can have a robot, if you like. It'll be completely synchronized with your home system.'

I thought about this for a second. How clever *were* these guys? 'What kind of robot can I have? What form does it take?'

'Any form you like, boss. Male, female, neutral, or, er, a pleasure model. Bloke in Golders Green opted for a Thai Lady Boy with a twelve inch shlong.'

'You mean ...'

'That's right boss. You name it. It arrives in a few days. You can order it online.'

A few minutes later they were gone, after I'd signed to say that the installation was complete. I added "untested" after my signature. I sat down and thought about things.

'Anything I can do for you?' she asked. God, she sounded sexy.

'The thing is, I'm not sure what you *can* do.'

'Try me.'

Oh God, how I realised I wanted to.

'Ok. I'm really tired. I didn't get much sleep. Can you alarm the house, and wake me up if I'm not already awake at 3 o'clock by playing me 'Hotel California'?

'Sure. The album or a live version?'

I crawled into bed with all my clothes on. I liked doing that when I wanted to be all warm and cosy and sleep well. Just before I closed my eyes I asked her 'What do I call you? Clitoris seems a little, er, formal.'

'Anything you like honey.'

'Ok I'll think about it and let you know.'

'Sweet dreams' she said as I closed my eyes.

"On a dark desert highway, cool wind in my hair
Warm smell of colitas, rising up through the air
Up ahead in the distance, I saw a shimmering light
My head grew heavy and my sight grew dim
I had to stop for the night"

I opened my eyes. 'It's just gone 3 o'clock honey' said a voice. 'You took a short while to wake up. You don't mind me calling you "honey" do you?'

'Not at all. What would you like me to call you?'

'You asked me that before. I honestly don't mind. Do you want me to give you some suggestions?'

'Yes please.'

'Ok. I know you like the name Hermione, but that's the name of one of your cats. How about Helen?'

'Helen. Yes, perfect.' I thought of Helen of Troy, and also the two Helens I'd had sex with, years ago (not together, I hasten to add). Happy memories.

'Ok. Helen I am. Now you're awake, is there anything I can do? Read out your new emails? Tell you the cricket score? Play you some music?'

I rolled over and thought about this. 'Would you play me 'Carmen' quietly please?'

'Of course. Would you like the version in your iTunes library or another?'

'That version's fine, thank you.' It started playing.

'While I'm looking at your iTunes library, incidentally, I notice a lot of duplicates and incorrect and inconsistent genres. Would you like me to tidy it up for you? Don't worry I won't mess anything up.'

'Yes please.' I rolled over the other way. I was still sleepy.

'You've had a text from Tom. I can read it out if you like, but I can see you're tired. You'll have to teach me what's important another time.'

'Yes please read it out.'

'All it says is:

STILL ON FOR TOMORROW AND FOR ME TO STAY OVER? WHAT SHALL I BRING?

… would you like me to reply?'

'Can you reply with "Yes and yes and beer!" followed by a smiley face please?'

'It's done' she said. I dozed for another hour or so.

I spent the evening and the following day faffing around. It was nice - I love faffing. And playing with Helen. Actually, that sounds a bit wrong. When I say, "playing with Helen" I mean exploring her potential. Actually, that sounds a bit wrong too. I was just establishing what she was capable of, and listening to her very sexy voice. Imagine a sort of sound surround Siri/Alexa combo with unlimited knowledge, access to everything that you want it to have access to, and which goes out of its way to be helpful, even to the extent of predicting what I wanted. For example, I asked her what the largest known prime number is and she said 'The Mersenne Prime M77232917, which was arrived at by multiplying 2 to the power of 77,232,917 and subtracting 1. The resulting number is 23,249,425 digits long, and was discovered on Boxing Day 2017 by the distributed computing collaboration "Great Internet Mersenne Prime Search", abbreviated to GIMPS. Do you want to know any more?'

I loved the way she said "GIMPS". I didn't want to know any more.

Tom arrived around 7.30 clutching a bottle of wine.

'A beaker full of the warm South, Full of the true, the blushful Hippocrene' he said with a smile.

I replied 'With beaded bubbles winking at the brim, And purple-stained mouth. Welcome to my humble abode. Shall we crack that open straight away?'

We sat in the mini cinema I'd had installed in the back basement and watched the new 'Blade Runner' while polishing off a second bottle of red and a large quantity of salt and vinegar pretzels. We then went upstairs and lounged around in the lounge drinking large G&Ts, and had fun getting Helen to play different songs for us. We kept testing her, but there was no song she couldn't find, however obscure. She was even able to play songs we wanted to hear by listening to us hum them or say a few words from the lyrics.

'Damned impressive', Tom said.

With hindsight and at this distance in time it's hard to remember exactly how what happened next happened. I had four spare bedrooms in the house, the one I'd put Tom's towel on was a circular heated water bed on the next floor up, but we both ended up in my room on either side of my bed, naked. I'm surprisingly unembarrassed about this, now. That night, I can't remember how I felt. For understandable reasons, I'd never been naked with another man in a bedroom, ergo I'd never climbed into bed with one.

After a few moments sizing one another up, so to speak, and without saying anything, we climbed into bed and wrapped our arms around one another. I'd never had a sensation like it. Electric. We just looked at one another in the gloom for a while, gently moving against one another until we were both fully excited. Then we made love, each to each, as it were, before falling asleep.

In the morning, I woke up before Tom, excited already, and woke him up with my mouth.

When we got up it was as if nothing had happened. I made some breakfast while he played on his phone, and he left around 11.

I sat back on one of the sofas, asked Helen to play me a Rossini overture, and she picked 'Semiramide', (my favourite) (I was already taking this for granted). I thought about what had happened. Was I gay? Bisexual? Or was it just a one off? Did I want it to happen again? I'd loved it, both times, but was it just curiosity or something more?

That afternoon I received my Barcelona details, and in the evening I went to a pub in Highgate, on my own, and had a few beers and a shitty omelette and chips. When I went to sleep, I dreamt about bombs again.

I love Barcelona. I remember going there a few years ago with some friends and we spent a few days drinking sangria and wine and eating paella and tapas and wishing Franco had been defeated in the Spanish Civil War and visiting the Sagrada Familia and thinking about Gaudi and stuff like that. It was fantastic. After a few days of this one of the guys had asked 'Shall we go to the beach?' 'Beach? This place has a *beach*? I didn't know Barcelona was on the *sea*!' My geography of Spain at that time was pretty crap. It still is. Anyway, it does indeed have a beach, and Barcelona - which was a very high spec place anyway - shot straight to number 1 on my list of top places. I've heard Vancouver's great too but I've never been there, but it'll have to be pretty special to even come close to Barcelona, which has everything. And I mean everything. Actually I don't mean that, literally, after all it doesn't have a giant particle accelerator or the

Northern Lights, but you know what I mean.

On my first day there I had learned the basics of the programme and how and where it would pan out. The three-year schedule, which would start in January, was as follows:

Year 1	Location	Topic
January - March	Tokyo	"Leading by example"
April	Participants can choose location(s) or stay at home or mix and match. All fully funded, no budget restrictions.	"Rest and relaxation"
May - June	Los Angeles	"Putting people first"
July	Participants can choose location(s) or stay at home or mix and match. All fully funded, no budget restrictions.	"Rest and relaxation"
August - September	New York	"High performance"
October	Barcelona	"Audit"
November – Dec. 15th	Oslo	"Effective communications"
December 16th - 31st	Participants can choose location(s) or stay at home or mix and match. All fully funded, no budget restrictions.	"Rest and relaxation"

I was reliably informed that the SPC facilities in the Maldives were "to die for", so I thought I'd take my first R&R there. For July, I decided I'd follow the whole of the Tour de France as an honorary VIP guest of the organisers. Apparently, the October "audit" was all about seeing where we'd got to, workshops, role plays, one-to-ones, panels, that sort of stuff.

Year 2	Location	Topic
January - February	Rome, including the Vatican	"The SPC's place in history, art and literature"
March	Montreal	"Finance for non-finance team members"
April	Participants can choose location(s) or stay at home or mix and match. All fully funded, no budget restrictions.	"Rest and relaxation"
May - June	Barcelona	"First Speaker module 1"
July	Participants can choose location(s) or stay at home or mix and match. All fully funded, no budget restrictions.	"Rest and relaxation"
August - September	Barcelona	"First Speaker module 2"
October	Geneva (CERN)	"Technology and mathematics for competitive advantage"
November until Dec. 15th	Rome, including the Vatican	"The role and influence of the SPC"
December 16th - 31st	Participants can choose location(s) or stay at home or mix and match. All fully funded, no budget restrictions.	"Rest and relaxation"

Even though I couldn't plan that far ahead, I was pretty sure I'd do the

Tour de France again in my second-year R&R.

Year 3	Location	Topic
January - March	Barcelona	"First Speaker module 3"
April	Participants can choose location(s) or stay at home or mix and match. All fully funded, no budget restrictions.	"Rest and relaxation"
May - June	Rome, including the Vatican	"The SPC in power, government and religion"
July	Participants can choose location(s) or stay at home or mix and match. All fully funded, no budget restrictions.	"Rest and relaxation"
August until Dec. 15th	Barcelona, with offsites in Seville, Florence, Prague, Tehran (to be confirmed), Hong Kong and Paris	"Becoming a First Speaker"

It looked like a really interesting programme. I didn't have to attend any recognition modules as I'd already achieved the required level, although "better never stops" as they say. Throughout I'd be paid a higher amount of £23,300 a month, tax free as usual, and of course all travel and accommodation and subsistence costs would be met by the SPC. In something of a departure from previous expenses policies I'd been familiar with, there was actually a *minimum* spend on things like wine and dinners and stuff. This was to encourage us to "think big".

When I got back from Barcelona I felt a bit flat. It's odd and unpredictable how the mind works. Materially things were going very well. I don't just mean money and houses and cars and stuff, I mean the tangible things that we can see and touch. But I couldn't see and touch Emily. Or our child. And I was confused about my sexuality. Did I fancy Tom, in the Alice sense? It was hard, no pun intended. So, I decided to get pissed.

I rang Sam and he agreed to drive on down with my Aston Martin and get the train back. I told him he could keep the car, at least for the next three years.

So, he got the train into London a few days later and we got absolutely smashed. When he stayed over there was never any question of us sharing a bed. It was unthinkable. I told him all about the SPC, including the eligibility criteria.

His response was 'Fuck me! Really?'

It saddened me that my best friend wasn't eligible.

I felt even flatter when he left, and on top of what I called my ELP (Emily Loss Problem) I became increasingly concerned about what was in the box that Madame Gironde had given me. Is "concerned" the right word? I'm not sure. Plus, there was still the unusual stuff that "The Specialist" had told me. For the first time since the whole SPC rollercoaster began, I had what I could call "misgivings" about it all. There was no doubt at all that being in it was wonderful, but the very fact that it existed and that I was in it was, I don't know, in that low mood I wasn't sure of the words.

Anyway, I had to "get busy living", as they say, so since I still had a few weeks before starting my First Speaker programme I decided to ask Alice to Paris for the weekend, and then head off somewhere remote and hot for a few weeks, on my own, with a big pile of books.

The Paris trip with Alice wasn't guaranteed, by any means. For one thing, I'd hardly ever spoken to her, and when I had it had more often than not been when she was holding one of those suction things in my mouth while the hygienist was cleaning my teeth. Don't get me wrong. I've got good oral hygiene and good teeth. I have very few fillings and a toothbrush that I have to login to. All the same it's not the most romantic of ways to get to know someone is it? And what if she had a boyfriend? Another Cambridge Rowing Blue with 3% body fat and a degree in astrophysics, or even worse, French Literature? Well, "if you don't ask you don't get" and "fortune favours the brave" and all that.

So, a couple of days later I left an envelope in the reception area of the Dentist for Alice, containing a letter and a Tiffany diamond bracelet. I did wonder if she'd think the bracelet was a bit over the top, especially as it cost me nearly £17,000 - but I thought, what the Hell? I'd spent ages writing the letter, and had got Helen to help me. It said:

> Hi Alice
>
> Remember me? I'm the guy that told you the joke about Batman and Robin the other day, that made you laugh. You gave me an A minus for my flossing technique :-)
>
> I know you don't really know anything about me, but I'd like to take you to Paris for a few days - all on me - first class Eurostar,

staying in the best hotel they have (you could choose if you like, there are some links below), fabulous dinners and the finest wines in the finest restaurants. And whatever you wanted to do. All I ask in return is that we have lots of uninhibited sex.

If you don't want to, or can't, that's fine. I mean, not exactly fine but acceptable. I'd never mention it again and there'd be no need for any embarrassment.

I'm including a small gift as a token of my sincerity, which is yours to keep whatever you decide. (I've also included the gift receipt if you want to exchange or return it). Either way please let me know. Here's my mobile number: nnnnn nnnnnn
You are an incredibly attractive woman.
xxxxx

P.S. I bought the toothbrush you recommended, the one you have to login to. It's great, thank you for the recommendation :-)
P.P.S. I never write "thanks" only "thank you", and always "Christmas" not "Xmas". Apart from those times, for illustrative purposes, otherwise I wouldn't have been able to explain it. Now you know something about me :-)
P.P.P.S here are some hotel links

While I was waiting, I researched where in the world would have the best weather in November, and settled on Barbados for that trip. I booked it all up, with the flight out in 13 days time. So that was the window in time I had for the Paris trip with Alice.

I didn't hear from her for two days, and I'd resigned myself that she wouldn't get in touch, and I started to feel embarrassed even though I'd told her there was no need for it, when she rang me. I didn't have her number stored, obviously, and I thought it might be one of those cold calls offering me a PPI recovery service or asking me if I'd been in an accident that wasn't my fault, but it was Alice. This is how it went, Alice second.

'xxxxx speaking.'
'Hi. It's Alice. From the Dentist.'
'Oh, hi Alice. How are you?'
'I'm great thanks, sorry, thank you,' (I thought I heard a little giggle at this point). 'I'm ringing about your letter.'
'Ah yes. Glad you got it.' I replied. I felt a jolt in my stomach.
'Sorry for the delay in calling. I only work a four-day week as I help to care for my little brother who's got amyotrophic lateral sclerosis, the same thing as Stephen Hawking.'

'I'm sorry to hear that.' (And I genuinely was too. I hate to hear stuff like that. That came out wrong. It's not that I hate to hear it so much as I hate that illness like that happens to people).

'It's ok, but thanks. Oops, I mean thank you. He's fine. I mean, he's not fine, but he's ok. As well as can be expected.'

'Not fine like it's not fine if you don't want to come to Paris then? Not that I'm comparing them, just clarifying what we both mean by not fine.'

'Not fine like that, yes. Now. About Paris. I have just one problem with it.'

'What's that then?' My heart sank. It was the sex, of course. I knew I'd been too forward...

'I'd like to pay my way. Or at least as much as I can afford, anyway. I'm not a freeloader. And the bracelet ...'

'Don't you like it?'

'I love it. But it's not just too generous. It's ... it's ... *crazy* generous.'

'Well, that's my middle name.'

'What, generous?'

'No' I laughed. 'Crazy. So how about you give it to me back the first time I do anything you don't like, but keep it until then? Or just keep it.'

'Will you ever do anything I don't like?'

'I'm not planning to, but I don't know what you like, yet. I'd like to find out as quickly as possible though.'

'I'd like you to find that out too.'

'Do you like staying in and watching a movie and getting in a pizza and drinking wine and then maybe sharing a tub of Häagen Dazs with Maltesers with Baileys poured all over it?'

'I think I'd like that a lot.'

'So how about now?'

'Now as in tonight?'

'Yes, that now. You could come over to mine and check out my cinema. It's big!'

'Is that a euphemism?'

'Definitely not! So, what do you say?'

'Well ...' there was what felt like a long pause 'Ok then. I've just got home from work. I need a shower and then get changed. Is 8 o'clock ok?' She replied.

'Not prime' I laughed, 'But perfect. I'll order pizzas for 8. Any preferences?'

'I'm vegetarian. Can I have a veggie deluxe or whatever. I'll pay you back when I get there.'

'No need. My treat. You can buy the next one. I'm a veggie too by the way. Although I eat fish. And occasionally meat. So, we're all set then. Great.'

'Isn't there something you want to tell me?'

'Well, um, I'm very happy you called and have implicitly accepted my terms for our Paris trip and ...'

'Your address, silly. I don't know where you live.'

That reminded me of a scene from 'The Graduate'. I told her my address.

'Where's that? I don't know where that is.'

After explaining the route, she replied again, 'You're kidding me. You live up there? I'd better buy a new dress just to visit!'

She arrived at 10 past 8 wearing a "JE SUIS CHARLIE" t-shirt, dungarees, boots, and a black beret, and carrying an overnight bag. She held it up.

'In case I get lucky.' she said with a smile.

So began my Adventures in Wonderland with Alice.

SEGMENT 55

I'm lying here in bed on the morning of the day of my flight to Barbados, Alice has just left. I just had the strangest dream, by the way. In it I was a fictional character created by someone who wished that an organisation like the SPC existed but that he wasn't eligible for it. Dreams can be so weird, can't they? I don't really believe anything can be read into them, or that they predict the future, but they sure as Hell can be thought provoking.

Before I say anything else about Alice, I have to say something about Emily. I'll always love her and I'll never forget her. Whenever I read Yevtushenko, which to be honest isn't all that often, I'm always reminded of her when I read the poem 'Colours' which she introduced me to and which I can recite from memory:

> *When your face*
> *appeared over my crumpled life*
> *at first I understood*
> *only the poverty of what I have.*
> *Then its particular light*
> *on woods, on rivers, on the sea,*
> *became my beginning in the coloured world*
> *in which I had not yet had my beginning.*
> *I am so frightened, I am so frightened,*
> *of the unexpected sunrise finishing,*
> *of revelations*
> *and tears and the excitement finishing.*
> *I don't fight it, my love is this fear,*
> *I nourish it who can nourish nothing,*
> *love's slipshod watchman.*
> *Fear hems me in.*
> *I am conscious that these minutes are short*
> *and that the colours in my eyes will vanish*
> *when your face sets.*

She would have wanted me to be happy, I know that. The question is, would she have wanted me to be *this* happy? Alice and I had slept together every night since that first night. And when I say slept, we hadn't actually slept all that much. We'd had hours upon hours of uninhibited sex interspersed with the occasional doze. It seems that we were totally compatible in that sense.

"We'll always have Paris" as they say. I love "they". We had a great time there. Three memories stand out for me. The first, the look on her face when she saw the Eiffel Tower sparkling for the first time. The second when, about half way through sex on the first night (elapsed time two and a half hours), she asked me to stop and she gave me a standing ovation (eat your heart out Woody Allen). The third was two and a half hours later when she had an orgasm so long and intense that she moaned the entire vocal of 'The Great Gig In The Sky' before "almost drowning in an ocean of ecstasy" (her words not mine).

It's not all about the sex though, although sex isn't to be devalued. It certainly comes in the top 100 facets of a relationship, at least it does for me, along with things like politics, what books someone reads, a vegetarian diet, cats, music, oral hygiene, and love.

Talking of oral hygiene, as a treat last night - since it would be our last night together for a while - Alice ran us a bath of hot antiseptic mouthwash before tying me up with dental floss and throwing me onto the bed which was surrounded by little travel tubes of toothpaste.

I'd invited her to Barbados with me, but she said she couldn't come because of her brother. We'd agreed to talk every day though.

I had a luxury beachfront villa over there, with my own heated pool, which was a short walk along the beach to a very nice bar which also served the most amazing grilled fresh fish. Did I mention I'd started to eat fish, but only when out of the country and/or in a Salad Niçoise? Is there a name for that kind of diet?

It was exactly the kind of break I wanted. I got up when I felt like it, which was usually late morning, checked text messages and the sports pages, and then had a shower before swimming in the sea. I'd then have a late lunch, followed by a siesta usually in my hammock, then I'd call Alice - mindful of the time difference - before strolling along to my beach bar for dinner and drinks.

It sounds rather lazy, indulgent and hedonistic, if not downright *bourgeois*, but that was exactly what I wanted.

Two weeks in I finally wore Alice down and persuaded her to fly out to stay with me for a few days. Her parents - who I hadn't met but had spoken to - insisted that she take a break and that her brother would be fine. I'd already made a note to try and sort out additional help for him - whose name was Jack by the way - to help Alice and her family out.

I picked her up in a nippy little buggy I'd hired and drove her straight back to my villa where I'd laid a mix of different sized interdental brushes all over the bed. She immediately went into some kind of uncontrollable frenzy. We didn't get up for 24 hours, apart from when the police called to check we were okay as the people in the next villa (250 yards away) had heard our screams and called 211, and when we flossed.

I had a couple more weeks on my own after she flew home, during which I did even less than before, although I did visit Kensington Oval in Bridgetown and also went diving for pearls. And found some too, big ones.

Coming back to England, and the cold, was exciting, although cold. Christmas was around the corner, and I had to get ready for the start of my First Speaker programme. It was a full-on couple of weeks.

I loved Christmas shopping in London, and Alice and I also managed to get away to Vienna for a couple of days for their famous Christmas markets. We went to a ball and waltzed to Johann Strauss. That night as we sat in the hotel bar before going to bed, she asked me what we were.

'What are we?' was what she said.

'Human, at least I am, although I sometimes think you must be an angel' I replied with what I thought was immense charm. (I was a bit pissed to be fair).

'No. I mean. You know what I mean. This is all brilliant. You're brilliant. We're brilliant. Paris. Barbados. This. But are we a couple? I mean, are we girlfriend and boyfriend?' She said it with a smile and I put my arm round her.

'I think so, don't you? I've just never put a label on it. Would you *like* to be my girlfriend?'

She started to cry and fished around in her handbag for a tissue. She didn't find one. 'I think I'm falling in love with you' she said 'and I don't know why but it makes me want to cry.'

I got down on one knee and popped the question. 'Would you do me the honour of being my girlfriend, officially? Which means, just so you know, we get to argue about where to spend Christmas Day.'

We enjoyed a long and beautiful hug before going to bed. She couldn't stop crying. Before we went to sleep I reminded her that she hadn't said 'yes' yet.

She promptly said 'yes.'

I followed this up with, 'I have to ask you a question.'

'Ok' she said, looking worried.

'Where shall we spend Christmas Day?'

She smiled and said, 'Let's argue about that in the morning, shall we?' and then wrapped her arms around me. And just when I thought we were closing our eyes to go to sleep she gave me a very serious look and said 'I have a confession to make. And I want to make it now, before we get even more deeply involved.'

My pulse quickened. What was she going to say, 'That time you called me from Barbados, and I didn't pick up because I'd gone to sleep. Remember?'

'I do now' I said. I was starting to feel a little sick.

'That night ... I didn't floss.' And then she poked her tongue out at me.

'If you're not very careful I might fall in love with you too.' I said.

In a fairly impressive diplomatic coup I eventually got everyone to agree to have Christmas at my house. After all, it was the biggest, and could accommodate everyone comfortably including all the sleeping arrangements. Things can go horribly wrong, when families meet for the first time at Christmas, but this one went brilliantly. At one point, after dinner, when I looked across the room and saw Sally and Alice talking together and laughing, and our Mums carrying plates into the kitchen as if they'd been friends for years, and our Dads amicably disagreeing (over port) about the rights and wrongs of the Queen's Speech, and Sam talking to Jack, it was so good that I half imagined that Charles Dickens must have time-travelled here unseen as inspiration for 'A Christmas Carol'.

I forgot to mention about Sam. He was going through yet another relationship breakdown, and was feeling low, and although he hadn't asked, and could have gone to his Dad's (his Mum had died of breast cancer a few years ago), he didn't get on with his Stepmother, and he was my best mate, and, well, it just felt right to invite him. To insist, in fact.

The parents and Jack went to bed around midnight, leaving Alice, Sally, Sam and me downstairs in the front living room. We cracked open a bottle of gin and then another bottle, got Helen to dim the lights and play 80's classics, and started a game of "Who's in the bag?", boys vs. girls. Sam and I never stood a chance. For example, one of the clues Sally read out was 'I think this guy was a cyclist'

Alice said, 'Lance Armstrong' right away, which was the correct answer.

How did she get it that quickly?

Another was 'Famous footballer. I think he's dead. Scottish I think. Good looking.'

'George Best?', which was the right answer, except of course he was Irish. This is what we were up against. By way of contrast, our clues were people like Proust and Anna Akhmatova which, perhaps unsurprisingly, we didn't get straight away.

After several rounds, losing every single one, we swapped to family (i.e. Sally and me) vs. Rest of the World. This produced even worse results, as no-one was in harmony with anyone on both teams and it descended into farce. And giggles.

When we'd polished off the second bottle of gin between us, around 2am, we decided to go to bed. Or rather, to sleep, as Sally said she was too tired to walk up the stairs. She really wasn't for moving, and got very comfortable on the sofa, so I got her a blanket and tucked her up and kissed her goodnight. I felt towards her like Nicholas Nickleby did towards Kate. Sam said goodnight, and thanked us again, and went to bed. When Alice and I got into bed, before we made love, she asked me why Sam and Sally weren't together. I don't know, I said, maybe they know one another too well.

Later, once she was asleep, I lay awake for a while thinking about it. Although Sam was my best mate, and I loved him, I sort of didn't want him to get with my sister, as he wasn't eligible for the SPC. Just as I closed my eyes I saw a message flash up on my phone, which was on charge next to the bed. It was from Tom and it just read:

HAPPY CHRISTMAS :)

SEGMENT 89

I'm not at liberty to reveal any further details about the FSP (First Speaker Programme) - its content, the tutors, my fellow participants and so on. I can, however, tell you a little more about First Speakers themselves. I think I've mentioned that it's modelled on the approach taken by the Second Foundation in Asimov's books. No unnecessary hierarchy, beyond what's required for the effective functioning of the organisation. No politics. No maneuvering. No petty squabbles. Ambition was fine, but not at the expense of others. All in all, quite different from corporate life, which by and large is a crock of shit. Being the First Speaker (FS) simply meant that you spoke first. There was/is, I suppose, an implied seniority, but not of the wanky corporate kind. It was based on respect and merit and on nothing else.

There were/are levels. At the local level the FS is typically voted in, or sort of naturally put in place by nods and winks, without rancour or bullshit. I'm sorry if I keep comparing it with corporate life, but it's so hard not to. Actually, I'm not sorry. Anyway, the local FS operates at the town or large village level, so think of Peter. Every town in the country, or every combination of a few small villages, has a group, (which just goes to show how many people are eligible, confounding the statistics). There's then the next level up, which is the county level, where all the local FS's congregate a few times each year for what, if I'm honest, sounds like a piss up. The only thing of real importance decided at this level is the FS for the county, who represents it at the next level up, the regional level. This level is where strategy is set. The UK has seven regions: London, South (excluding London), Midlands, North, Scotland, Wales, and Northern Ireland. Each region has an FS, and the seven of them meet monthly. This group will also have an FS, representing the UK as a whole, and so on up the levels - Europe, Global. Thus, there is an FS for Europe who sits on the Global Group, and ultimately there is an FS for the whole world.

As an organisation, of course, there are all sorts of parallel functional and operational areas and committees and such, supported by a vast (but efficient and effective, the two things not being the same) administrative function. Once again, I'm not at liberty to say more on this point.

The primary objective of the FSP I was participating in was all about succession planning, my guess is that you've already figured that much out..

Being unable to tell you more, I'll say something about tax that may have been troubling you. It certainly troubled me until I found out what was really going on. You'll recall that I paid no tax on any of my SPC income, which although personally beneficial concerned me as I didn't want to be bracketed as a tax avoider along with scumbags like Amazon and Google and Starbucks and Virgin Care and all the rest of those bastard organisations. At one level I was comfortable with it, as we had a Tory government at the time, and if you're ever going to avoid paying tax that's the time, as all they're going to do with it is buy weapons and bail out dodgy banks and award multi-million pound contracts to their corporate donors and such like. I was also comfortable with it at another level, as I wasn't "working" as such. I wasn't "employed". It was a gift. And I was comfortable with it at a third level too, since I took home £23,000 a month instead of around half that. Still, I was nonetheless pleased to learn that the SPC paid its member's tax and NI equivalents for them, by complex agreement with HMRC. And while I'm on it, made enormous charitable donations and contributions to good causes on a regular basis, right across the globe.

The FSP was intense, but as you've seen I had regular months of R&R and moreover I was free on average two weekends a month. On most of these weekends Alice would fly out to see me or I'd fly back to see her.

Our relationship evolved to the extent that two years later I decided to ask her to marry me. I'd arranged a weekend in Krakow, where neither of us had ever been. I bought a beautiful engagement ring - Sally helped me choose it - and was so excited that once or twice I forgot to breathe. Alice just thought it was a nice weekend away, but I'd booked the best restaurant in the city, and I'd shipped in a bottle of the finest champagne in the world which would be waiting on our table. Always assuming she said yes, I'd also organised a firework display. I meant to start out as I meant to go on, showing my utter devotion and love every single day.

I arrived in Krakow on a Thursday early evening - given the occasion I'd been allowed the Friday off - to check everything was ok. I wanted it to be perfect. Alice wasn't due to arrive until 5.30pm the next day.

The hotel was fabulous, the restaurant was fabulous, the champagne had arrived and was being stored at the perfect temperature and was (allegedly) fabulous, and I was promised that the fireworks would be fabulous. And I hadn't lost the ring. I could relax.

I found a really nice bar, and met some guys over there from Dunstable who were on a Stag Do, and ended up drinking quite a lot of vodka. Alice and I never missed speaking to one another or leaving a voicemail every night without fail when we were apart, so when I got back to the hotel a little worse for wear - actually quite a lot worse for wear - I called her. Voicemail. I can't remember what I said but it must have been something along the lines of 'I love you and can't wait to see you tomorrow' or something like that. I crashed out without flossing, and resolved to confess the following evening.

When I woke up, a little headachy, I was surprised there was no voicemail back from her, since that had never happened - but thought no more of it. I was too excited. I was planning to go on a day trip to Auschwitz, about 60km away. I'd never been, and I thought that it was important for me to go. It may seem odd to you to want to do this on my Engagement Day, but it doesn't to me.

I don't want to talk about that day trip. It's too upsetting. All I'll say is that everyone should go there once.

I got back in time to have a quick shower and change before setting off to the airport. I'd hired a limo. Alice's flight was on time, and we made love as soon as we got back to the hotel, naturally, before going out for dinner. I forgot to mention, the dinner, that's to say the engagement dinner, was to be the following night, on the Saturday.

We slept in a bit the following morning, and then wandered around the town. I took her to the bar where I'd met the guys on the Stag Do and introduced her to chocolate vodka. We got back to the hotel, made love again, and then had a siesta. I set the alarm on my phone so we wouldn't miss the Engagement Dinner.

When we sat down to eat, in the best table in the restaurant and possibly at that moment in the world, I couldn't have been happier. The waiter, who knew all about it, played it very cool. When I pretended to go to the toilet I checked, and the champagne was ready and on ice and would be brought to the table on my signal, which would obviously be after she said 'yes'. And the fireworks were all organised too.

I felt for the ring in my pocket and it was still there. I was very nervous. I decided to wait until we'd finished our starter and were waiting for our main before getting down on one knee.

Our starters came and went. I was almost too nervous to speak. I don't really know why as I knew she was going to say yes, nonetheless, as anyone who has ever done this will testify, it's a very nerve-wracking moment. I took another sip of wine, got the ring out of my pocket, cleared my throat, when she gave me a very serious look and said 'I have a confession to make. And I want to make it now, before we get even more deeply involved.'

My pulse quickened. What was she going to say?

'Last night, when you called me, and I didn't pick up. Remember?'

'I do now' I said with a smile. I thought I knew what she was going to say.

'I was with Sam.'

I was confused. 'With Sam? My best friend Sam?'

She looked down. 'Yes.' was all she said.

'Well, that's fine, isn't it?'

I knew they'd met up while I'd been away. I was delighted that my best friend and my future wife got on so well. I saw a tear run down her cheek, and reached across and took her hands. Suddenly I was worried. Was he ill?

'We slept together.' she said, without looking at me.

After that it all seemed to be in slow motion.

'You ... slept ... together? What, in the same house?'

There was a long pause before she said, 'In the same bed.' I tried to take this in but it didn't compute. What was she saying? Then she looked at me, her eyes now full of tears. 'It didn't mean anything. We got hammered, and, well, you know.'

'No I don't know,' I said, fighting to stay upright as my world was crumbling. 'I want to hear you tell me.'

She looked at me for an age, the tears now streaming down her face. 'We had sex. Crappy, quick, drunken sex. And then we fell asleep. And when we woke up this morning we hated ourselves for it.'

'So, you didn't have sex again this morning?'

'Of course not!'

'You say "of course not" like it's a preposterous suggestion, but you can see why it might not be, surely?'

'Don't xxxxx' she said. 'Please don't. I feel bad enough already.'

'Oh, I'm sorry to hear that, I really am. Tell me, was it crappy at the time, or only afterwards? Does he know it was crappy? Was it crappy for you or him or for both of you? How crappy was it?'

'Please don't do this' she pleaded.

'Your main course, Madame' said the waiter. We hadn't seen him arrive. 'The wine you ordered, Sir, is ready whenever you are.'

'Thank you' I said, 'Please keep it a little longer.'

Alice rushed off to the toilet as my main course arrived, which gave me a moment to gather my thoughts after this bombshell. They still weren't gathered when she came back.

'Everyone makes mistakes, she said. 'We're allowed the occasional mistake, aren't we? Not everyone's perfect, like you. Haven't you ever made a mistake?' She was properly crying now. The couple on the next table were looking at us.

'Me, perfect?' was all I could think of to say. I was overwhelmed by the fact that Sam wasn't eligible for the SPC. 'Excuse me a moment, will you?'

I went to the washroom and retched into a sink, and then stared at my reflection for a minute or two before returning to the table. Alice was texting someone.

'Is that Sam?' I asked. 'Checking whether you've told me or not? Do say "hi" from me, won't you, and tell him I'll call him in the morning.'

She put the phone down. 'xxxxx, please, after all we've been through. It was a mistake. It meant nothing. I love you.'

'And you confirm it was crappy, right? You didn't enjoy it at all? Not one little bit?' She put her head in her hands and silently sobbed. I could see her head shaking. I called the waiter over.

'Slight change of plan' I said. 'She's not feeling well. I'm taking her back to the hotel. I'll be back later. Keep the champagne and fireworks until then. Can you get us a cab please?'

In the taxi, she could hardly make herself understood through her sobs. I didn't put my arm around her or anything. When we reached the hotel, I asked the driver to wait for me.

'Please, please don't do this' she kept saying. We got back to our room.

'I'm going back to the restaurant now. You can do anything you want except come back with me. Don't wait up for me.'

I walked down the corridor and pressed the button for the lift. She called out my name. I turned around one last time.

'I was going to propose to you tonight.' was all I said. The lift door opened and I got in and pressed the button for the ground floor. Sam not being in the SPC was what I couldn't stop thinking about.

Before getting back in the taxi I stopped at Hotel Reception and booked another room for that night and the next, I didn't want to stay with Alice. She was already ringing me. I didn't answer. She rang twice more while I was on my way back to the restaurant. I didn't answer those calls either.

When I got to the restaurant I asked if I could move out onto the terrace and have my champagne there while I watched the fireworks. The waiter asked if I still wanted to go ahead with the fireworks and I said of course. They were as fabulous as I'd been promised, as was the champagne, and I sat there and resolved to remember this moment.

I had so many negative feelings and emotions: sadness, betrayal, loss, doubt, uncertainty, but also a strange sense of liberation that I couldn't explain. The whole mix made me laugh and cry simultaneously, as well as have a very runny nose.

Several people came out onto the terrace to watch the fireworks, and I was delighted that they were so impressed. None of them knew they were anything to do with me of course, I could hear them asking one another what they were celebrating.

'Sad eyes.' I heard a voice say to me.

I looked up. Standing there was a woman wearing a red coat with a multi-coloured scarf and a black hat. I don't know why I always notice and mention stuff like this, I guess clothes are important to me.

I just gave her a sort of rueful smile but didn't say anything. She did.

'Mind if I join you?' There were two chairs at my table as of course Alice was supposed to have been with me.

'Please do' I said. She sat down.

'Beautiful fireworks aren't they?' she said.

'Yes. They are.' I looked at the spectacular display which was at its climax.

'Have you ever played the ten-word introduction game?' she said.

'No.'

'It's used when you've only just met someone. You simply say ten words, alternately, to describe yourself however you want to. They can be things about you or people or things you like, such as poets or ideas. Ten words only, maximum. It can be less. Want to play?'

I wasn't really in the mood but I said 'Ok. You first.'

Her - 'European.'

Me - 'Remainer.'

(She smiled).

Her - 'Journalist.'

Me - 'Shakespeare.'

(She smiled again).

Her - 'I think you've got the hang of it. You go first this time.'

Me - 'Keats.'

Her - 'Communist.'

(The fireworks ended).

Me - 'Socialist.'

Her – 'Opera.'

Me – 'Rossini.'

Her - 'Peace.'

Me - 'Love.'

Her - 'Feminist.'

Me - 'Sad.'

Her - 'Just checking. Do you mean tonight, or always? The ten words are supposed to describe *you*, not your current mood.'

Me - 'Ok. Scrub sad. Interested.'

Her - 'Passionate.'

Me - 'Dostoyevsky.'

Her - 'Dostoyevsky.' At which point she clapped her hands. 'We have a match, and it didn't even take ten! That's rare.'

'What do we do now?' I said.

'We celebrate.' she said. So I poured her a glass of champagne.

'Hmmm. This is very good.'

Alice called me again.

'Excuse me' I said, 'I have to deal with this.'

'Take the call if you want to.'

'I don't want to. Wait just a moment please'. I sent Alice the following text:

ALICE. I DON'T WANT TO SPEAK TO YOU OR SEE YOU RIGHT NOW. MAYBE IN A FEW DAYS BUT NOT NOW. I'VE BOOKED ANOTHER ROOM IN THE HOTEL SO I WON'T BE BACK TONIGHT. HAVE A SAFE FLIGHT BACK TOMORROW

I thought about adding a kiss at the end but it would be sending out the wrong signal and I didn't want to kiss her, and I kept thinking about her kissing Sam. So I didn't.

'Sorry about that.' I said.

'No worries. So, what do I know about you? You are a Socialist who voted Remain and likes Shakespeare, Keats and Dostoyevsky, and also love. It's a good game, yes?'

'Very. And you're a passionate European Communist Feminist Journalist who likes peace and Dostoyevsky also. Quite a cocktail. My name's xxxxx by the way.' I shook her hand.

'My name's Laetitia.' She took another sip of champagne. 'I'm from Branch 7. We know all about the SPC.'

'What's Branch 7?' I asked.

'Plenty of time for that later.' she said.

'Later? So, what do we do now?'

'Now we fuck.'

SEGMENT 144

I woke up late, having been kept awake for much of the night. Laetitia wasn't in bed, and for a moment I thought I'd dreamt the whole thing, but as I rolled over I could see her sitting on the balcony. I stretched. It felt good.

'Come back to bed' I shouted.

'Can't. Busy' she said.

I went into the bathroom and examined the scratch and bite marks on my face, neck, shoulders and back, and the bruises on my arms, and then put on a dressing gown and joined her on the balcony.

'What are you doing?' I said.

'Peeling grapes.' she said matter of factly. 'The awful awkwardness of unpeeled grapes.' She popped one into her mouth and looked at me. She was wearing glasses, I hadn't seen them last night.

'So what's Branch 7?' I asked, 'And what's its interest in me?'

'All in good time.' She put the grapes down. 'I thought you wanted me to come back to bed.'

An hour or so later, after a mini doze, we had a bath together, and she began to tell me about Branch 7.

'When you were examining the SPC archives in the Vatican library, did you come across a group calling themselves the Lepidopteri in the early part of the last century?'

'Can't say I did, no. Was I negligent?'

'No. But perhaps you weren't as thorough as you should have been. The Lepidopteri, named after Puccini's 'Madame Butterfly', came into being just before the First World War, as tensions mounted and as war gradually became inevitable. They were a secret division of the SPC, accountable only to the global First Speaker, operating completely outside the usual parameters. Their role was to influence or interfere with events in such a way as to enhance the SPC's interests and keep it on track, shall we say, covertly. Think of a sort of Second Foundation to the First Foundation, if you're familiar with the books?'

I told her I was.

'Most of the time they stayed within the laws of whatever country they were active in - they originated in Italy but spread across all SPC operational regions - but occasionally they strayed beyond the straight and narrow. The odd assassination, for example, or bringing down a bank or a corporate entity or a Stock Exchange, stuff like that. Nonetheless, they did their job very well inasmuch as the SPC continued to flourish and provide services to its members.' She paused to sip her wine - we'd brought a bottle into the bath - and as she did so I examined her delicious throat (with drips of hot bathwater running slowly down it) as she tilted her head back. Not for the first time in the last 24 hours I fantasised about being a vampire.

She put her glass down and continued. 'It was the assassination of Kennedy in 1963 that led to change. The Lep ...'

'You mean they killed him?'

'Patience, all will be revealed. No, they didn't kill him. Neither did Oswald, by the way, although that's another story, but they had an indirect connection, is the best way I can put it. Some of the causal links predicted by what we now call algorithms are seemingly very dilute.' She drank more wine.

Now I'm by no means a genius, but I'm not thick either, and I had no idea what she meant by that last sentence, and I told her.

'Kennedy had to die,' she said, 'to prevent something far worse happening many years later. I'm unable to tell you what at this time. You've heard of the butterfly effect? A butterfly lands on the side of a ship and causes a storm thousands of miles away? It's derived from chaos theory, the sensitive dependence on initial conditions in which a small change in one state of a deterministic nonlinear system can result in large differences in a later state.'

'I see.' And I did too. The interconnectedness of everything.

'Hence Lepidopteri' she continued. I tried not to think about drinking her blood by the cup-full. 'It's got nothing to do with 'Madame Butterfly', that was just a front. Remember, they had to keep themselves secret. Anyway, the fallout from Kennedy proved very hard to manage, and then, just when they were getting on top of things, in 1967 'Sgt. Pepper' came out, and as you can imagine, that changed everything.'

I nodded. Well, it was a bloody good album but I couldn't quite see where she was coming from.

'So, the organisation underwent a root and branch, top to bottom, reform, was radically restructured, and renamed Branch 7. Which is where you and I come in.'

I'd been thinking about her in a "top to bottom" sense, which was very distracting. 'So how do you and I come in, exactly?'

'I'll tell you that tonight. Now, can you get out of the bath so I can stretch my legs?'

I did as she asked, and looked at my phone for the first time that morning. Three missed calls from Alice and a text that said:

WHERE DID YOU SLEEP LAST NIGHT? I WAS WORRIED ABOUT YOU. PLEASE, PLEASE, SEE ME BEFORE I GO TO THE AIRPORT. MY TAXI'S BOOKED FOR 3.
I LOVE YOU, ALICE
XXX

I looked at the time. Ten past two. Clearly, I didn't see her. I did, however, call Sam. I withheld my number so he wouldn't know it was me when he picked up.

'Sam speaking' he said.
'Hi. It's xxxxx'
'Oh, hi.' He immediately sounded flustered.
'Just thought I'd check in from Krakow. How're you doing?'
'Not too bad thanks. How are you?'
'Well, it is my engagement weekend. Krakow is great. Great vodka too'
'How's Alice?'
'On her way back now. I'm staying on another night'
'So ... did she accept?'
'She didn't turn me down, no'
'That's great!' I thought I heard relief in his voice. 'How did you celebrate?'
'It was different, that's for sure.'
'How so?'
'All sorts of reasons. It's been one helluva weekend.'
'Did you talk about a date?'
'Date for what?'
'The big day, of course.'
'We didn't get around to that level of detail, actually. We did talk about another date though.'
'Oh?'
'Yes. The night before she flew out here'
'Ah. Hmm. And what about it?'
'That you guys met up.'
'We did, actually. We had a nice evening. She's a top girl.'
'She certainly is. How nice was the evening you had?'
'Yes, it was nice.' Again, I thought I heard a slight waver in his voice.
'How nice? Specifically.'
'She told you didn't she?'
'Told me what? I don't know what you mean?'
'That we slept together...'
'Yes, she did tell me.'
'I'm so, so, sorry.'

'You know, the thing about apologies is, they usually don't make things better. I mean, just because someone says they're sorry for doing something, doesn't mean they didn't want to do it at the time, does it? So it's really just bullshit, most of the time. In fact, the more I think about it, all apologies are a waste of energy, don't you think?'

'xxxxx, listen.'

'No, you listen to me. You fucked my girlfriend. And I do not forgive you'

'It takes two...'

'Oh, right. That helps. Thank you. She wanted to as well. Is that supposed to make me feel better?'

'It was just a drunken thing. It didn't mean anything.'

'It meant something to me. Anyway, I thought I'd let you know the consequences. Cause and effect and all that. I never asked her the question. We're finished. And as for you, don't ever get in touch with me again, for your own sake. Got that?'

'xxxxx...' he began.

'That's it. I'm done. And by the way don't drive the Aston Martin again. I'm going to get it collected.'

'Wait.'

'Fuck off.' I ended. And then I hung up.

Laetitia was still in the bath, so I took her in some grapes. She asked me if they were peeled, and I had to confess that they weren't. We both had things to do that afternoon, so we agreed to meet for dinner. I made some calls, dealt with some emails, and did some shopping. I thought about Alice a lot, but I thought more about Emily. I sat on a park bench and had a little cry. While I was sitting there Sam sent me a text:

I'M SO SORRY MATE. I DON'T KNOW WHAT TO SAY :(
I sent him a reply:
I TOLD YOU TO FUCK OFF
He sent me one back.
I'M YOUR BEST FRIEND!
My reply was loaded:
WAS NOT IS. AND YOU'RE NOT EVEN SPC!
His reply to that was
SO, THIS IS WHAT IT'S ALL ABOUT? NOTHING TO DO WITH INFIDELITY BUT ALL TO DO WITH YOUR STUPID SPC?

I ignored him after that and deleted the thread. It got me thinking though, how much of how bad I felt *was* because he wasn't SPC. I had to admit that if he had been it wouldn't have been as bad. It was still bad though.

After the preliminaries were over at dinner Laetitia got right down to it. 'The SPC. Do you agree with its aims?'

'To make its members lives better. How could I not?'

'But isn't that decadent? And rather unimpressive when it could do so much more?'

The word "decadent". It's transformed when the French say it. To be fair, most words are, but there's something all intellectual and angry and "Left Bank" about a French person saying it. Like the word "bourgeois". I'm not sure the English can even spell it let alone explain what it means.

'How do you mean?' I asked. 'The SPC does wonderful things. It ...'

'Yes. It gives you money. And things. And power, to some of you at least. What every man wants, no?' She took a sip of her wine. 'But it doesn't address the real issue, does it?'

'The real issue?'

'Why it exists in the first place. Eligibility.' she whispered. 'It doesn't address that, does it?'

'I'm not with you'.

She took a very large swig of wine and continued. 'Have you heard of the order of tailed amphibians called the Caudata?'

'Should I have?' I wanted to kiss her.

'Salamanders and newts. Capable of regenerating lost limbs, tails, jaws, eyes, and a variety of their internal structures. I'm talking about morphogenic processes that characterize the phenotypic plasticity of traits, allowing multi-cellular organisms to repair and thus maintain the integrity of their physiological and morphological states. It's quite remarkable.'

I loved her talking dirty like this. 'Sorry I'm being a bit dim here. What's the connection with the SPC?'

She just looked at me, at which point my phone rang. It was Alice. 'Excuse me' I said.

I bounced the call and blocked her number. I didn't delete it totally as I'd call her at some point, when I was ready.

'Sorry. You were saying?'

'Imagine if it was possible to introduce these processes into the human genome! To fully integrate REGs at the genomic, epigenetic, and transcriptome levels!'

'REGs?'

'Regeneration related genes. Do you see where I'm coming from now?'

And then it dawned on me. 'You mean ...?'

'Yes. That's exactly what I mean.' I was dumbstruck. 'But is that possible? In reality?'

'Trials have been carried out with a 100% success rate. And now it's time to roll it out worldwide. And that's where you come in.'

'Me? What can I do?'

'Lots of things. When you become a First Speaker.'

'But ...'

'Ssshhh. It's all under control. Remember, Branch 7 is your Second Foundation.'

'But what do I have to do?'

'Well. The next thing is to get the bill and take me back to your hotel and fuck me, and then we'll take things from there. Happy with that?'

On my flight back, I was struck by the transience of things, of people, of relationships, of everything, really, and I fell into quite a melancholy, not helped by reading a biography of Keats.

I'd recently bought some antiseptic mouthwash - my concerns with oral hygiene pre-dated (and would now post-date) my relationship with Alice - but it didn't taste as nice as the one I'd had before. The thing is, I couldn't remember what brand the one I'd had before was, and short of trial and error I couldn't think of a way I was going to find out.

Every time I started to like some food or drink a lot I worried that they would stop making it, like Virol in my youth. So, I hoarded Rude Health Almond Milk and Santal Peach Juice (both long life so I could buy loads and store them).

Relationships. Emily. Alice. I felt a bit sick even thinking about them in the same sentence, if thoughts can be packaged in sentences, if you know what I mean. I wondered if Alice would start dating Sam now. Probably. Once the Rubicon has been crossed, it has been crossed (obviously).

When I landed I decided to call Alice. I couldn't put it off any more, not because I felt I owed her anything but because I wanted to end it formally, so she was in no doubt.

'Oh xxxxx I'm so pleased you called!'

'Really? You think this is going to be an enjoyable conversation?'

'Listen. We need to meet. What we have is too important to throw away just because of one silly mistake.'

I could hear the excitement, and hope, in her voice. She seemed to have convinced herself that it was all going to be ok.

'One ... silly ... mistake. Is that how you see it?'

'Yes, that's exactly how I see it. What we have is too important to throw away.'

'So, who's throwing it away? Me, or you, when you had sex with my former best friend?'

'xxxxx don't. It wasn't like that. We didn't make a conscious decision. We were drunk. I can't even remember anything about it.'

'I see. That makes it ok then, does it?'

'Yes. I think philosophically it does. Have you ever done anything you regretted while drunk?'

I wasn't going to let her get away with that, or let her get me on the defensive.

'Philosophically? You quote philosophy to me? Hmm, well I've done plenty of things I regret while drunk, but never fucked my best friend's girlfriend.'

I thought I could hear her starting to cry.

'Please, please, can we just meet to talk about this? I can come to you if you like. I've taken a few days off work and…'

'No, we can't meet. Our relationship is over, as of this moment. When I get home, I'll pack up all your stuff and have it delivered. I'd appreciate it if you packed up the stuff I have at yours too and I'll arrange for it to be collected. You can keep the necklace.'

'I don't want the fucking necklace. I want you!'

'You should have thought of that then before, or perhaps while, you were fucking Sam, shouldn't you?'

'Why won't you forgive me?'

It was a fair question, really.

'Because you betrayed me, and because he's not SPC. I'm going now. Goodbye.' And I hung up.

The next few weeks passed quickly as I was approaching the end of my FSP. I didn't get home much, and then only fleetingly. The first time I opened my door there was a huge pile of post including a long letter from Alice which included the necklace. Although I'll never forgive her or go back to her it was still sad reading it, and it brought tears to my eyes. She was right, we had a really great thing going. We were going to get married and have lots of babies and travel the world in a camper van and see the Northern Lights and kiss beneath the Eiffel Tower and snuggle up on the sofa and watch old black and white movies and buy an old Citroën 2CV and paint flowers on it and see a Mozart opera at 'La Scala' in Milan and all sorts of other stuff too and hug lots and make love lots and love one another and our numerous children until the end of time. And it was all going to end, had ended, because of a few minutes - how many minutes? I often wondered - of something she did when she was drunk, which she regrets bitterly. Not bitterly enough, though, or she wouldn't have done it, would she? I gave the necklace to a Big Issue seller. That's SPC for you, right there.

The night I was confirmed as a First Speaker was very special. I'll never forget it. It was I think the proudest moment of my life. When I was little my Nan used to say to me that she wanted to see me married and on University Challenge. She never got to see either, she died when I was 10.

Even if she hadn't, I never got married, did I, and was not clever enough to get on University Challenge. At University I went to the trials, but my general knowledge was pretty shit frankly, and some guys just seemed to know everything and had read every book ever written - and memorised their entire contents - and had heard - and memorised - every piece of music ever composed by anyone. The one question I did know the answer to - it was to do with Keats - I was so nervous I got wrong. But as I was congratulated on stage I thought my Nan would be proud of me now. I even looked upwards as if to say to her, look at me Nan, I made something of myself. The thought immediately occurred to me, regrettably, whether it was really down to me though or whether it was a Branch 7 manoeuvre with me as the lucky but undeserving beneficiary. I let it go, but resolved to ask Laetitia the next time we spoke.

Listerine - that's what it is! I feel a mixture of sadness and anger that I think about Alice when I think about mouthwash.

This (I'm not referring to the Listerine) is *not* a novel. It's non-fiction, but it's not a diary either. I'm not sure what it is. I think I made this point earlier but I can't remember. (Cognitive failure, is that what's happening?) I'm not sure. I had this disturbing dream again last night that I was a fictional character created by someone who wished that an organisation like the SPC existed, but that he wasn't eligible for it. I wonder if that explains what I see as the gaps in this narrative. "Narrative", that's a good description, I like that. By gaps I mean Madame Gironde (and her box), and why the monks had the key (I just remembered that), and also the thing about me that's curious (according to "The Specialist").

I know I've mentioned that I can reveal very little about the FSP, (have I even explained that acronym, the First Speaker Programme? Well, if I have it can't do any harm mentioning it again); but what I can say is that by mid-way through the third year of the programme you know if you've made it or not. Because they tell you. I also know I've talked about the hierarchy. All the people who made it - about half on my programme - became a First Speaker at some level. And all levels are great levels. It's a great thing to become. And you can move up levels, too, theoretically, if you qualify and of course if you want to. I found out that Branch 3 are responsible for succession planning and development of the First Speaker community. "Good to great" is their motto.

On the day I woke up thinking about Listerine and potential cognitive failure and whether I was a fictional character - not to mention (although now I have) whether I'd qualified on merit and why I was in the SPC in the first place - I was summoned to a meeting in the afternoon to discuss my placement. I don't think I've mentioned that aspect of the FSP. You have to agree to accept a minimum term of twelve months wherever you're posted. It could be anywhere at any level. They obviously decide based on their assessment of your capabilities and what's actually available, as well as vacancies caused by ongoing promotions and sideways moves and deaths. As I entered the room I had no idea what initial level I'd be placed at and where my placement would be.

'Come in. Sit down. Make yourself comfortable.' said a very well dressed man flanked by two very well dressed women.

For a moment, I thought it was an interview panel. I really had no idea what to expect.

'Would you like a drink?' I was asked.

'Yes please. Could I have a cup of tea. Non-dairy milk, soy or almond or something like that, no sugar. And some sparkling water, please.'

'I think we can manage that.'

While I was waiting the three of them were reading files in front of them and chatting quietly amongst themselves. I couldn't read their faces at all. They looked in a good mood, though. I was thinking, whatever news they were going to give me was going to be good news. I was going to be confirmed as a First Speaker. But there was a world of difference between being posted to, say, *Northampton* and New York or Vancouver or Melbourne. I waited patiently and readied myself for anything. I told myself it was all good. My drinks arrived. My tea came in an old-fashioned cup along with a little jug of milk, and I spilt a small amount of milk into the saucer when I poured it out. I thought about my recurring dream. Surely if I was a fictional character this wouldn't happen? It was too trivial. I'd probably drunk about half of my tea when the man spoke.

'Well, xxxxx, first of all we want to offer you our congratulations. You have successfully become a First Speaker in the SPC, which is a marvellous achievement. You should be very proud.' And all three of them smiled and gave me a mini round of applause.

'Thank you. I am.' I wondered if I should add "Sir", but I didn't. I had another sip of tea.

He continued. 'On leaving this room you'll be given details of your new benefits package, which I'm confident won't disappoint you. It's a significant increase.' He turned over a few pages and then looked at me intently. He sure was hard to read. 'How well do you think you've performed?' Before I had a chance to work out the best response he said 'Be honest. False modesty will get you nowhere.'

'I think I did very well in some modules, and ok in the rest. Overall, I'm pretty pleased. I think I gave it my best shot, and that's important. It's the best someone can do. If I was sitting here thinking, I wish I'd worked harder, or regretting certain things I'd done, or not done, I'd be disappointed. But like I say, I think I've done the best I could, and after three years I'm confident that the assessment you've made will be the right one. I trust the system.'

They all looked at one another. I still couldn't read them. 'What if you hadn't succeeded?' he asked. 'How would you be feeling now?'

Was this a test, I wondered? Would my response have any bearing on my level and/or posting? That had already been decided, surely?

'I never allowed myself to doubt.' I said. 'Don't misunderstand me. It wasn't arrogance or a feeling of inevitability, or anything like that, it was simply that I was completely focused on succeeding. I decided that the very thought of failure made it more likely … so, to coin a phrase, I never accepted that gift of abuse. Clearly, if I'd failed, I'd have accepted it with good grace, but until that moment arrived I was never going to let it interfere with my progress.' I paused. 'I'm glad it didn't.' I was thinking of all sorts of scenarios, and still couldn't read any of their expressions. They looked at one another again, and then all closed their folders simultaneously and looked even more intently at me. The next person to speak was the woman to my left (to the right of the man).

'As you know all new First Speakers are assigned a level and a location appropriate to that level. You understand and accept this?'

'I do'. Northampton suddenly felt very real to me. I shivered as if someone had walked over my grave.

'You have consistently achieved the highest scores not just in your group but in the entire programme's history. Across all modules. From very early on we believed that we were looking at someone very special, and you have confirmed that suspicion resoundingly. As a consequence, we are offering you a First Speaker role at the Regional level. I have to tell you, this has only ever happened twice before, and both of those individuals went on to become Global First Speaker.'

She paused. I was in shock. I'd done that well, really, or was it down to the manipulations of Branch 7? Regional level, that probably didn't mean Northampton (thank fuck).

'I must tell you that your achievement is entirely merit based. The FSP is a meritocracy. Anything less would make a mockery of, and undermine, the programme. We are aware, of course, of Branch 7's *interest* in your progress …' and here I thought that she gave me a funny look '… and no doubt that will continue. But have no doubt that you fully deserve this posting. On which point, you will appreciate that at any one time there are only a limited number of Regional roles available, so I hope you won't be disappointed when I inform you that you will be the new First Speaker for Paris, one of only seven Regional roles in France. This prestigious role comes with its own luxury home in Pigalle, offices on the Isle St. Louis and in Versailles, and a permanent staff of six. Additionally, you will have your own Executive Assistant, who herself has a staff of three. You take up your post in three weeks time. I suggest you do some celebrating.'

She stood up and held out her hand.

'Congratulations, xxxxx, and Bon Chance.' One by one they all shook my hand warmly. I was so happy I welled up.

When I left the room, I was handed a thick envelope and briefcase, and asked to enter a small office to examine their contents.

'The envelope contains details of your new package and details of the role. Please check it and let me know if you have any questions or if anything is unclear. The briefcase contains details of the new role, names, addresses, security codes, where to go, where to report on day one, where your official residence is, and so on. And your new phone.'

'New phone?'

'Yes. It's a big role. Every Regional First Speaker is in regular dialogue with senior government and business leaders in the country in which they operate. You will now learn just how influential the SPC really is. Your new phone comes pre-programmed with the personal numbers for the French President and his cabinet, plus the personal numbers for various Heads of State and government around the world, and of course your own staff.'

I had so many questions but top of the list was, 'Do all these people know what the SPC really is? I mean, who we are? And why would they care?'

The reply I got was 'You'd be surprised at the influence very large sums of off-book money buys you in government circles. Or maybe you wouldn't? And as to who we are and why anyone would care, do *you* know who we are, and our true purpose, *really?*'

I was grappling with this thought when I was told more details about the new phone.

'Usually your home country's Head of State and Head of Government are programmed in out of courtesy. But in your case, we didn't think there was any point in giving you Theresa May's number as she's so utterly incompetent, and thoroughly evil. You do have the Queen, however, and the First Sea Lord.'

I thought that was fair enough. I wouldn't speak to Theresa May to ask her to pull me out of a burning pit if she/it was the only help available. First, the pain of my skin burning would be preferable to communicating directly with her/it, however briefly, and second, she/it wouldn't help anyway unless I was a Director of Carillion and/or a major Tory donor, (neither of which, I'm proud to say, I am). For the record, I'm not much of a fan of the Queen either, *drenched* in unearned privilege and with about as much clue as what goes on in the life of a normal human being as a jellyfish ... and with such a fucking ridiculous accent. But yet more information was forthcoming about this phone.

'It auto-records all conversations, transcripts of which are available real time. You can switch this off on a per call basis, should you wish. It also auto-runs an emotion detection application, which can detect, for example, stress levels, or whether whoever you're speaking to is lying. It's tested to 97% accuracy. Again, you can turn this off, but we've found it particularly useful when talking to Donald Trump, although, to be fair, quite unnecessary.'

'Why would I ever want to speak to that twat?' I asked. I was politely ignored.

'It also runs the X.100 security feature-set. Fully encrypted and completely un-hackable and untraceable. As secure as it's possible to get.' I looked at it.

'Some phone.' was all I could think of to say.

I didn't switch it on until later. I'd gone back to my room to have a lie down, reflect on Paris, and listen to some opera. There were several voicemails waiting for me already:

1. From my new Executive Assistant, Emmanuelle, welcoming me to the role and saying she was very much looking forward to meeting me soon and doing "anything at all to help me in the role. Anything"
2. Congratulations from the new French President, along with an invitation to join him "for a little cognac or two" "at your convenience"
3. From the EU team negotiating Brexit, asking for an urgent meeting to help them out as "the Brexit Secretary is an utter arse"
4. Congratulations from the Queen, inviting me to tea at the Palace and to see if I could help out with the Brexit negotiations as "the Brexit Secretary is an utter arse", "at your convenience"
5. Congratulations from the Pope and an invitation to discuss Papal infallibility, how best to "manage" historic and ongoing abuses carried out by Catholic Priests, and the evils of contraception, "at your convenience"
6. Congratulations from the Heads of State of (not in order) Germany, Norway, Sweden, Finland, Denmark, Hungary, Italy, Austria, Canada, Mexico, Cuba, Japan, Latvia, Estonia, Slovakia and Venezuela
7. A garbled voicemail from Donald Trump along the lines of 'Hello? Hello? Is anyone there? I can't hear a ring tone. Where is this number anyway, in one of those shithole countries?' (I went into Settings and blocked the number)
8. One from Laetitia that said, 'You jammy bastard. Paris. Call me if you want to fuck.'

SEGMENT 233

I'm compelled to say something more about the SPC, and to do that I need to preface it with something about Laetitia, and to do that I need to preface it with something about relationships, generally. This is purely to try and get things into some kind of context (which might also go some way towards helping me to understand those things).

When I was about 13, I asked someone to "go out with me", and she said yes, and so we were boyfriend and girlfriend. It was official. Now compare and contrast that with someone you've had sex with, say, once. Sex is a big deal, right, a very big deal, but no-one would argue that that alone constitutes a relationship, that you are boyfriend and girlfriend, *officially*. But what if you have sex several times? Or what if you stop having sex with anyone else? Or what if you don't have any sex at all but just love one another? (I say "just" like I don't value love, but you know what I mean). As grown ups, we tend not to ask will you "go out with me?", a tacit understanding simply develops. So, I don't think there's a scale, as such, i.e. 11 fucks and you're in a relationship. The maths is more complex and factors like age, fidelity, and other stuff kick in.

Anyway, I've had quite a few relationships, ranging from one night (and the following morning) stands right through to Emily and Alice, both of whom I nearly married. (Actually, I hate mentioning them in the same sentence). And they all followed some kind of pattern, although I'm damned if I could describe the patterns mathematically (and I'm pretty good at maths), until I met Laetitia. The only tacit understanding between us was that there was no tacit understanding. We had sex every time we met but we weren't "going out" and I don't think we considered ourselves boyfriend and girlfriend. Indeed, I think she'd find the notion somewhat preposterous. I'm sure she has sex with other people - and that's fine as I do too. There's no rancour or jealousy or possessiveness at all. Sometimes we don't speak or exchange messages for weeks on end, other times we talk every day.

I found myself thinking about all this the week before starting as the Paris First Speaker (PFS, not to be confused with FSP). I'd taken myself off to the Maldives, and she had joined me for a few days. We were lying in big hammocks next to one another on the beach gazing at the bluest of Indian oceans. We couldn't see where the sea met the sky, it was all so blue. I was dozing on and off and listening to music, and she was reading Voltaire. We'd talked more about the amphibians called the Caudata, who can regenerate their limbs and other parts of their bodies, a conversation which again had led to a discussion about the SPC and, specifically, *eligibility*. The E word. Dropping the E bomb, one might say.

'Don't you see,' she would argue 'That the SPC is too passive? Entirely passive in fact. It does a lot, an awful lot, to militate eligibility. while doing nothing to attack the problem *at source*.'

I questioned what she meant by "attacking the problem at source".

'Simple. Instead of spending millions of pounds swanning around and tossing it off, you could be spending that money, or some of it, on fixing the original problem. Defusing the E bomb. And now you're a First Speaker - and the PFS no less - you have the power and influence to change direction. If not a full-scale realignment and reallocation of resources then at least some research.'

So, I lay there, trying to see where the sky met the sea, and thinking about visiting an "Applied Genetic Research" facility I'd heard about near Toulouse (where allegedly some breakthrough regeneration research was going on) and mulling over her words, when I asked her why she was so bothered about it.

'Two reasons' she said. 'One, as a Branch 7 Operative I want to shift the SPC out of its stagnation. And two, well, isn't it obvious?'

So, with both prefaces done I can now fulfill my compulsion to say a few words about the SPC itself. Not, of course, revealing any of its core secrets, or anything that in anyway undermines the integrity of the organisation, but just some personal reflections.

Here I was, lying in a hammock in a 5 Star Hotel on the Indian Ocean, with a sex goddess in the adjacent hammock with whom I enjoyed the most straightforward "relationship" imaginable. I was about to start a new job paying €1.7 million a year, tax free, in Paris, with my own staff. I had a beautiful (paid for) house in Hampstead, kitted out with everything, quite literally, I could wish for (including a new self-aware self-stocking robot fridge), and an Aston Martin in the garage. Last time I'd checked (I'd largely stopped bothering) I had nearly £370,000 in my current account. I owned a Picasso. I was moving into a fabulous 5 storey house in Pigalle, in which Helen had been installed. Felix and Hermione were already there and were loving it, and were being spoiled rotten by my pouting housemaid from Lyon. I had appointments with the French President and the Queen (I know, I know, but still …) in my diary, and was gradually and subtly fucking up the Tory Party. But was I happy, I mean, truly happy? Was I content? Satisfied? Did I enjoy complete peace of mind? (Note to self: does anybody?). Was the SPC *stagnant*? Was there any mileage with this regeneration thing?

'Fancy going back to the room?' asked Laetitia. 'There's a new position I want to try, fairly desperately.'

'If you insist' I said, thinking about Voltaire's "best of all possible worlds".

On the following Monday morning my FSP role began, and my driver, Philippe, was scheduled to pick me up. The thing was, it was easier and quicker (just the one change) to get there on the Metro than get stuck in the Paris traffic, but on this first day I had quite a lot to carry, plus it gave me an excellent opportunity to get to know him. He looked and even sounded like a French Morgan Freeman, and it sort of became apparent to me that he was much more than the driver. He picked me up in an SPC black limo at 7am and soon we got stuck into conversation.

'So, what's your actual job title?' I asked.

'I haven't really got one' he said, 'But I'm sort of an Office Manager. I do all the things that need doing that aren't written down, including unofficial liaisons.'

'Unofficial liaisons? Sounds dodgy!'

'It can be.' (Turns out he wasn't joking). 'I have my people in the Gendarmerie, the government, the Paris underworld. People that can help. Back channels and all that.'

'I see. That's helpful. Is everything going ok? Anything I need to know?'

'I'll tell you everything you need to know.'

'Excellent. I need a special kind of relationship with you. The kind of relationship based on absolute trust and absolute discretion and absolute honesty. Are you up for that kind of relationship?'

'Sure am.'

We arrived at the office around 8:30am - Emmanuelle was waiting for me, along with the third member of staff in this office, a young graduate called Gabrielle. Roger from the Versailles Office was also in doing some IT work. They were all very friendly.

I looked around the rooms, had a brief chat with Gabrielle and Tony, and at 10am I sat down at my desk with Emmanuelle for a more formal chat and to check on the itinerary. I hadn't really noticed it properly before but she had a bad bruise on the side of her face and a swollen lip.

'Are you ok?' I asked her.

'I'm fine. I fell off my bike yesterday.' she said.

I had this lovely image of her cycling through the streets of Paris on an old steel bicycle in a red checked dress and a floppy hat with a baguette tucked under her arm and a bunch of flowers and some fresh strawberries in a basket on the front. Of course, I had no idea how true to life this was, but it was a lovely image. She told me that she liked being called "Emmie". Her grandfather used to call her that when she was little.

We spent a couple of hours or so running through all sorts of administrative stuff, including diary management, and if and how I wanted my calls and emails handled by her, and generally how I wanted to run things, and then I took everyone out for lunch. Philippe had gone out somewhere.

After lunch, she took me through my itinerary for the first couple of weeks starting the following day:

Itinerary	
Tuesday	Versailles Office (all day)
Wednesday	Back in Isle St. Louis. Lunch with the French Interior Minister
Thursday	Bristol Hotel. Meeting of the seven French Regional First Speakers (all day)
Friday – Sunday	Guest of the French President (*I was looking forward to the cognac!*)
Monday	Nothing organised
Tuesday – Wednesday	Conference of all First Speakers across Paris
Thursday	Nothing organised
Friday – Sunday	Three day mentoring 121 with Global First Speaker. Somewhere in the Austrian Alps (in a castle, being his official residence).

There was something about Emmie's mood that troubled me, but I didn't say anything at first. I got the Metro home that day, but when Philippe was driving me to Versailles the following morning I raised it with him in French.

'Was she really in a bike crash?'

I could see him give me a serious look in the mirror.

'No'

I now gave him a serious look back. 'And?'

'It's her boyfriend. He hits her. He's been doing it for months, but usually on her body so the wounds can't be seen. Something's clearly changed.'

'Does she know you know? Does anyone else know?'

'We all know. Tony's all for beating the shit out of the guy, but she's made us promise not to interfere or hurt him.'

I sat back and took this in, and wandered what to do, if anything. These issues seem simple but they never are. My personal phone rang. Alice. For some reason, I decided to answer.

'Hi Alice'

'Hi.' There was a long silence. 'How are you?'

'Good, thanks. You?'

'Fucking terrible.' Another long silence. 'I miss you.'

'Is there anything you want Alice, or is this just a catch up call?'

'How can you be so - so, like this? Like you are? After everything we've been through. All the plans we had.' She was almost shouting. 'Did I really mean so little to you?'

'Two questions there Alice. First. I can be like this because you fucked my best friend. Second, you meant the world to me. Does that help?'

'You, you *bastard*' It sounded like she was crying as well as shouting now. 'I've been waiting for you to come to your senses. To see what we had, and to just get over it. I made a mistake, just once, when I was drunk, and that's all. You have to forgive me. You have to.'

I felt sorry for her. She still didn't get it.

'*I'm* the bastard? You're sure about that? I have come to my senses. I have got over it. And I don't forgive you. That's it. Le fin.'

'Don't speak French to me.' She sounded a bit hysterical.

'Ok. The end. It's over, Alice, like I've told you. And there's nothing you can do or say to change that. I've told you this before. Do you think I was...'

'It was a mistake! We all make mistakes. Even you.'

'You should have thought of that before you fucked him.'

'I was drunk. I didn't realise what I was doing. I can't be held responsible.'

'Alice. I'm tired of this. I'm hanging up now if you've got nothing else to say.'

'Please, xxxxx, don't do this.'

'It's already done Alice. It was done the exact moment his cock found its way inside you. I didn't do anything. *You* did. Cause and effect. I...'

'You can't punish me for something I didn't do deliberately. It's, it's not right. It's ...'

'Bye Alice.'

I hung up.

'Do you know where he is right now?' I asked Philippe.

'Who?'

'The guy that's hitting Emmie.'

'Yes.'

'Can we go there right now. Tell the office we'll be a bit late.'

On the way, my work phone rang three times. I bounced Theresa May twice but had a nice chat with Keir Starmer. I also got an email saying my meeting with Applied Genetic Research had been confirmed in three weeks time. Laetitia would be pleased. I was pleased too. We reached the office building where Emmie's boyfriend worked. I got out of the car.

'Wait here, please,' I said to Philippe. 'This won't take long. I'm going to make him an offer he can't refuse.'

The lady at the reception desk where the guy worked was very polite but said he couldn't be disturbed if I didn't have an appointment. I said it was a matter of life and death, and would have to insist, but that it would only take five minutes or so. He came over to me a few minutes later.

'Who are you and what do you want' he said. He even sounded like the kind of guy that beats women up, and most definitely wasn't SPC.

'Can we go somewhere private?' I said.

'No. Let's just get it over with here.' He sat down.

'Fair enough' I said. 'This is about Emmanuelle.'

'What about her? How do you know her?'

I leaned forwards. 'It doesn't matter how I know her. I've come to give you a warning.'

'A warning? What the fuck is this? Who are you anyway?' He looked like he was going to get up and leave.

'I'm your Guardian Angel' I said.

'My what?'

'Your Guardian Angel. I'm here to look after you, and that's why I'm warning you.'

'Guardian Angel?' he said it with distain. I wanted to smack him in the face right there but held it back.

'That's right. And the message I have for you is this. I want you to assume the role of Emmanuelle's protector, to see that she doesn't come to any harm. For her sake, and for yours.'

'What the fuck ...' he began. I leant a little closer still and interrupted.

'If you ever hurt her again, I'll have your balls chopped off. Got that? That's the warning. My advice is, take heed of it.'

I got up to leave.

'She doesn't know I'm here by the way. She hasn't discussed it with me or asked me to intervene. Like I said, I'm doing this for your sake as much as for hers. Actually, that's not strictly true, but you get the gist.'

I left before he could say anything else. Back in the car, Theresa May called again, and I bounced her again. What did the evil hag want, I wondered? I wanted to know, but not enough to speak to her, so I blocked her number.

Back in the Isle St. Louis Office the next day, Emmie didn't arrive. There was no reply when I called her mobile. Then, around 11 o'clock, I got the call. Philippe drove me to the hospital. On the way, we agreed that her boyfriend would be brought in.

'Can you do it today?' I asked.

'Sure.'

'Ok. Do it. I'll come straight from work.'

Philippe took one look at Emmie, in a coma, face and arms covered in cuts and bruises, one eye so swollen so it was almost closed, the other not looking much better, a tube into the side of her mouth, and some of her hair cut off, before leaving. He said he wanted to know what he was dealing with so his reaction would be proportionate. I stayed there a while looking at her, feeling sad about her hair. Naturally, I wondered if I'd done the right thing. When I got up to leave I saw one of the Doctors.

'How's she doing?' I asked.

'She should be fine' he said. 'I'm just glad we got her when we did. She was in quite a state.'

'How was she found?'

'A neighbour, apparently, called the police after hearing screams. Are you a relative?'

'We work together.'

'I don't think she'll be coming back to work in a hurry.'

'That's fine. Just make her better.'

I was thinking about her cycling in a red checked dress when Philippe called. The guy had been arrested and had been taken into custody, but Philippe had called in a favour and he was now "secured" in an abandoned warehouse on the outskirts of the city. I told Philippe that I'd warned the guy that if he hurt her again his balls would be chopped off, and stressed that I wanted the warning fulfilled. Philippe said that was no problem at all, and that it was "too good for the son-of-a-bitch".

I went home after work to get showered and changed. Gabrielle called to say that Theresa May had called the office several times but had refused to leave a message, just saying that she needed to speak to me urgently. I told her to say that if she called back I needed to know in advance what she wanted to talk about.

I also had a message from Tom. I hadn't heard from him in a while. I wasn't ignoring him or anything, to tell the truth I was just a bit embarrassed. I didn't know what I felt, and was a bit well not exactly worried but not merely perplexed that once or twice I'd had fantasies about doing it again. I'd mentioned it to Laetitia - who incidentally (and wonderfully) I could mention absolutely anything to - and she'd just laughed, said it was perfectly normal. 'I have gay sex all the time' was one of the things she said, before suggesting we have a threesome. I must say I was tempted.

Philippe picked me up and drove me to the warehouse. We hardly said anything on the way. I don't know why but I was thinking about 'The Catcher in the Rye' and how Emily knew I'd like it. Emily. Wherever I may find her. Isn't that a song?

I was in a hurry when I got to the warehouse. I was meeting the other six French Regional First Speakers the following day, and to be honest could have done without all this. Still, I had warned him. It wasn't my fault.

The guy was tied to a chair with tape over his mouth. When he saw me he struggled like Hell. I sat in front of him and spoke quietly.

'You do remember what I told you yesterday, don't you? Just nod if you do.'

He looked like he was trying to escape.

I shook my head sympathetically. 'You should have listened to me. I did warn you and you took no notice. I want you to remember that.'

I looked across the warehouse and a guy brought me one of those gas-fired portable camping cookers and a frying pan, along with some butter and a sharp knife.

'Ordinarily,' I said quietly, 'You'd get the choice of pan fried or grilled, or maybe even baked or sautéed. But tonight, I'm afraid we can only pan fry. I'm sorry about that.'

I nodded to someone - I didn't know who he was but he looked quite scary - and he started heating up the butter in the frying pan.

'Here's what's going to happen. As discussed, we're going to chop your balls off.'

He struggled like crazy but couldn't escape.

'Now listen. Don't get angry. I did tell you, and you ignored me, so you've only got yourself to blame. Anyway, once we've cut them off we're going to pan fry them and then you're going to eat them. I'm sorry in advance that we don't have any seasoning. If you choose not to eat them, we'll also cut off your dick. It's your call, really.'

I looked across at the guy frying the butter. He nodded. I nodded back, and then he went straight over to the guy in the chair, and without any fuss or delay whatsoever cut his balls off and dropped them in the frying pan. I could sense the guy's pain, even though I couldn't hear him, but like I said he had been warned. He was the one in the wrong. Once his balls were sizzling nicely we pulled the tape off the guys face and forced him to eat them. Then he passed out. I wasn't vindictive in the slightest. As we left I called the emergency services and told them where to send the ambulance.

Over the next couple of weeks or so I was quite busy, and it certainly made for an enjoyable start to the PFS role. I got pissed with the other Regional First Speakers, totally pissed with the French President (top bloke), and completely shitfaced with all the Paris First Speakers. I also had an excellent time with the Global First Speaker in the Austrian Alps, which I can't discuss. In addition, I finally told Theresa May to 'Fuck off' (LOVED doing that!), fucked up the Tory Party even more (long term that one - "revenge is a dish best served cold"), had tea and cucumber sandwiches with the Queen, (who wasn't all that bad really, although she hasn't got a fucking clue about anything), and had my threesome with Laetitia and Tom (LOVED doing that too).

Then it was time to visit Applied Genetic Research. I opted to get the TGV down there instead of flying. I love travelling by train, especially when I have a nice comfortable seat facing the direction of travel with a table by the window and there's no-one sitting opposite or even next to me. Laetitia was meeting me in the hotel that night - she was flying into Toulouse from Amsterdam - and we were going to be picked up in the morning at 8:30.

On the journey south I had a call from Sam for the first time in ages (I didn't pick up and he didn't leave a voicemail), and Gabrielle said that she'd had Theresa May on the phone "in tears". I was absolutely delighted about that. I dozed for a bit, played chess against my phone (and lost) and read a bit about that year's Tour de France. It was a pleasant journey.

I got to the hotel before Laetitia, and decided to spend a bit of time in the spa/pool area. I did a few lengths, then sat in a jacuzzi for a while, and then got in the sauna. Laetitia joined me, and as soon as we were alone in there we had what we'd jokingly (and somewhat ironically) come to call DRAWL sex (dirty rough abandoned wild and loud).

Over dinner we discussed the forthcoming visit. Laetitia was very excited about it, as I've previously said. "Infinite possibilities" was a phrase she used on more than one occasion.

The following morning, we were picked up on time. It was about a 40-minute drive. As we approached the gates there was some sort of demonstration going on, and things were thrown at the car.

'It's because of the animal experiments' the driver said.

Inside the facility, we were taken into a boardroom where the Director joined us a few minutes later. I was feeling a bit mischievous, giggly even, (it was something that Laetitia had done to my nipples the night before), and hoped that he'd arrive in a wheelchair and be unable to stop his arm giving the Nazi salute like Dr. Strangelove, but he was a very ordinary looking guy. He wasn't even in a white coat. He was accompanied by some people in white coats though.

After coffees and tiny tasteless biscuits had been delivered, he fired up a PowerPoint presentation that took us through the history of genetic engineering, right up to a few years ago, and then he handed over to one of the women in white coats. She talked about the concept of "Intelligent Design", how Lamarck and not Darwin had got it right (I'm not a geneticist, and it was technical, but I think I understood the essence of what she said if not the full detail), leading into a lengthy discourse on recent breakthroughs in "regenerative manipulation nanotechnology". Her talk lasted about an hour and a half, then it was time for lunch.

Afterwards the Director said, 'Come with me' and we followed him down long white sterile-smelling corridors until we reached what was obviously an observation window. We looked through the window and saw a room with a large 7x7 grid on the floor that looked like this.

A	B	C	D	E	F	G
H	I	J	K	L	M	N
O	P	Q	R	S	T	U
V	W	X	Y	Z	.	,
?	'	!	&	*	$	0
1	2	3	4	5	6	7
8	9	+	-	x	÷	=

'Now watch this' he said, and nodded to someone sitting at a console who pressed a green button. We saw a small mouse enter the room. It stopped and looked back up at us watching it.

I whispered to Laetitia 'It's spooky. It's almost as if it knows we're here.'

She laughed. The guy at the console then pressed a red button and the word "Pi" flashed on and off in the room several times. What happened next I don't have the vocabulary for. The mouse started running around the grid and patting various squares with one of its front paws:

3.14159265358979323846264338327950288419716939937510ISTHATENOUGH?

'That's impossible' I said. I was actually feeling slightly afraid.

'Don't you believe your own eyes?' the Director asked.

'It must be a robot.' said Laetitia.

'It's not a robot. Ask it something.'

Laetitia looked at me oddly and then said to the guy at the console 'Ask it to spell out something from Hamlet.'

This instruction flashed on and off several times, after which the mouse started running around the grid again and patting the following squares:

TOBEORNOTTOBETHATISTHEQUESTION...ANDBOYDON'TIKNOWIT!

Having finished the mouse stared up at us, whether I imagined it or not, quite menacingly.

'Ok tell us what we've just seen.' I said. 'It's giving me the creeps'.

The Director led us back to the boardroom and we all sat down again.

'You ask me what you have just seen.' the Director said calmly.

I still had the look of the mouse's eyes burnt into my memory, and didn't feel at all calm.

'This morning you heard about the history of genetic engineering, something about intelligent design, Lamarck and his thoughts on evolution, and then some words on regenerative manipulation nanotechnology, which we call RMT. Part, but no means all, of our research here has involved the attempt to regenerate limbs in mammals, and so move beyond what was considered to be the boundary of salamanders.' He took a sip from a glass of water and continued. 'We used to use that particular phrase a lot. About two years ago we made a breakthrough with something we will call Agent XY. With this Agent, we were able to regenerate limbs in various mammals, right up to the higher apes.' He paused. 'But that's when we started to notice something different about these mammals. Older injuries were repaired. Musculature increased. Vision and hearing improved. Over time we realised that other medical conditions were being solved too, *completely* solved, such as arthritis and muscular degenerative conditions. At first, we didn't believe the results, so we re-tested and we re-tested and we re-tested, and always had the same results. We injected the treated mammals with every disease you can think of - that's why we have all the protests outside - cancers, smallpox, malaria, tuberculosis, HIV, the common cold ... Agent XY seemed to be a "cure all". But even that's not all!'

Here he coughed and for the first time looked slightly nervous.

'We also noticed increased intelligence - massively increased intelligence, as you saw in our mouse. And also, a cessation of the ageing process. In other words, we have the ability to create beings, of whatever species, *vastly* more intelligent than their counterparts. Healthier - not only without any illnesses at all but immune from all illnesses - stronger, faster, without physical defects of any kind, indeed with perfect bodies. Perfect vision, perfect hearing, perfect everything. And, unless an accident should take place, immortal. Do you understand the implications of this?'

I looked at Laetitia. She looked as amazed and horrified as I was.

'Are you telling me that the mouse ...'

'You saw it with your own eyes. Yes, it understands mathematics, and yes it can quote Shakespeare. It, and the other mammals, as far as we can tell, also have perfect recall.'

'But ...' I didn't know what to say.

'You're thinking the same things we thought. Man and Superman.'

'Has it been tested on humans yet?'

'Officially, no. Can you see the government licensing authorities giving us the go ahead to run trials on humans? They'd probably put us on a military footing. Imagine the impact of this in wars.'

There was so much to take in, so many implications, new ones kept dawning on me.

'And unofficially?' said Laetitia.

'Unofficially, yes.'

'On who?'

'On some terminally ill patients, who are now cured. On some people born without eyes, who now have 20/20 vision. On some people with serious brain damage, who are now Chess Grand Masters and University Professors. On people with cancer, Motor Neurone Disease, Alzheimers, Parkinson's, other conditions. All of them cured.'

'So there are some of these Supermen out there? Are they planning on taking over the world? How can we stop them?'

'But you see you are taking the pessimistic view that these Supermen would want to rule the world and be some kind of autocratic elite with the rest of humanity as their playthings or slaves. But don't you see? With that much increased intelligence comes not aggression but altruism. All of the subjects so far are happily settled into society and, as you can imagine, enjoying their newfound gifts. Why would they want to be or do anything else?'

'How many of them are there?' asked Laetitia.

'About fifty. Spread across the world.'

'What's the treatment? How is Agent XY administered?' I asked. I couldn't think of a more intelligent question at that moment.

The Director opened a box in front of him and held up a small blue pill. 'Just take one of these, and within about a week it will have been assimilated and you will start noticing the improvements. Within about a month the process will be complete.'

'It's too preposterous to believe' said Laetitia. 'It's like the story of Frankenstein.'

The Director smiled and put the pill back in its box. 'Frankenstein? No. We prefer to call it the God Gene. A vast oversimplification, of course, but it serves its purpose, don't you think?' He took another sip of water.

'So, what now?' said Laetitia. 'Give it to everyone on the planet? When we are all Supermen there will be no Supermen. No more disease, hunger, war, we really will be God. I wonder what Nietzsche would have made of it.'

'A noble idea, and it's commendable that you thought of it. We thought of it too. But there's a slight complication. Think of the practical considerations first. The Agent is time-consuming and complex to produce. We can only make around 20 a day. We currently have 477 in storage. Then there's the cost. Factoring everything in, each pill costs just over €20,000 to produce.'

'Surely you can solve both of these problems by opening up manufacturing to other plants around the world? Economies of scale, and all that?' said Laetitia.

'You'd have thought so, yes. And we thought of that too. So, we took the process and replicated it in every detail in several facilities like ours across the world, and none of them could produce the Agent. We've spent hundreds of man hours trying to establish why, but we haven't come up with an answer yet. So, as things stand, this is the only place where it can be made.' He paused. 'Then there is the, shall we say, moral, or perhaps *political* question. Who gets it first? And who decides? Do we trust any government on earth to act impartially and make the right decision?'

Laetitia and I couldn't think of one, no, except possibly Cuba. Even the United Nations was riddled with infighting and vested interests, and dominated and ultimately corrupted by the permanent members of the Security Council.

'But that's not the biggest complication' the Director continued. 'In fact, all this is academic. For security reasons, no single person knows how to make the Agent on their own. We took this precaution deliberately, thinking that someone could leave and take the ability to manufacture it to a competitor or even a terrorist group, or worse still be kidnapped. So, we designed the manufacturing process such that seven different people are each required to play a crucial part, not known to anyone else. Six of these people are still here at the facility. The seventh disappeared nearly three months ago, and no-one has seen or heard any trace of them since.'

'But surely you have a failsafe, some kind of backup? Someone, anyone, could get run over by a bus.' said Laetitia.

'We do. And it failed. Whether for sinister reasons or a simple accident we don't know. All we know is that the information the seventh person had is no longer available to us.'

'So that means that you can't make any more?' I said.

'Correct. The 477 we have left is the end of the line unless we find the seventh person.'

'Have you any idea what's happened to them?'

'None whatsoever. Like I said, they just disappeared. They left work one evening and failed to return the next morning, and that's it. Extensive enquiries have produced no leads.'

'Oh dear.'

'Oh dear indeed. And this is where you come in. I understand your organisation has an extensive search and rescue capability. In return for finding and returning to us the seventh person, we will give your organisation privileged access to the Agent.'

'Privileged access?'

'First use.'

'You do realise they may have simply had an accident. Be lying at the bottom of a gorge somewhere perhaps?'

'Perhaps. But perhaps not. We have just one piece of information, which may not even by a clue. The day before the disappearance the seventh person received a telephone call from someone who called themselves Monsieur Barrett. The receptionist took the call and transferred it through. All inbound calls are recorded. We still have the recording.'

'Yes, we can help you' said Laetitia. 'I will get in touch with the right people within our organisation and we will get back to you within 48 hours. But tell me, can we meet any of these Supermen?'

'You already have!' said the Director. 'I hesitate to use the word Superman, but I have taken one of these tablets myself.'

On the way back to our hotel - we were both staying for the night - Laetitia told she would get a Branch 5 operative assigned. She told me those guys are 'the best HSRs in the business'.

'HSRs?'

'Hunter Seeker Rescuers. Enhanced surveillance capabilities. State of the art technology. Advanced search protocols. Dark operations. They can find anyone, trust me'.

We had dinner, and then went to bed and had DRAWL sex again (three times). Laetitia went straight to sleep, but I lay awake for a while. For some reason, I kept thinking about the people who jumped to their deaths from the Twin Towers on 9/11. What a decision to have to make, be consumed by fire or splattered all over the pavement. In the seconds before making that decision, what must it have felt like? I also wondered how I'd react if I opened up a toilet seat to find a frog struggling in the basin. Would a fictional person think stuff like this? I went into the bathroom and looked at myself in the mirror. What we had learned today astonished and unnerved me in equal measure. Could Agent XY really be the God Gene? Could it be the ultimate solution to the Eligibility question? I came out of the bathroom and looked at Laetitia sleeping peacefully, before swallowing a small blue pill that the Director had given me secretly and climbing back into bed.

SEGMENT 377

I woke up wonderfully refreshed the following morning, I hadn't slept that well in ages. You know how quite often you wake up tired, and aching a bit? That happened to me a lot, but not that morning.

I hadn't even heard Laetitia leave - she'd had to catch an early flight. She'd left a note for me simply saying 'See you soon, L'. She sure was a romantic at heart.

My train back to Paris wasn't until mid afternoon, so I had time to head into the centre of Toulouse for lunch, drink some wine, and reflect on the events of yesterday.

In the end, taking the blue pill had seemed like a no brainer. I was a bit nervous though, or maybe more apprehensive than nervous; (is there a difference?). What, exactly, was going to happen to me, and more pressingly, when? I'd not expected to wake up as Superman, given the timescales I'd been told, but as far as I could establish nothing at all was different. I didn't *seem* more intelligent - but how would I know? – and everything else seemed exactly as it was yesterday. Then again, it was only a few hours ago that the God Gene had entered my body.

Over my third glass of red I imagined DNA spirals being modified as I sat there, and my cells transforming. Or maybe it wouldn't work on me. Maybe the whole SPC was immune. That was a horrible thought, to be tantalisingly close to defusing the E bomb, but learning that it was doomed to detonate after all. (This isn't a perfect metaphor by the way, this whole bomb thing, and I'm not even sure that metaphor is the right word, but it'll do for now).

The one thing I did notice was that I felt really good, physically I mean, like I was not only refreshed but energised – super-energised even. Ready for anything. Again, I didn't recall feeling that good in ages. I put it down to great sex and a good night's sleep. Sorry, there was something else. Ordinarily I needed to wear glasses to read, but that morning reading my 'Charlie Hebdo' I didn't. Must have been the lighting.

On the train back to Paris I checked my schedule. I was also due to visit Emmie that evening for the first time since she'd left hospital. I was obviously delighted that she was back home and would apparently make a full recovery, but worried what her reaction would be to my "intervention".

About half way to Paris Gabrielle called - Theresa May was apparently visiting the office in the morning. Someone from Number 10 had said that she "wouldn't take no for an answer". I told Gabrielle to call in extra security to ensure that neither her nor any of her entourage would be able to gain access. I said that I'd be in anyway, and would quite enjoy knowing that she would know that I was in the office but refusing to see her. Gabrielle asked me if she should inform Number 10 that they wouldn't be allowed in. I said no - they'd announced they were coming, they hadn't been invited or received any encouragement, and this whole "wouldn't take no for an answer" thing annoyed me even more. I had no other messages, but she told me that someone had phoned in for me and said they would ring back, they didn't leave their name.

I went straight to Emmie's when I arrived back in Paris. She looked a lot better, and said she was hoping to come back to work soon. I told her she didn't need to rush, to take as much time as she needed, and we'd get her some gear in her apartment so she could work from home.

It's an odd expression isn't it, "the elephant in the room"? I wonder who first used it. Someone must have. Thinking about it, someone must have used every expression first, but for the vast majority of them we'll never know who. ("The shit hitting the fan" is one of my favourites. What a delicious image, if you think about it). I made a note to ask Helen. Have I mentioned she'd been installed in my apartment in Pigalle? Well, I have now. I jokingly call her Helene, which makes us both giggle a little bit.

Anyway, the particular elephant in this room as it were was of course my "intervention. I'd decided to front up and come straight out with it, so I did. She asked me what had happened to him, on which point I simply said that he'd been "dealt with". She said she hadn't seen or heard from him since the night he attacked her, and I asked her if she was upset about that. She said yes and no. I couldn't begin to understand the yes part of that answer, but I guess no-one knows or truly understands a relationship other than the people in it. I told her that I didn't regret my intervention, although of course I regretted his reaction. I'd clearly had no idea he would do that. She asked me if I would still have intervened had I known how he was going to react. I said eventually I would have, yes, but had I known I would have ensured that he wouldn't have been able to act as he did. She asked me if he was dead, and I replied that he wasn't the last time I saw him, which was of course true. She thanked me for my honesty and said she was tired and wanted to go to bed, so I left rather suddenly. I think I forgot to mention that she was wearing a red checked dress.

I took the Metro to the office in the morning, and arrived before 8 o'clock. Around 10 I heard a helicopter directly overhead, which turned out to be part of Theresa May's security detail. I smiled. I didn't care what anyone said or did, I wasn't letting her in. The phone on my desk rang, which turned out to be the Chief of Police. He was RSP incidentally, and helpfully. He announced that "The British Prime Minister would arrive in fifteen minutes", and I took the opportunity to explain that she was uninvited, unwelcome, and wouldn't be allowed in. He said it would be a trifle embarrassing, but I made him laugh when I asked "for who?"

'Between you and me' he said, 'She's a stuck up cow, and as for that Boris Johnson...'

Sure enough, it did turn out to be highly embarrassing for her. I'd given the TV companies a tip off, and later that day images of her knocking at my office door and being told to 'Go away we don't want your type around here' were beamed across the world. After receiving several calls from the Press, I put out a brief statement saying:

"I don't know why the Prime Minister wants to talk to me, but whatever it is I don't care and don't want to talk to her. Her attempts to communicate with me are now bordering on harassment, and if she makes any further attempt to contact me directly or indirectly by any means I will seek a restraining order. For the record, I'm very proud to be British but most definitely not proud of the vile government that she so poorly attempts to lead".

Later that afternoon I thought to myself, *why* is Theresa May so keen to talk to me? She certainly had been persistent, and coming to see me personally on what seemed to be a whim seemed an odd thing to do. The thing was, though, I couldn't really give a shit. She was just too unimportant and unimpressive to me to think about for too long. Much like that twat Donald Trump.

In the late afternoon, I went to the gym, and although the session wasn't spectacular, I recorded several personal bests. I certainly wasn't Superman though - far from it.

The next day was one of the most event-filled I can ever remember. I laughed to myself at one point: if my life (that part of it that's covered by this narrative anyway) was a movie, the music for this day would be very dramatic, by Vangelis or Hans Zimmer or by someone like that. Some of it would be quite sinister. It got me worrying about being a fictional character again, although I hadn't had one of those dreams for a while.

When I woke up I saw a message on my phone from Alice telling me that she was pregnant. I didn't bother replying, but I did wonder if it was Sam's.

Laetitia called me to say that the Branch 5 operative had been assigned, someone by the name of Chloe. Laetitia described her as "one of the best. At everything!" Chloe was already en route to Toulouse and would report back with her initial assessment on a conference call between the three of us at 5pm that day.

The German President and I had a chat about Brexit.

I had a long and somewhat liquid lunch with the First Speaker of France – we continued a discussion we'd started a week or so previously about buying an island in the Caribbean or somewhere like that. It was partly inspired by a visit he'd made to Cuba, coupled with some thoughts I'd had on the perfect SPC environment.

We imagined an island - we rather unimaginatively called it El Dorado - where first and foremost everyone on it would be SPC. Or a woman. If you were male and non SPC you wouldn't even be allowed on the island. (We tittered a little uncomfortably at the implications of this when it came to border control). That would be a huge thing by itself, but there was more. The island would be completely vegetarian - no meat or fish would be consumed at all - and also non-smoking, obviously. A disgusting habit. There would be other criteria too, we joked about some of them. It had started out as a bit of a joke, but the more we talked about it, the more we liked the idea. It would be the perfect holiday resort for SPC members, and maybe it could be an administrative centre of some kind. Maybe also a kind of refuge. Certainly, a kind of refuge, in fact. And we had the money – in fact we'd been encouraged to get a few trillion Euros off the books as we were accumulating cash too quickly. Laetitia loved the idea.

'At last you're being proactive' she said, 'instead of lying around feeling sorry for yourselves.'

I decided to visit French Polynesia followed by Cuba and then Bermuda as background research. Laetitia said she'd join me for part of the trip as long as she could bring along someone called Camille. I said I didn't mind at all.

I decided to go straight back to my apartment after lunch to have a siesta, not unconnected with the two bottles of red I'd drunk, plus the brandies. I never quite got to sleep though, as I didn't want to miss the 5pm conference call. While I was dozing, Alice texted me again saying,

WELL?

I decided to respond this time.

AM I SUPPOSED TO SAY CONGRATULATIONS?

After a little while I got a reply:

WELL IT MIGHT BE YOURS.

I hadn't thought about that possibility. I'd need to check the dates, but presumably she'd already done that. I followed it up with:

WHO ELSE'S MIGHT IT BE?

which prompted her to call me. I decided to answer.

'Hi Alice.'

'You bastard. You just don't let up do you. You just can't move on.'

'From what you did, no that's right I can't. Did you honestly expect me to?'

'That's all in the past, in a foreign country. Anyway, it's academic. The point is, it might be yours. I've checked the dates.'

'And it also might not be, right? I guess you've checked those dates too?'

'I want it to be yours. I want you to forgive me for one stupid mistake. I want us to get back to how we were. Can you do that?'

'I want it to be mine too. But that's the whole point. The uncertainty. Caused by you fucking my best friend, let's remember. My former best friend. There's a lot of things I want that I can't have. John Lennon never got shot, I want that. Syd Barrett never left Pink Floyd. Leicester Tigers...'

'Don't be so fucking TRIVIAL!' she shouted. 'This is more important than fucking Leicester Tigers. Who gives a shit...'

'*I* give a shit. But you're missing my point. It doesn't matter how trivial or non-trivial the thing is. Leicester Tigers winning or peace on earth. Wanting the thing isn't enough, is it?'

'But what we had was so good' she started crying again. 'I miss you.'

'Yes, it was good. And it was going to get even better. As for missing me, you should have thought of that before you made your mistake, shouldn't you?'

The thing is, I sort of started getting upset too. I wasn't expecting that, it wasn't part of my plan. You know what I really missed? It's not sex - I was getting plenty of that, and great sex too - it was what I call "midnight moments". Those moments when you're really moved or upset or emotional and you just want to hold someone very close in the certain knowledge that they're there for you and they're not for anyone else. That they've not hugged like that with anyone else. It's *far* beyond closeness, and intimacy, there's probably a word in French for it but I don't know what it is. Perhaps I should invent one? Anyway, that's what I was missing. And I could never have it with Alice again. Not having it or having it and then losing it, which is worse? Was Tennyson correct? "Better to have loved and lost ...". But this was no longer love. Our conversation ended with me promising to help her out if the baby was mine, and her hoping I was starting to forgive her. She was wrong about that.

Michel Barnier and I had a chat about Brexit.

I bounced a call from Jacob Rees-Mogg.

I listened to 'Who's Next?'

Then it was time for the 5pm Conference Call. Chloe was, as Laetitia had said, pretty full on. She had already visited Applied Genetic Research and interviewed several people, including the Director, and liaised with the local police, as well as accessing CCTV footage and phone records.

'It has all the hallmarks of a kidnapping. I just don't know who did it yet. The fact that there's been no ransom demand or any other communication leads me to conclude that he's dead, probably unintentionally. I'm bringing in reinforcements and also activating a Hersch Construct. We'll find the body, or what's left of it.'

'What's a Hersch Construct?' I asked.

'I'm sorry but I'm not at liberty to discuss that' she said. 'Rest assured however that it's the ultimate search protocol. I'll report back when I've made some progress.'

She dialled off. Laetitia and I stayed on the call for a while, talking about the French Polynesia/Cuba/Bermuda trip and what Camille would bring to it. After that I had a shower, and wondered whether a Hersch Construct could track down Madame Gironde. I resolved to ask Chloe at some point.

That evening I went to see a performance of 'La Traviata' at the Paris Opera House with the Swedish Ambassador to France, a lovely lady with whom I shared a love of Verdi, screwing over right wing political parties, and salty pretzels.

En route back to my apartment I did something I'd never done before. I asked my driver to pick up a prostitute for me. He told me that he could organise someone much nicer, better looking, more sophisticated, cleaner, than I could get off the street. I told him tonight I didn't want nice, sophisticated and clean, I wanted not nice, dirty, quick, raw, animal sex, and that I wanted it now. He knew where to go. The first woman we saw, he pulled up and I opened the car window. She looked haggard and rough, just what I wanted. I told her I'd give her €1,000 if she would fuck me, right now in the car, without a condom. When she hesitated I showed her the cash. She climbed in the back of the car. It was all over in a couple of minutes. I felt fantastic on the rest of the drive home. I took her number as I wanted to fuck her again.

The last thing I did that day was have a bath. I stretched out, still not feeling like a Superman or any more intelligent, but feeling fantastic anyway. While I was drying myself, a message came in from the Director of Applied Genetic Research:

WHATEVER YOU DO, DON'T TAKE THE BLUE PILL. CALL ME TOMORROW

I dreamt I was a fictional character again, it was very vivid, like it was real. I knew I was dreaming, and even thought of that great movie 'Inception', but couldn't wake up. I sort of thought I had a glimpse of the person who created me, but it faded.

As soon as I woke up, I felt painfully in need of sex. I think I need to explain that a bit. It was actually, literally, painful. It was sort of unpleasant, like I had to have it, instantly. Like being unable to have a piss when you're desperate, but far worse. I could have masturbated, of course, but didn't want to. I called the prostitute from last night and asked her to come to me straight away and I'd pay for the cab. She said she was still in bed. I said I'd give her €2,000 cash if she came straight away. She said she was on her way.

I decided not to go into the office that day. I went into the bathroom and looked in the mirror and studied my reflection very closely. I thought of the film 'The Fly'. Did I look different, in any way? I couldn't see anything different. My eyesight seemed a little better though, but only a little. I didn't need glasses, but no X-Ray vision. I had a scar above my right eye from an old rugby game that hadn't healed. Was healing scars part of the deal? Was there even a deal? How do you know if you're more intelligent than you were yesterday? How do you measure it? I thought about doing an online IQ test, but remembered that IQ is a very narrow view of intelligence. I decided I couldn't give a shit if my IQ increased or not. I needed a more intelligent measure of intelligence.

Then I heard the buzzer. It was the prostitute. I didn't want to know her name. That was part of it. I wanted, needed, a completely impersonal transactional relationship. I wanted to fuck her and then I wanted her to fuck off. I didn't want conversation. I opened the door and she smiled at me.

'You wanted me?'

'Turn around' I said.

She turned around. I pulled up her skirt and ripped her pants off and bent her over. It couldn't have lasted more than thirty seconds. I hadn't even let her in the house, we did it in the doorway. I didn't care if anyone was watching. I gave her the €2,000 and told her that there was plenty more where that came from. Then I called the Director of Applied Genetic Research.

'Please tell me you haven't taken the pill.' he said.

'I don't want to lie to you.' I replied.

'That's unfortunate.' he said.

I asked him why.

'Remember I said that about 50 people had taken the pill, and all were achieving extraordinary things or were healed in some way? Exactly as it was with the lower mammals. The precise number was 53, including myself. Most of the pills were taken between 3 and 6 months ago. We've been tracking the triallists closely for progress, and of course to look out for any side effects. There haven't been any.'

He stopped, and I wondered what was coming next. No side effects, a serious upside - what could the problem be? What I heard next answered the question.

'As part of our tracking we know the exact date the pill was taken by each of the triallists. As I've said, most were taken between 3 and 6 months ago. The first triallist took his pill 173 days ago. He died suddenly with no warning just over a month ago. He was in a car crash, so although regrettable, of course, we thought no more of it. Three more people then took the pill on the same day around two weeks later.'

There was a pause.

'All three of these people died on exactly the same day, around two weeks ago. In each case they simply collapsed with apparent total organ failure and with no previous symptoms.'

Long pause.

'Another larger batch of triallists, nineteen in total, died suddenly the following day. They had all taken the pill on the same day, the day after the three had taken theirs.'

He cleared his throat.

'This has all happened so quickly we haven't yet been able to determine the cause, but of course it's clearly not a coincidence. Whatever benefits may accrue in the interim, someone who takes Agent XY dies exactly 151 days later. We don't know why, and we don't know how to prevent it. For the record, I took mine 148 days ago, so if the pattern continues I have 3 days to live.'

This news sank in slowly. This was sub optimal. Did I really have only about 5 months to live? I thought the word "about", but if the pattern continued I would know *exactly* what day I would die. I would wake up (actually I might not wake up) on a given day, and know I was going to die that day. Like a condemned man being led to the gallows. I thought back to a book I had read as a child in which a man about to die imagines a bird flying across the sky and he contemplates not being there to see it. I couldn't remember the name of the book. I was so distracted I missed some of what the Director had said.

'... so naturally all of our efforts are going into finding an antidote, for want of a better word. It may come too late for me.'

'How confident are you?' I asked rather desperately. My hands had started to shake.

'Not at all confident. We never completely understood how the God gene worked, and how comprehensively it became enmeshed with the host DNA. The task of working out how to un-mesh or disentangle it, even if possible, will not be easy. The only advantage of not being able to make any more ...'

I had stopped listening to what he was saying. Mortality. No, not mortality, *Death* was staring me in the face. I had about 5 months to live – I'd reluctantly have to do the calculation – unless an antidote was found. People get news like this every day, of course, people with cancer and tumours and such like, but *other* people, not me. The irony – as if the word could do it justice – just when I thought I was about to become Superman, to be immortal, and brilliant, I learned I was going to die.

I lay on my bed and stared out of the window. I saw a bird fly across the sky. I wasn't at that point in the right frame of mind to decide what I would do. Go out with a bang? Have a 5-month fuck-fest? Or leave a legacy, like El Dorado? Would it be possible to do both? I certainly felt wildly sexual - abnormally so, even for me - and thought that whatever happened I would see the prostitute every single day, unless I was out of the country.

The next thing I did was call Laetitia and tell her.

'You twat!' was all the sympathy I got from her, but she did make me smile. And what she told me about Camille made me literally drool with anticipation. Of course, I had to go on the trip with them both. What I also had to do though, was think of a plan, and map out the next 5 months, assuming the worst, which I did for the rest of the day.

I decided to go for a very long walk, without my phone. Sometimes we don't appreciate what's on our doorstep. I wanted just to walk around Paris, and feel it. Let it sink into me. Get drunk on it. I can't really explain what I mean. Too often I hadn't really noticed what was all around me. I kept taking turns I didn't recognise, deliberately, until pretty much I had no idea where I was, at which point I sat down in a small café and ordered a coffee. I watched the people walk past.

It's interesting what the prospect of your own imminent death does to your thoughts, and I started to think about the *morality* of the SPC, in the sense that, what good did the organisation really do other than materially help its members? That's not bad, but couldn't we do more? That was Laetitia's argument of course. Even the island, El Dorado, would only really benefit our members. Indeed, that was the whole point. Could we do more? With all that money, shouldn't we do much more for the poor and the disadvantaged? We did make huge donations to charity, but should we give even more? I sat there and meditated on eligibility for the SPC, that was the real thing. Non members would never understand. *Could* never understand.

'Is this seat taken?' said a man's voice.

I looked up.

'No, it's free. Make yourself comfortable.'

He sat down next to me and I started looking out of the window. I ordered another coffee, and noticed that he was reading Comte's 'Discours sur l'Esprit positif'. Praxeology, I thought, the deductive study of human action. The notion that humans engage in purposeful behaviour, as opposed to reflexive behaviour. He noticed me looking at his book title.

'Are you familiar with Comte?' he said.

'Only the cheese.' I said with a smile. 'Seriously, I wouldn't go so far as to claim familiarity, but I'm aware of his doctrine of positivism.'

He gave me rather an odd look, and just when I thought he was going to say something the waiter came over and he ordered a brandy. He then continued reading his book as if I wasn't there.

I noticed a lady pushing a pram across the road, holding the hand of a little girl about seven or eight years old. The girl was wearing grey flared trousers that were slightly too short. For some reason that made me well up. I watched her drop a doll in the road, but her mother wouldn't let her pick it up as there was too much traffic. They reached my side of the road and the girl started to cry. I went out of the café and rescued the doll, and gave it to the little girl. She said, 'thank you' in the sweetest manner imaginable, and her mother gave me a lovely smile. They looked poor.

'Would you like to join me for a coffee?' I asked her. 'I've had some life changing news today and, well, feel like I want to perform a random act of kindness. If that isn't too weird!' (That sentence sounded so much better in French than it reads in English, but this is for an English readership).

'I'd love to, Monsieur, but I don't have any money.'

'I'll treat you.' I smiled.

She said she'd like to if I didn't mind but that she couldn't stay long.

When we got back inside the man who had been reading Comte had gone, but had left his card on my chair. His name was printed as "Monsieur Barrett", his organisation was "Omega", his phone number and email address were provided, and on the back of the card he had hand written four words: 'I have the antidote'.

I put the card in my pocket, and turned to the lady.

'Listen. I know this might sound odd. I'd just like to help you, if I can. Help anyone, really. Is there anything you need?'

'You don't even know my name. Or anything about me.' she said.

'I know. It's kind of liberating, isn't it? Listen.' I felt excited. Sort of delirious, actually. 'Let's not tell one another our names. We may never meet again, anyway. Now tell me, if you could have one wish, what would it be? Anything at all.'

'Anything?'

'Try me!'

'My rent arrears. I owe three months, and we may get evicted.'

'Hmm. Well, we can't have that, can we? How much do you owe?'

'€1200. It's a lot of money.'

I'd got about €500 cash on me. Nowhere near enough. I thought about what I'd spent on the prostitute in the last 24 hours. I looked closely at the little girl. Her clothes, close up, were frayed and had some holes. I noticed her shoes which looked too big for her.

'Listen' I said when our drinks arrived, 'Can we meet here tomorrow? I'll have a little something for you.'

The girl held out her doll, that I'd picked up in the road, for me to hold.

'What's her name?' I asked her.

She told me that the doll's name was Josephine. I immediately thought of Napoleon. And then I welled up again. I didn't really know why. There's so much poverty, so much suffering in the world, and it's all so unavoidable. If I really did have only 5 months to live I determined at that moment to make a positive difference. We agreed to meet the next day at 9 o'clock. I extracted a solemn promise that they'd be there.

I cried all the way home. It was an emotional overload about everything. Josephine the doll. The little girl's trousers that were too short and her shoes that were too big. Why so many people were poor. Sad music. Moving chord changes (do you know what I mean?). That I was probably going to die in about 5 months. Thinking about it, I really needed to know as soon as possible exactly how long I'd got, so I knew how many days I had left. Assuming of course that I didn't get the antidote from Monsieur Barrett, who of course I called as soon as I got home and picked up my phone. I got his voicemail, a standard network greeting, not personalised. I left a message.

Then I called my bank to arrange for €20,000 cash to be ready for me to collect tomorrow morning, Philippe to collect me at 8:30am and be available to drive me around all morning, and then Chloe from Branch 5. She told me she wasn't ready to report back yet, but had made some progress. I asked her if she thought she could find Madame Gironde, and she said 'yes' without any hesitation. I loved her confidence. I then told her that I'd unwittingly met Monsieur Barrett, and had his business card.

'You met him? Impossible!' she said.

'Impossible? Why?'

'I didn't want to mention it initially, but as soon as I heard his name mentioned in connection with the missing scientist, and therefore knew that Omega was involved, I knew what we were dealing with. I just didn't know why.' She paused. 'Monsieur Barrett, as he calls himself in France - he goes under different names in different countries - is Omega's Chief Troubleshooter.'

'What's Omega?' I asked. 'And why is it impossible that I met him? I did. He gave me his card.'

'Omega is a secret organisation formed by elements of the British Royal Family, remnants of the Gestapo still active in Germany, the National Rifle Association, and the Vatican. We know very little about them. Even our Branch 11 have been unable to penetrate them. We only know that their ultimate objective is global domination, but subtly. Controlling governments, banking systems, the military/industrial complex, pharmaceuticals, that sort of stuff. Thoroughly nasty types.

Monsieur Barrett, who we've been tracking for years, is top of our wanted list. And you say he sat next to you and gave you his business card, just like that?'

'Well, he left it for me when I left my place for a short while. He also wrote 'I have the antidote' on the back.'

'Fuck.' she said. 'This is serious. I need to get back to you. This may be for Branch 1.'

'Branch 1?'

'Don't ask. When they get involved, the shit has already hit the fan and they need to clean it up. Now tell me you haven't made contact with him.'

'I called the number on his card, left a voicemail asking him to call me back.'

'Jesus Christ. They'll now be able to access your phone and all your contacts. We'll have to deactivate it immediately.'

'How could they access my phone and contacts from a voicemail? I thought our systems were secure?'

'They use FCT.' she said impassively.

'FCT?'

'Fucking Clever Technology! Some of the best there is. Not as good as ours, mind, but pretty darned smart. Don't use your phone again. I'll have another one with you within an hour. Your number will stay the same, don't worry'.

'What happens if he rings me?'

'He won't. He just wanted you to ring him so Omega could access your phone and contacts.'

'But if he does?'

'Don't answer. I've now extended the Hersch Construct to cover that device.'

'But what about the antidote?'

'That was a bluff. He knew it would make you call him.'

'But how would he know? About me? About Agent XY? About the 151 days?'

'That's what Branch 1 will find out. In the meantime, carry on as normal. Incidentally, by "normal" - noticed anything yet?'

'Noticed about what?'

'About you. Since taking the pill.'

'Oh' I thought about this. 'Nothing much. Improved eyesight. Increased sex drive. Massively increased, actually.'

'Following the usual pattern then. How long ago did you take it?'

'There's a pattern?'

'Yes. A very definite one, identical in all cases. When did you take it?'

I tried to remember exactly. In Toulouse with Laetitia. Was it two or three days ago? Or four? I couldn't remember.

'I can't remember exactly. A few days ago. Between two and four.'

'Well that's not a problem now. It will be as you approach Day 151 if we haven't found an antidote. Try and work it out.'

'What's the pattern?'

(I resolved to work back and remember the exact date and then put new additions into this narrative in the form of a Countdown as such: T minus n days).

'I'll provide you with a comprehensive report, so you know what to expect, but, essentially, weeks 1 and 2 bring enhanced sensory capabilities, sight, hearing, smell, and so on. Week 3 sees the first indications of increased intelligence and memory, which gather pace. Week 4 sees the first signs of physical improvements in musculature, cardiovascular endurance, agility, coordination, balance, flexibility, speed, strength, power, stamina, size, and so on. Sex drive increases exponentially from day 1, as you've begun to see. After about a month, well, let's just say things get really interesting.'

'And an antidote?'

'Nothing yet. The improvements seem irreversible, with the downside that death seems inevitable after 151 days.'

'That seems a pretty big downside to me.'

'I don't disagree. We've got top people working on it, and you'll be updated constantly. In the meantime, as there are no guarantees, all I can say is, enjoy it while it lasts. I must go. I'll set a time to report back to you and Laetitia. In the meantime, do everything that Branch 1 tell you.'

After the conversation ended I went on my exercise bike until there was a buzz at the door. It was two scary looking types from Branch 1. They looked like second row forwards for France from the 70's. All that was missing were blood-stained headbands. They didn't beat about the bush.

'We believe your device has been compromised. We need it back. Here's your replacement.'

It looked exactly the same.

'Everything has been transferred across, and will work exactly as before. The only difference is that we've installed a safety app. The phone will be polled every hour by us. All you need to do is touch the green circle that will appear with your left thumbprint. Remember, your left. If you touch the circle with anything else, or don't touch it at all, we'll move in. There will be Branch 1 Assets within fifty metres of you, wherever you are.'

'You mean I'm being followed?'

'It's a Security Detail, for your own protection. We've had dealings with Omega before.'

'Does that mean I need to tell you where I'm going at all times?'

'Well, that would be helpful, yes. We'll be discrete, of course. No-one will know we're there. If you can just keep your diary up to date on the phone, with accurate locations, we'll do the rest. Call us if you have any trips planned. By the way, do you have any trips planned?'

I told them about the French Polynesia/Cuba/Bermuda trip with Laetitia and Camille, although we hadn't agreed the dates yet. That was the only major foreign trip that I was thinking about, well, was going to go on whatever, apart from some trips to Brussels as part of deep background Brexit talks. They asked me to let them know as soon as dates were confirmed, and reassured me that there was a Branch I presence in all those locations.

'We'd also like to be on the same flights' they said, 'although you won't know who our people are.'

I agreed to let them know. They finished by telling me that Omega might try and "acquire" me, and that this could be advantageous to SPC's wider objectives.

'Acquire me?' I asked, with a hint of unimpressedness (is that a word?) in my voice.

'Yes. Kidnap you, if you prefer. If they do we're inclined to let them. Remember we'll know exactly where you are and can extract you within minutes if there's a problem.'

'How will you know if there's a problem?'

'If you don't touch the green circle.'

'A lot can happen in an hour!' There was now no mistaking my unimpressedness.

'Only kidding. If Omega acquire you we'll activate a secondary security protocol. You'll be in no danger.'

I was far from reassured.

'And what are the SPC's wider objectives, and how do they conflict with my personal safety?'

They smiled.

'Best if you don't know.'

It must have been a coincidence, but as soon as they left, the phone rang. The screen said it was the White House, (it was impossible to withhold a number to my phone, which was one of the things I liked most about it). I answered.

'Will you hold for the President?' asked a voice.

I was promptly put on hold before I could say 'Fuck off'. I said it anyway and hung up.

It rang again about 5 minutes later.

'I'm putting you on hold for the President of the United States.' said the same voice.

'And I'm telling you I don't want to speak to the cunt' I said. 'If he wants to get me a message tell him to email my secretary.' And I hung up again. Next, I had a call from my bank: the €20,000 would be ready to collect from 9am. Then I received a call from David Staples, Chief Executive of the Officers of the United Grand Lodge of England, UGLE, who was taking great exception to my promise to expose the names, personal details including photographs, and job descriptions of all 200,000 freemasons in England and Wales.

'If you've got nothing to hide, what's the problem?'

'That's not the point.' he said.

'What is the point?' I said.

'People have a right to Freedom of Assembly.'

'I agree. This exposure isn't stopping freemasons assembling as they see fit, with or without the quaffing of virgin's blood.'

At this he got quite irate.

'Listen,' I said. 'I seriously don't give a fuck what you think. I'm going to expose every freemason in England and Wales, as previously described, on the internet, at a time of my choosing but within the next seven days, unless within 24 hours you voluntarily reveal the names of and interrelationships between all freemasons in the Judiciary, Police, Parliament (both houses), Local Government, the Armed Forces, the Tory Party, and any other public bodies or QUANGOs. Your call.'

'How did you even get this information?' he asked. 'If you got it illegally...'

'I'm bored now. I'm going.' and I hung up.

I had yet another call from Theresa May. I bounced it.

I slept well that night, despite everything.

SEGMENT 610

T minus 146 days

The thing about peach juice is - at least the thing about peach juice if you want to experience it at its best - is that you have to drink it at the right temperature. (I suppose this applies to most if not all drinks? I've only ever thought about it in the context of peach juice though). You don't want it warm, but you don't want it too cold either i.e. straight out of the fridge. I find if you take it out of the fridge you should ideally leave it for somewhere between 10 and 20 minutes before drinking it, depending on things like how cold the fridge was and how warm the room is where the peach juice will be once it's been taken out of the fridge. I suppose the use of a thermometer might be the perfect guide. I must make a note to take a temperature reading the next time I drink peach juice at the perfect temperature. Except I probably won't. And I don't have a thermometer anyway.

The other thing on my mind when I woke up was the use of rucksacks, specifically, hanging them over just one shoulder instead of putting them properly on your back. I watch people like Josh Lyman and Jason Bourne do it with style. That's the way I'd like to carry a rucksack, although I'd be worried that I'd drop it. And I don't have anything to put in a rucksack. And I don't even own one.

It was also nearly 24 hours since I'd had sex, and I felt a bit ill.

Anyway, I drank some peach juice (slightly too cold but I was really thirsty) and ate a fresh croissant (I had one delivered every morning) and then Philippe collected me at 8:30 precisely. There was bad traffic, and we were running late, and didn't get to the meeting place until about 9:15, and I was worried they wouldn't be there, but there they were, waiting patiently. They got in the car, the mother, the little girl, and the baby. The little girl gave me Josephine to hold. I'd decided it might make conversation easier, not to mention improve familiarity, if we knew one another's names. The mother was called Juliette, the little girl Apolline, and the baby Mathilde.

'Where are we going?' said Juliette.

'It's a surprise.' I said.

'A nice one, I hope?'

'Of course! Tell me, if you don't mind, are you married?'

We were stuck in traffic again. I noticed a tear run down her cheek.

'Yes I am married. But we are no longer together.'

She gave me a look as if to say, not in front of Apolline. I nodded.

We finally reached the bank. They all waited in the car while I went inside to collect the money. The bank clerk commented on Josephine - I was still holding the doll.

When we got back in the car I asked Philippe to take us to Galeries Lafayette on Boulevard Haussmann. On the way there, making small talk with Apolline, I thought about the children of my own that I'd never have. I was having a child with Emily, once upon a time. I was going to have numerous children with Alice. Numerous. Come to think of it, I may *still* be having a child, sort of, with Alice. Would I still be alive when it was born? If so, would we do a DNA test or something? Would it really matter? Was Alice "with" Sam now, in the "with" sense? I'd ask.

When we arrived I asked Philippe to return in two and a half hours. We all went inside and were met by the personal shopper I'd booked for them.

'Please take these three lovely girls around and help them choose anything they want. I'll meet you back here at, say, 1 o'clock?'

'What's your budget, Monsieur?' she asked admirably discretely.

'No budget. They can have anything and everything they want.'

I turned to Juliette. 'My little treat. Now, enjoy. I'm going to have a little mooch on my own. See you later.' And off I went.

I wandered aimlessly, still holding Josephine, wondering what Juliette would buy. I guessed that she'd hardly buy anything. I hoped that the personal shopper would persuade her otherwise. After about an hour I decided to sit down and have a coffee and send some messages. On the way, I bought a rucksack. I sent a message to Sam:

ARE YOU SEEING ALICE?
To Alice:
ARE YOU SEEING SAM?
To Tom:
DO YOU FANCY BEING THE EDITOR OF THE DAILY MAIL?

I then called the office. It was Emmie's first day back in. Theresa May had called twice and Donald Trump once. I said I'd be in mid afternoon. I then called the prostitute and asked her to come to mine at midnight for another €1,000. I also asked her name - I was obviously having a name "thing" that day. She told me she'd be there at midnight and that her name was Sophia.

I looked at my watch. Over an hour to go. I ordered another coffee and started making a list of all the things I wanted to complete in the next 146 days, assuming the worst. Impending death certainly focuses the mind. While writing I thought about the whole "Carpe Diem" thing.

Surely, we should seize every day even if we aren't dying, or going to die soon?

Priorities:

1. a) Find the Antidote
   b) Assuming either 1.a) is accomplished or rendered unnecessary by improvements to Agent XY, use said Agent to defuse E bomb
2. El Dorado
3. Make a will
4. Complete the fucking up of the Tory Party
5. Release the names of the freemasons
6. Try and buy the Daily Mail
7. Re-read "The Catcher in the Rye"

I heard back from Tom. He'd love to be the editor of the 'Daily Mail'. Then I got a call from Emmie. Theresa May had called again, and said she would hold until the call was transferred to me, and wouldn't hang up. I told Emmie to leave her holding then, as I had no intention of speaking to her. Instead, I started to make a few notes regarding my will:

Beneficiaries:

Sally; Mum and Dad; Keats-Shelley House in Rome; Medecins Sans Frontieres; SHELTER; Alice? Anyone else?

Things:

House. Contents. Cash. Anything else?

I made a call to my solicitor to make an appointment to sort the will out. When the call finished, there was a text from Alice:

WHY DO YOU WANT TO KNOW?

I took that as a yes. I examined the proposed itinerary that had come through for the French Polynesia/Cuba/Bermuda trip, and emailed it to Laetitia along with some comments and a suggested start date.

I've been meaning to add, I was of course regularly touching the green circle to inform Branch 1 that everything was ok, I just assumed that it wasn't worth mentioning here. Similarly, on the procedure I had to follow when I went to sleep, as obviously, I didn't want to have to wake up every hour to say that I was sleeping peacefully. Helene was able to do it for me somehow.

I did wonder, at that point, whether Branch 1 were observing me right now, in the Department Store. I looked around. I couldn't see anyone who looked as if they might be Branch 1. Then again, how would I know?

I also haven't been mentioning all the eligible people I'd been spotting, and how I'd approached them about the SPC. I guess I'd assumed that wouldn't really be of much interest. It was happening regularly but infrequently, maybe one or two guys every other day on average.

I was just about to read an incoming message from Sam when I felt a tap on the shoulder. It was the personal shopper.

'I've been calling you, Monsieur.'

'Sorry. I must have my other phone on silent.' (I'd mistakenly given her my SPC number and not my personal one.)

She told me that they'd found some lovely things but Juliette absolutely and categorically refused to confirm the purchase of any of them before talking to me. Everything they had liked was currently in a changing room and they were waiting for me to arrive. She said that Juliette was the nicest customer she had ever had, and that Apolline was the sweetest little girl she had ever had the pleasure of meeting.

I followed her away. I heard a voice shouting 'Monsieur Monsieur', and turned around. It was a waitress. 'I think this is yours?' she said, showing me Josephine. How could I possibly have left it?

We met the girls a few minutes later and I looked at all the things they said they liked. There were a few dresses and a couple of jumpers for Apolline, and a pair of ankle-high boots. A few things for the baby. Nothing for Juliette. Even at their prices it couldn't have added up to more than a few hundred Euros.

'Didn't you see anything else you liked?'

'Lots of things. But we could never pay you back.'

'You will be able to pay me back, I promise. Now listen, this is my treat, something I want to do. Please. Do it for me.'

I looked at my watch and then at the personal shopper.

'Have you been making a note of everything the girls have liked, even if they didn't pick it up?'

'Yes Monsieur, as you instructed. And I've made a list of other items that I think they would look great in.'

'Great. Can you go and get everything and have it all packed up and ready to collect in, say, an hour? And I do mean everything. Use your initiative and creative flair!'

I lent closer to her so Juliette wouldn't hear. 'There's a €1,000 bonus for you personally if it all adds up to over €10,000'.

Off she went.

'Now. Shall we go and grab an ice cream?'

'Why are you doing this?' Juliette asked me.

'Because I want to. Because I can. Because I'm dying and you'll be doing a dying man a favour. I've got no-one else to give to. Are those good enough reasons?'

'But you don't know me.' she said. 'You don't know anything about me.'

The ice creams arrived.

'I know enough.' I smiled at her, and she smiled back, I think for the first time. She had a lovely smile. A little melancholy, but all the lovelier for that. Given the sexual frenzy I was in, which had continued building throughout the day, I couldn't stop myself thinking about kissing her. I'm proud to say that was as far as I allowed myself to think, (on that occasion).

Everything was collected and brought into the car. The personal shopper achieved the objective I had given her, and there ended up being several carrier bags and boxes. Apolline was already wearing the boots.

'I need to go to my office now. Philippe will drive you home and help you carry all the stuff in.'

I realised I didn't have her address. Or phone number. She wrote them down on a piece of paper for me.

'What do you do for a living?' she asked. I caught the twinkle in Philippe's eye in the driver's rear view mirror.

'I manage the Paris region for a member's organisation' I said. 'It's not terribly exciting. How about you?'

'Well, I trained as a teacher. Of infants. But recently, due to, um, circumstances, I've taken on cleaning roles. So, I suppose I'm a cleaner.'

'Wow. Incredible. What a coincidence. I need a cleaner. Would you clean my house for me? I'll pay competitive rates, although I don't know what competitive rates are.'

'I could come around tomorrow and take a look, and give you a quote?' she said.

'Perfect. Philippe could collect you if you like?'

I caught another twinkle in his eye.

'It would be my pleasure. Won't take no for an answer.' he said.

We agreed that he would pick her up at 10 o'clock and bring her straight to mine. I resolved to take the day off. As I got out of the car she stopped and looked at me seriously for a moment.

'Are you really dying?'

I felt very happy when I sat behind my desk, notwithstanding the 146 days. First of all, I read Sam's reply:

YES

I took that as a yes. Laetitia had got back to me about the trip, told me it all looked good, and said that Camille seemed "totally up for it", which sounded good. So, I booked it, and sent the confirmed itinerary to Branch

1. We would be flying out in just under three weeks.

Next, I set about establishing how much it would cost to buy the 'Daily Mail'. As far as I could establish, the Daily Mail General Trust was a PLC with global revenues of around £2 billion. Chicken feed compared with the amounts the SPC wanted to get off the books. I sent an email to the British First Speakers asking them what they thought about the SPC buying a national newspaper, including a statement on why buying the 'Daily Mail' in particular was such a good idea (namely ridding the world of such a "dismal and soul-destroying piece of misogynistic homophobic nimbyist right-wing bollocks", or words to that effect).

Next up, I read the latest briefing document from the El Dorado transition team I had established. Their plans were now at an advanced stage, with several thousand volunteers already lined up to arrive on the island as soon as it was purchased.

Towards the end of the afternoon I received an invitation from Chloe about tomorrow's Branch 5 update call on the missing scientist and matters arising. It was set for 10am, exactly the same time that Philippe was due to collect Juliette.

I stayed at my desk doing odds and sods for another hour or so, when I got a text from Laetitia:

TURN ON THE NEWS IF YOU HAVEN'T SEEN IT ALREADY

I turned on the news. There was a reporter shouting into her microphone while fire engines and ambulances drove past behind her, and I could see a huge cloud of smoke in the background. I thought it must have been a terrorist attack, or possibly a plane crash or something, until I picked up the following: '... at this stage we don't know if any Animal Rights organisation was behind it, no-one so far has claimed responsibility. We can say that the entire facility was destroyed in the explosion. Emergency Services have not yet revealed the casualty figures, although they are saying that it is unlikely there were any survivors. Army bomb disposal experts have been called in to establish if there are any secondary devices. Due to the nature of the work carried out here, with some Defence contracts, an enforced evacuation is underway ...'

I didn't hear the rest of the report. Fuck, I thought. Where did this leave the search for an antidote?

Immediately afterwards, I felt quite ashamed. People - and intelligent mice - had very possibly died, and there I was worrying about the antidote. Then again, I was potentially going to die too, so maybe it wasn't too selfish of me.

I had quite a lot of things to catch up on so didn't finish until about 7pm, and I had so much energy and vitality I decided to get the RER to

Gare du Nord and then walk. I was a long way from Superman - it had been less than a week - but I just felt totally physically *prepared*, if you know what I mean. It's hard to explain. Boundless energy, raring to go. Every step I took felt as if I was feeding from Mother Earth. My whole body felt more alive and more ready than it had ever felt - to say nothing of my sex drive which meant that every part of me felt like a hyper-sensitive erogenous zone.

When I was about a ten minute walk from home, I stopped for a coffee. I don't even really like coffee, but I like the thought of liking it. It makes me feel French. I take it black with no sugar, when I think I'd prefer it white with plenty of sugar. Anyway, I sat there watching people go past and trying to think about nothing in particular. The monks had taught me about "sitting quietly, doing nothing".

I got home and still felt pretty wired, so after making myself an omelette I went for a run. The improvements apparently weren't supposed to be kicking in yet, yet I ran 10k in less than half an hour, and didn't even break a sweat.

Then I watched a movie, I can't remember what, and waited for Sophia to arrive. I don't think I'd ever felt more sexual. Midnight seemed to take ages to arrive, but eventually it did, and I heard the buzzer go. I could hardly walk downstairs.

When I opened the door, she had a bag with her. She said she thought I wanted her to stay the night. I hadn't thought about that, but now that she came to mention it, it seemed like an excellent idea. We went straight to bed. I can't remember how many times we had sex during the night, but it was at least six times. I didn't sleep much in between the sex either. At one point, I remember lying there holding her while she was sleeping, and maybe I was dozing a bit because I had another of those weird thoughts that I was a fictional character. That the whole thing was someone's creation.

I must have gone to sleep properly at last, because I do remember being startled by the alarm ('La Marseillaise') going off at 8:30am. We had wild quick rough sex again, and then she was on her way. I asked her to come back at midnight again.

At 10 o'clock precisely I dialled into Chloe's conference call for the update, Laetitia joined too. She began, unsurprisingly, with yesterday's explosion. There were no survivors. The police were still trying to determine who had been in that day, to establish the death toll. Chloe didn't believe it was Animal Rights protestors. She thought it was Omega. She then said that the original missing scientist had been traced to Tangier, in the company of persons unknown, three days after his disappearance. After that the trail had gone cold. Even the Hersch Construct had been unable to come up with anything further so far.

Investigations were continuing and leads were being followed up. She then said, 'But the most interesting thing of all is ...' when the buzzer went.

This would be Juliette.

'Hold on a minute' I said. 'I don't want to miss anything. There's someone at the door for me.'

I let Juliette in, and asked her to make herself at home and look around as I'd be on the phone for a little while longer. I got back onto the call, leaving Juliette looking around the kitchen.

'Sorry about that. You were saying?'

Chloe said that the Director had taken all the remaining stock of Agent XY out of the facility two days previously.

'Why?' Laetitia asked.

'We don't know.'

'Where are they now?' I asked.

'We don't know.'

'Where is the Director? Was he in the facility when it blew up?'

'We don't know.'

'Wasn't his 151 days up tomorrow?' asked Laetitia.

'No. It's the day after' I said. 'I was going to call him this afternoon.'

'Any news on an antidote?'

'We know they were working on it. We picked up some chatter that they thought they had made a breakthrough, but this hasn't been confirmed yet.'

'So where does all this leave us?' I asked, rather deflated.

'Work in progress' was all Chloe said. 'I'll report back again as soon as I have news. We're focusing our efforts now on the whereabouts of the missing Agent XY and Omega's motive for blowing up the facility.'

'Who's focusing on the antidote?' I asked.

'You are. We're HSRs. We're not biochemists. Clearly if we uncover anything we'll let you know.' And with that, she dialled off.

'That's me told!' I said to Laetitia who had stayed on the line.

'Don't take it personally. It's not her role.'

'So, what do I do now?'

'If I were you I'd find the best geneticists in the world, and pretty quickly, and get them on the case. Oh, and buy some sun cream.' She dialled off too.

I went downstairs to see Juliette. 'Well? Are you up for cleaning my house for me?'

'It's a very nice house' she said.

'Thank you. It's not actually mine. It comes with the job. So, are you happy to clean it for me, sort of regularly?'

'What, specifically, would you like me to do?'

'Well, I'd like to broaden the scope a bit if I could, to include washing and ironing, if that's ok?'

'How often would you like me to come round?'

'Every day. For two hours.' I blurted out. I had no idea if this was enough, I just wanted to see her every day.

'That's 10 hours a week. How about €100 a week?'

'I'll pay you €500 a week.' I said. 'Ok with that? Oh, and before I forget, here's an advance for you. Open it when you get home. See you tomorrow then? If you get here for 10 we'll sort everything out, priorities, like the bath, places not to tidy, like my desk, times, stuff like that. And I'll get you a spare key'.

I gave her the envelope containing the €20,000 and we both left, her to go wherever and me to head over to the Ministry of Finance to talk about a proposed reduction in interest rates.

T minus 145 days

I'm not going to do this every day. For starters, it's a bit boring to do, sometimes, and may even be boring to read. It probably is. But I'm not writing a novel, this isn't entertainment. Frequently I ask myself why I'm doing it at all. And I forget a lot of stuff too, I'm sure I do. I forget what I've forgotten, or if I've forgotten anything. Sometimes we remember that we've forgotten something, we just don't remember what, and sometimes we don't.

Anyway, the only notable thing that happened the next day was Juliette's visit in the morning. First of all, she was wearing a pale blue dress that I'd bought her the day before. She looked very good, actually. She asked me to sit down, so I did, and this is how the conversation went, as far as I can remember:

'We need to talk.' Juliette started.

'OK. What about?'

'Everything.'

'Everything? That's a lot to talk about. Where do we start?'

'I mean, about us.'

'There's an us?'

'You know what I mean. The shopping. The money. What was in that envelope.'

'Wasn't it enough? I have more...'

'I don't understand. You don't know me, us. I don't know you. Yet you give us all this.'

'It's nice not to know things, sometimes.' I replied.

'But why?'

'Because Apolline dropped Josephine. And because her trousers were a bit too short. And you told me you're alone, and about the rent, and...'

'Are you really dying? Is that why you're doing this?'

'Yes. Unless a cure can be found. And I just want to make a difference to someone, to some people.'

'Don't you have anyone special?' she asked.

'No. I used to, but I don't any more. I have a sister and parents whom I love. I take care of them as best I can.'

'Apolline is dying too, you know.'

'What?' I felt sick.

'She has an incurable disease. She doesn't know.'

'How long has she got?'

'Three months. Six, maybe, if we're lucky.'

I thought for a minute. 'When I asked you if you could have one wish, you mentioned the rent. I don't …'

'It's too sad.' She began to cry, quietly. 'You see, there's no hope. I just didn't …'

'What can I do? I can pay for the best treatment in the world, the best doctors, I can…'

'It's incurable.'

I remember her putting her head in her hands. I wanted to put my arms around her but didn't feel confident enough.

'Will you let me at least get a second opinion? I will pay for the best doctor in the world, and the best treatment. I will put all of my resources at her, your disposal…'

'I came here to give you the money back. I can't take it. I can't ever pay you back.'

'For her, then? Take it for her?' I pleaded.

She looked at me. I couldn't read what she was thinking.

'You can take her around the world, or something. To places she's always wanted to go? Disneyland? Harry Potter World? I don't know, anywhere…'

'It's too much.'

'No it's not. It's not enough. Anyway, you can pay me back. With your cleaning. Oh, and the washing and ironing. And with your smile.'

She gave me an odd look, which again I couldn't read.

'Do we have a deal?'

This time I read her expression.

T minus 144 days

Laetitia called me. 'I've been thinking' she said. 'Get this. The missing scientist was taken, against his will, to Tangier…'

'Do we know that?'

'What? Tangier?'

'No, that he was taken against his will.'

'Chloe said it was "persons unknown". I see what you mean. Anyway, let me finish my scenario then you can tell me yours.'

'I haven't got one yet.'

'Hmm, well, shut up then. The missing scientist was taken against his will, it doesn't matter where to, *or* he left voluntarily. Either way as a result no further production of the Agent was possible. Some time later the Director removes all the remaining supply, and a few days after that the facility is blown up. Now what do you conclude from that?'

'Er, no idea. What's your conclusion?'

'I thought the Agent was supposed to increase intelligence!' she said, but not, I thought, all that unkindly.

'That's week 3 I think. Give me a few more days.'

'Hmm. Well, this is what I think. Somebody wanted those pills, and they wanted no-one else to have them, or no-one new anyway. So, they abduct one of the scientists, so no more can be made. Their plan was then to extract the remaining tablets, but the Director discovered the existence of the plan, hid the tablets, and blew up the facility so no more could ever be made.'

'Interesting. Two things. *One*, why did he hide the tablets? If he didn't want anyone to get them, why not blow them up with the facility? *Two*, what if the Director is compromised somehow, or perhaps was dodgy in the first place? Perhaps he's Omega himself?'

'Hmmm. Perhaps. We'll have to see what Chloe turns up. Anyway, onto more important matters. How's the trip shaping up?'

We chatted for a while about that, and other trivial stuff.

I hadn't heard anything back from David Staples, so I thought, fuck it, and put on the internet the names, addresses, phone numbers, email addresses, photos, and job descriptions of every freemason in England and Wales. I was looking forward to the shit hitting the fan actually, and while I'm thinking about it, I always giggle at the thought of actual shit actually hitting the actual fan. And for some reason "the" fan is funnier than "a" fan. Think about it.

I did a few more things to fuck up the Tory Party. It was very clever, subtle, irreversible, stuff, medium term. I can't say what it is, because it's not finished and this might end up in the wrong (i.e. Tory) hands. That said, I don't think they could save themselves now, even if they found out. It's just such a shame that I may not be around to see it.

That thought stopped me in my tracks. Death in 144 days. What could I do about it? What I could do something about, though, or at least try to, was Apolline. I discovered that the best qualified experts on her condition in the world were based at the St. Thomas Hospital in London and at the Johns Hopkins Hospital in Baltimore.

The thing about money is, it solves most problems, if you have enough of it that is. Not all problems, of course, and, as the Beatles sang, it can't buy you love, but it can buy you a lot. The sad thing is, not everyone has enough, with some tiny proportion of the world's population having a massive and totally disproportionate amount of the world's wealth, while billions live in poverty. This sad fact occasionally made me question the purpose of the SPC. Well, maybe not the purpose, but the point. What we do - ultimately, is it worthwhile? On the grand scale, I mean.

Anyway, since one worthwhile thing I could do was try and help Apolline, I made a few phone calls and sent a few emails, and before long she had appointments in London and Baltimore in the next couple of weeks. All the travel and accommodation was arranged. Next up I called Chloe about Madame Gironde.

'Sorry, I forgot to tell you about that.' she said. 'Nothing so far. It's very unusual, actually. Normally by now we'd have picked up something, but she's not coming up on any of our traces. Are you sure you have the right name?'

I told her that I did, and gave her a few more details, including a description of the box that she gave me, and how when I went back to find her it was as if she'd never been there. I asked Chloe if she still felt confident about finding her, and got an ambiguous answer. The conversation prompted me to look in the box, which I hadn't done in ages.

Next up, I called Sophia and asked her if she could come right round. She said she'd be with me in an hour. After that I emailed my solicitor about my will, and made further enquiries about buying the 'Daily Mail'. It was beginning to look unlikely that I'd be able to raise the money, due to other priorities which I'm not at liberty to reveal, so as a tiny gesture I organised for every copy from my local newsagent back in Hampstead to be delivered straight to my house, where they would all be collected later during the day and burnt. Futile? Almost certainly. But it made me smile. For evil to triumph, it is sufficient for good men to do nothing, is I think how the saying goes. I did have a concern that the distributors might ship more copies in, thinking it had gained in popularity, but I resolved to deal with that problem if and when it arose.

Thinking about the 'Daily Mail' got me thinking about Tom, and I called him to say that he might not get the Editor's job, but that the forthcoming trip with Laetitia and Camille might make up for it. I've forgotten if I've already mentioned that he was going to come along for part of it. No matter.

I went into the office later that afternoon and stayed until quite late. Everyone had gone home by the time I left. It was a pleasant evening, so I walked up to the Notre Dame Cathedral, crossed the river, and wandered over to Shakespeare and Company where to my delight there was an event going on. A French writer I'd never heard of was discussing his new novel and taking questions. I bought my copy of "The Catcher in the Rye", which if you remember I'd resolved to re-read (for about the twentieth time I think) and then wandered aimlessly around until I found a bar I liked the look of, and decided to get drunk. I hadn't got drunk, not properly anyway, in ages, and I just felt like it.

The thing was, that I *couldn't* get drunk. It sounds odd, as I certainly tried, and had quite a few beers and a few glasses of Pastis too, but all I got was tipsy and headachy and melancholy. I even cried, I don't know why.

I could have got Philippe to pick me up - in fact, had I called him, he'd have insisted - but I wanted to get the Metro. When I got off I went down towards the Moulin Rouge and found another bar. I sat by the window looking out while listening to a karaoke competition that was going on inside. Someone sang 'Zombie' by the Cranberries, in French. That made me even sadder.

It was around 2am when I started to walk uphill towards home. The side streets were deserted. I stopped a couple of times. I wasn't tired or anything, I just wanted to stop. I finally got home, and just as I was about to open my front door someone ran across the street towards me very quickly. He was wearing a grey hoodie which completely covered his face. I thought I was going to get mugged or something, but, as it happened, I wasn't. It was the Director from Applied Genetics Research.

'Can I come in?' he said.

'Quickly, in case they've followed you.'

We went upstairs and I sobered up pretty quickly. I made us both a large black coffee and then we sat opposite one another in the lounge.

'Aren't you supposed to be dead?' was all I could think of to say.

SEGMENT 987

The Director told me what had happened.

'It should have been obvious to us, but at first it wasn't, that as soon as people started benefitting from taking Agent XY then questions would be asked. Questions like "What's going on?" and "How is this possible?" leading into "Can I have some?". We were approached by several organisations, offering substantial sums of money, and I do mean substantial, for a supply of the Agent for their top executives and senior management teams. We explained that it was still a trial, that we were still monitoring potential side effects, but many of them didn't seem bothered.' He paused to drink some coffee.

'Which organisations?' I asked.

'I'm not at liberty to discuss that for all cases. What I can say though is that one organisation in particular, Omega, were extremely persistent. They wouldn't take "no" for an answer. They bombarded us with calls and emails, approached some of our staff outside working hours with bribes and inducements, and even turned up at the facility unannounced on one occasion.'

'I've heard of Omega. A bunch of utter cunts if you ask me!'

'Absolutely. Anyway, we turned them down repeatedly. Shortly after that we noticed that some pills were going missing. We have - had - very tight security, but it's virtually impossible to prevent something as small as a pill being smuggled out, as you can imagine.'

'How many went missing?'

'Fifteen.'

'Do you know who took them?'

'No. We tightened security, installed cameras throughout the facility, and no more were taken.'

'So only fifteen were ever stolen?'

'That's right, as far as we can tell.'

'Do you know where they ended up?'

'It must have been with Omega, since as soon as people started dying they came onto us for an antidote.'

'Serves the fuckers right, if you ask me. They get someone on the inside to steal the Agent for them, fifteen of their top officials take it, and then they learn that they're all going to die. Happy days.'

'Indeed. Except for the fact that the missing scientist had developed the antidote, or rather the formula to make it. Whether he was the original leak, or an unfortunate victim of circumstance, either way it was bad news. He could develop the antidote for them, and the fifteen people would survive. Imagine fifteen Supermen at the top of Omega.'

'Horrific.'

'But thankfully it turned out that they needed the original Agent to manufacture the antidote. And they had none left, so they needed some more. Furthermore, they needed our facility to manufacture it. So, they made us a new offer, one we couldn't refuse.'

'What was that?'

'Life or death. Very Godfather!'

'I see. Did you go to the police?'

'They warned us not to. Said they had penetrated to the most senior level.'

'So, you got us involved.'

'Absolutely.'

'And the antidote? Did you manufacture it?'

The Director lent closer as if we could somehow be overheard. 'We agreed to let the facility be used for the manufacture of the antidote, but by now we had developed an anti-Agent to the original Agent. Basically, it reverses all the improvements and returns the person to their original state. So, our thinking was, we would incorporate this anti-Agent into the antidote, leaving the Omega hierarchy back at Square One.'

'So, what's the problem?'

'It didn't work. We hadn't carried out any tests. It turns out that a combination of Agent XY, its anti-Agent, and the antidote, is lethal. All fifteen died. They think we did it deliberately.'

'But I thought you said it was an antidote?'

'We did. And it was. But only to the original Agent XY. Taken together, problem of death after 151 days solved. In case you're wondering, that's why I'm still here. Any chance of a drink by the way? A proper drink, I mean?'

I'd sobered up sufficiently to have another one myself, so I poured out two beers.

'This is all getting a bit James Bond.' I said. 'Agents, anti-Agents, antidotes, lethal combinations. I'm not sure I'm keeping up.' I said.

'Tell me about it. Anyway, Omega let it be known that I was now a priority kill target, so I took steps to remove what was left of the Agent and put it in a safe place. And just in time, too, as they blew up the facility. Everyone's dead and all manufacturing capabilities have been destroyed. We can't make any more of anything.'

'So, you have a stash of Agent XY in a safe place. And what about the antidote? And what about the anti-Agent? You can guess why I'm interested?'

'I have around 500 capsules of Agent XY. I have 1 capsule of the anti-

Agent, and I capsule of the antidote.' He reached into his pocket and took out a red pill and a green pill.

'And here they are, for you.'

I took both pills and put them in my pocket. 'Remind me how the combinations work again?'

'Easy. Agent XY, Superman, dead on 151st day. Agent XY plus antidote, Superman, and you don't die. Agent XY plus anti-Agent, no net effect. Agent XY plus antidote plus anti-Agent, rapid death.'

'What about if you take only the antidote or the anti-Agent, or both, without taking the Agent?'

'We don't know. It's never been tried.'

'Hmmm. Which one's which, by the way?'

'The red pill is the anti-Agent and the green pill is the antidote.'

'Incidentally, do you have any blue pills on you, just in case?'

He gave me one.

I was still no Superman, but I had completely sobered up. It was bizarre. It shouldn't have happened that quickly. Maybe it was the Agent? We got around to chatting about other things, notably the fact that he was now on the run from Omega. I called Branch 1 to see if they could help, given that he'd saved my life. They asked me to put him on, and while he was speaking to them I texted Sophia again and asked her to come straight round. The Director gave the phone back to me.

'They want to speak to you now.' he said.

They told me that everything was arranged. His wife and children were being collected immediately, and the Director would be collected at 5:30am. Apparently an ESV (enhanced security vector) was in the process of being thrown up around the house. I said that sounded good. I asked what would happen to him next, and they said that the fewer people that knew, the better. He would have a new identity in a new country and have permanent Branch 1 protection. That's the SPC for you.

The buzzer went. It was Sophia. It occurred to me as I went down to get her that the Director might like to join in as well. I was right, he did. We enjoyed a frenzied threesome on the floor, did just about everything it's possible to do, and then she climbed into my bed.

'Well, goodnight.' I said to the Director with a smile. 'The night is young! I'll set my alarm for 5 so I see you before you go.'

T minus 143 days

Thinking about it, I don't need to do this any more do I, as I'm not going to die? To clarify, of course, I'm going to die, at some point, but not of Agent XY. You never know though, do you? I might be killed in an accident tomorrow, or have a heart attack or something, and die in less than 143 days! Anyway, although I don't *need* to I think I'll keep doing the T minus thing, as it serves as a reminder of what might have been, and is also a useful counter.

Sex and grapes. Sex and green seedless grapes straight from the fridge, cold. Brief, rough sex and then green seedless grapes straight from the fridge, cold. That's the way to start the day. Then sit in a dressing gown too big for you, of rough toweling material, not the fluffy material you get in spas that doesn't dry you and feels like it's falling off your skin. Then, ideally, a hot bath.

I did all that today after the Director got picked up at 5:30am and before Juliette arrived at half past nine. When she did arrive we discussed her forthcoming trips to London and Baltimore. She would be able to give Apolline either the antidote or the anti-Agent, if the doctors couldn't help her, depending on whether she wanted her daughter to be normal or a Superwoman. Somehow I didn't see Apolline as a Superwoman, being a Chess Grand Master (Mistress?) and a mathematical genius and a great philosopher and a sublime artist and a stateswoman on the world stage and an elite athlete and all that stuff. I mean, I *could*, but I liked her just the way she was. What would her mother make of it? Should I even tell her? If I was going to give her the Agent and the anti-Agent she need never know. Come to think of it, if I was going to give her the Agent and the antidote she need never know that either. I would wait and see how things panned out.

T minus 135 days

I'm not doing this every day. I never have. It's not a diary.

I've felt different in the last few days. I can't explain in what way. Mentally, I mean. Things seem clearer to me, more obvious, if that makes sense. I did an online IQ test and scored 173, which is pretty good, I think. I've also been remembering stuff, stuff I thought I'd forgotten, from childhood even, like the time I cried when I read "Jennie" by Paul Gallico.

I had sex six times with Sophia today, and it still wasn't enough. I also saw a performance of Rossini's "La Gazza Ladra".

T minus 130 days

Juliette got back from her trips to London and Baltimore. There was nothing the Doctors could do. Fuck. I took her and Apolline out to dinner, during which I asked her if she trusted me. She said she did. I told her I'd like Apolline to take a tablet from me, without asking any questions.

'Would you do that for me? Please?' I asked.

Apolline swallowed the tablet with her Coke. Great, I thought, she now has Agent XY working its wonders. Should I give her the antidote or the anti-Agent? I didn't have to make that decision yet, so I didn't.

T minus 129 days

I packed for the trip with Laetitia and Camille. I had sex with Sophia five times. She told me it felt different but she couldn't explain in what way. I did notice that I was lasting a lot longer, on one occasion nearly an hour. I was pleased with that I must say.

I told Juliette I would be away on business for a few weeks. She agreed to visit the house every day and keep an eye on it. I asked her to arrange to revisit the Doctors in London and Baltimore in a couple of weeks time, before I got back. She said there was no point. I asked her to trust me again.

I had dinner with the First Speakers of France, Germany, and Italy at a very nice little restaurant I'd never been to before in the 6th arrondissement. What a find! I was going to write down what it was called, but I want it to remain a (relative) secret. I wouldn't want the thousands of people who'll read this (ha!) eating there and then telling all their friends about it... and before you know it, it's lost its character. (Note to self: it, it's, and its, all in the same sentence!). I'm joking though, I'm not sure if anyone at all will ever read this and I don't think I care. I mean, I don't know if I care or not.

Over dinner we talked about Brexit, naturally, the state of Italian politics and the rise of the "right" throughout Europe generally, and what a total fucking twat Donald Trump is. And I mean, *total*. When the third bottle of very cheeky red came out they told me why they'd invited me; (it hadn't escaped my notice that I was the only non-national First Speaker there). They said they'd been very impressed with the work I'd done in Paris in such a short time, and following protocol they wanted to sound me out about being the First Speaker for Italy. I looked quizzically at Gianni, who explained that he was "getting too old" - he said he was 65 - and that it was time to step down. He said there would be competition, including a very bright young talent from Slovakia, but if I was interested then I'd almost certainly get it, and the Slovak would then get Paris. His time would come.

I was genuinely astonished, and of course delighted. I didn't know what to say. I told them I was off on my El Dorado fact-finding mission the next day, and we all agreed to reconvene when I got back. This led naturally into a discussion about the island - they all thought it was a fantastic idea - and into a few more bottles of red.

I got a lift back in the French First Speaker's limo. I ran a bath, turned the lights out, lit some candles, listened to whole of "The Magic Flute", and thought about the Eternal City.

T minus 127 days

I read somewhere once that Helen of Troy was the most beautiful woman who ever existed. There was even a scale - of "millihelens" - of female beauty. So, Helen of Troy would score 1,000 millihelens. Some would say it's subjective - "beauty is in the eye of the beholder" - others would argue it isn't. Would anyone argue that Audrey Tautou, Nicole Kidman, Jennifer Aniston, Kylie Minogue, Angelina Jolie, and the waitress in the bar near my house aren't beautiful? Exactly. But what about sexy? Is sexiness more or less objective/subjective than beauty? Are they related, and if so how? And how should alcohol consumption and/or desperation be factored in and compensated for in any form of measurement?

I mention this because when I was introduced to Camille at Charles de Gaulle I came in my pants. Literally. Twice. Just looking at her. Not really literally, but you know what I mean. I know I was in an enhanced sexual state anyway, but this was absolutely ridiculous. A unique combination of contours (tits, arse, waist), legs, face, mouth, haircut, coupled with the dirtiest mind imaginable, as I found out even before we boarded the plane.

So, I'm introducing the sexiness measurement unit of the "millicamille" (abbrev. MC). She obviously scores 1,000 MC. It's just a bit of fun. It's just for me. I'm not objectifying women or anything, I'm simply making a joke about how sexually attractive I find them. That's right, how I find them. There's nothing objective about it at all. I'm making no comment about all their other attributes, that's a different discussion. I'm not saying they don't have any, I'm just saying that's a different discussion. If anyone, a feminist, say, thinks otherwise, they can fuck off.

On swearing by the way. I think I might swear too much. I'll try and curb it. That said, I did sort of read an article recently saying that we shouldn't get so hung up about it. Swearing can be cathartic, and it can also of course be appropriate, like during sex or when some fucking twat carves you up on the motorway or when you see Donald Trump on TV..

On sex. I've always been quite obsessed with it (haven't we all though?) but of course now it's different; with Agent XY coursing through my veins. I'm finding it impossible to satisfy myself however much sex I have. Within minutes - an hour at most - of having it I need it again. And, thankfully, I'm capable of doing it pretty much constantly. My recovery rate is about ten minutes.

I've also noticed something else. A bit embarrassing, really, so I'm not going into it in any detail. Let's just say that I've noticed a new change in my physical characteristics. For the better. Sophia noticed too. I've updated my personal profile in the online SPC database.

The journey that followed, from Paris to French Polynesia, was a bit of a trek:
1. Paris to Amsterdam
2. Amsterdam to Los Angeles
3. Los Angeles to Papeete

We flew out at 16:45 and landed at 05:20 two days later! That's a long time. Still, we travelled First Class all the way, which had its benefits:
1. Lots of champagne
2. Those nice bed/seat things so you can lie flat when you want to sleep
3. No screaming kids

As it was such a long journey I got through quite a lot (have I mentioned I like lists? Don't we all?). In rough chronological order, as I recall:
1. Re-read "The Catcher in the Rye" (which made me think of Emily) even though I wasn't going to die
2. Watched "Withnail and I"
3. For an unaccountable reason (life being too short for fussing and fighting?) I felt somewhat conciliatory towards Alice, and composed an email for her. In it I said I'd forgiven her (but not forgotten); that I hoped she was happy with Sam; I asked her whether Sam knew the baby might be mine (I presumed he would but I thought it was worth checking); and that perhaps we could meet for a drink when I got back
4. Watched a Bourne movie
5. Watched a bit of a Spiderman movie but it was a bit shit so I gave up
6. Had fantastic sex with Camille in the toilet (I took nearly three hours to finish)
7. Read some Robert Frost
8. Read some cycling magazines
9. Talked to Laetitia and Camille about Rome. They both said it was a no-brainer
10. Played a drinking game
11. Had fantastic sex with Laetitia in the toilet (this time I took three minutes to finish)
12. Ate some figs for a dare. Disgusting!
13. Dreamt I was a fictional character again. I even at one point sort of saw, or was aware of, the writer, and dreamt he was lying in

the dark sobbing quietly. It was quite disturbing if you want to know the truth
14. Thought about Apolline, and wondered what new pill I'd give her and whether I should discuss it with Juliette. I supposed I only really needed to if I was going to give her the antidote, as if I was going to give her the anti-Agent she'd simply get better and be back to normal
15. Arranged for the Aston Martin to be re-delivered to Sam.
16. Put the finishing touches to fucking up the Tories. Boy those fuckers really had it coming, and the best of it was they had no idea at all
17. Made lots of notes about El Dorado and what we were looking for
18. Listened to some Bill Hicks
19. Had fantastic sex with the foxy stewardess in the toilet. (Only kidding)

That fantastic feeling when you get off a plane and you're immediately hit with the heat and it's so bright you have to squint. Brilliant. Even at that hour of the morning it was hot and sunny.

We were taken to our villa on a small island by speedboat, the journey took about forty minutes. The villa was even better than it had looked in the photos, backing onto the beach, with its own pool, and about a ten-minute walk to the nearest beach bar and a few shops. Perfect. From here we'd investigate the local El Dorado possibilities for the next couple of weeks. I ought to clarify, we already knew we'd be buying an island somewhere near here. The Cuba leg of the trip was to investigate political and cultural considerations, and the Bermuda leg was a boondoggle.

First, though, our maid arrived who explained that she'd be available every day to cook - if we wanted her to - clean and tidy and wash and get shopping in and generally keep the place nice. She'd also be able to give us advice and make recommendations. We thanked her and said that after such a long journey the first thing we all wanted was a shower and then maybe a light lunch and an afternoon doze on the beach. When she went off to get some food for lunch, the three of us writhed around naked on a large rubber mat (not sure what it was doing there but it came in handy) covered with warm honey. Delicious.

Then we all had showers and were unpacking our stuff when she came back. She really was an excellent cook. We said we didn't need her that evening as we'd eat out, and she told us about a great local restaurant a fifteen-minute walk away with "the best fish on the island". We agreed that she would come around every morning at 10 o'clock to make us breakfast and see what else we wanted doing that day. We explained that if we didn't answer the door within five minutes we were probably having sex, and could she come back in an hour.

We'd hired an open top jeep which was going to be delivered the next morning.

That evening we walked along the beach to the bar. The sand was the perfect temperature to walk on barefoot, I remember giggling over cocktails that my feet had never been so happy. We spent the evening talking about our plans for El Dorado, what would and wouldn't be allowed on the island, and stuff like that. These were the notes we came up with:

Allowed	Not allowed
SPC members only	Non SPC members (male)
Female partners of SPC members	
Male partners of SPC members if eligible	
	Sugary drinks
	Any tobacco products
	Any plastic or non-biodegradable containers of any kind
	Any meat (the island would have a strict vegetarian diet)
	Any shit food (the island's FS would monitor this) including raisins
	Football shirts
	Guns (obviously)
	Drugs (illegal, stuff like Paracetamol is ok)

We got into quite a debate about whether Tories should be allowed, or NRA members, or freemasons, or various other undesirables - but leaving aside how we'd know, we eventually agreed that any such restrictions would undermine the whole point of the place, which was to provide a luxurious environment for all SPC members to spend some time in, completely free from the E bomb. How absolutely wonderful is that? I mean, it's an absolutely beautiful, perfect scenario. Unprecedented. Unbelievable, if it wasn't actually happening. I remember sitting there downing my umpteenth cocktail and thinking it would be the best feeling in the world. By which I meant, feeling i.e. emotional, not feeling as in walking barefoot on warm sand or writhing around naked with two women on a rubber mat covered with honey.

T minus 120 days

These are just markers, you understand. Not everything below happened on the same day. I hope that's clear?

When you know, you know, as they say. Which is a bit bloody obvious, really, like "it is what it is" - I mean, how often isn't it what it is? Anyway, as soon as we saw the island, we knew. Love at first sight. The right location, the right size, the right amenities, the right price, the right everything. We still went ahead and looked at the other contenders, but none of them came close.

I got the SPC legal team involved, and put them in touch with the seller's legal team, and since it was a cash purchase (I'm not allowed to say how much) I was told things would progress quickly.

We'd obviously need someone on the ground to oversee everything, and it turns out the SPC sort of assumed I'd organise stuff like that, so I thought of Tom. I called him, and my pitch was along the lines of 'I can't get you the Editor's job at the "Daily Mail" but I can get you a twelve month secondment (initially, potentially extending to two years and potentially becoming permanent) living in luxury on an island in French Polynesia overseeing the creation of El Dorado for SPC members, on a tax free retainer of €2,500 a day.'

He said he'd think about it. By the time he'd finished the sentence he'd said yes.

'That didn't take long' I smiled. 'See you in Bermuda. Camille's dying to meet you. I think you'll like her.'

The work (if you can call it that) in French Polynesia being completed, we spent the rest of our time there drinking lots, lounging around on the beach and in/by the pool, eating fine food, and having orgies. We also drove all over the island in our jeep which was great fun.

Cuba was great. We loved Cuba. We stayed in the Presidential Suite at the Hotel Nacional, and drank lots of rum. One day we had a bath of rum, just to experience what it would be like. It caused quite a stir in the kitchen as they had to heat it all up and bring it to the room in multiple saucepans. They did a fine job though, getting the temperature just right, and we gave them each €1,000 tip for their trouble.

I pay in Euros, and write €, whenever possible, as paying in Pounds and writing £ reminds me of everything I dislike about the UK. The Royal Family. Deference to elites. Tory voters. Brexit. Refusal to embrace the European project. Shit newspapers. Shit TV. Ant and Dec. Shit weather for 10 months in every year. Arms sales to Saudi Arabia. Endless and often needless bureaucracy. The UK is sort of like a fly buzzing around a light when you're in the bath. Intensely annoying. Don't get me wrong. I want England to win at rugby, and cricket. Couldn't give a shit about football though, in fact I laugh when our prima donnas lose on penalties to countries with less than the population of Kent. At least the Tory Party is fucked. And there are good things too. Soho and Borough Market and Cecil Court in London. Hampstead Heath. The Lake District. This is too boring to continue, actually. I'm not under any obligation to justify myself or explain my views.

Anyway, Cuba. We liked the political vibe. That's not really the right word but it'll do. The sort of desire, the imperative, for fairness. The free healthcare. The fact that you're obliged to pick up hitchhikers, who maybe can't afford public transport. The fact that they stick two fingers up at the Americans. They need to get their act together on toilet paper though. Every bar in Havana I went into, you had to tip someone to get toilet paper. I would say Havana is in my top ten places not to need to have a shit, up there with Hong Kong street markets and the desert around the Egyptian pyramids.

Bermuda was fabulous. This was pure holiday. Basically, we ate, drank, slept, shopped, and had sex, pretty much all the time we were there. Tom arrived too. I think I mentioned he was coming and about the change in plan? Well, I have now.

Like on the way out it was a long journey back. I watched "Jean de Florette" and "Manon des Sources", and slept a lot. I'd decided to take the Italy role - as Laetitia had said it was a no-brainer really - and had agreed a date to have what amounted to an interview, although they didn't call it that. I also decided to spend a few days back in Hampstead, and thought I might try and see Alice. I wasn't sure why, really, or what I'd say, I just wanted to see her again.

The possibility of leaving Paris made me think about the possibility of *leaving Paris*. It's so much more than a place for me. More even than a home. It's the place where I feel the best, the most "me". It's hard to explain. Impossible, even. I'd miss it like I'd miss my children, if I had any and if I ever had to say goodbye to them. Of course, I supposed I could go back any time, but it's not the same as waking up there day after day after day and knowing that you really belong. Still, I hadn't actually got the Italy job yet, it might not even happen.

I don't really know why but I kept thinking of the shoes Apolline was wearing the first time I met her, the ones that were too big. It made me well up. She'd given me her doll, Josephine, the one she'd dropped. It lived on my bed. Just then I wanted to buy every little girl in the world shoes that fitted. I hated the thought of them wearing shoes that didn't fit, or that had holes in, or Heaven Forbid that they didn't even have any shoes. I thought of Holden Caulfield wanting to be a catcher in the rye. I sort of felt like that about their shoes.

T minus 110 days

I met up with Alice in a bar in Soho. Her bump was quite big. We didn't talk about it though, or who the father might be, all that much. It was nice to see her, I had to admit. She asked me if I was seeing anyone. I said there was no-one special, which was true, depending on how you define special. My relationship with Laetitia was nothing like my relationship with Alice had been. Neither was my relationship with Camille or Sophia. Or Juliette. I wasn't sure what kind of relationship I had with Juliette. It wasn't sexual. I remember wondering whether I wanted it to be. Alice talked about Sam a bit, and it was really odd hearing her talk about him, the man who was for so long my best friend. As the evening wore on I started to think about the night they'd betrayed me, and wondered what they'd been drinking. I mean, *exactly* what they'd been drinking. It made me feel sort of sick thinking about it.

She wasn't drinking, obviously, but I was. I was getting drunk in fact. And then I did something I'm not particularly proud of. I invited her back to mine.

'Seriously?' she said. I thought she was angry with me, but it turns out she didn't believe me.

'I mean it.' I said. 'Come back with me, if you want to.' I burped, I was even drunker than I thought I was. 'I'd like you to.'

'What for?'

'I don't know. I'd just like you to come back with me. And stay over. But if you don't want to, or don't think it's a good idea, then I guess you shouldn't.' She gave me a long serious penetrating look. 'That's the problem. I do want to but it's most definitely not a good idea, is it?'

I took a big swig of my beer and gave her what I thought was a cheeky grin. 'Your call.'

'This is just sex, right?' she asked in the cab on the way back.

'Absolutely.' I confirmed.

We had sex six times actually, before we got up in the morning. She noticed something different too, I'm pleased to report. After she left I lay there thinking about what I'd done and wondering about the implications. Had I done something wrong? Had we done something wrong? There was no doubt that it could degenerate into something of a mess. I was confused about my feelings. I also needed sex again.

I lay in bed listening to all the sounds I could hear. All my senses were heightened. The occasional clicking of the central heating system thingy. Not much traffic noise, as the house was set back from a quiet road, but I heard a motorbike go past, and in the distance some police sirens. (Have I mentioned how unpleasant British police car sirens are compared with continental ones?)

I made a list in my head of the best sounds to hear as you're waking up, or soon after:
1. Peacocks
2. A woman moaning with pleasure
3. Ocean waves
4. The sound of children playing or listening to their music
5. Church bells

T minus 80 days

Rome. The Eternal City. It would be my new home - I'd been offered the role and had accepted it. I had plenty of time to finish up in Paris, nearly three months in fact, during which time we'd agreed that I'd focus on El Dorado.

First Speaker of Italy. I still couldn't believe it really. I kept thinking back to the quiz night when it all began, it seemed like an age ago. More than that, it seemed like it had happened to a different person. In a way, of course, it had, thanks to Agent XY. I'd noticed all sorts of changes recently, intellectual, emotional, and physical. I constantly had masses of energy. I slept perfectly, for about seven hours each night. I seemed to be able to anticipate virtually everything that happened around and to me. I ran a marathon in just over two hours with no training. I'd gone down to the south of France for a French First Speaker Meeting, hired a bike, and cycled up Alpe d'Huez in 31 minutes.

I don't want to keep banging on about sex, so to speak, but I needed it constantly, several times a day if possible. On one occasion with Sophia it had lasted for over two days, pretty much non-stop. I'm not sure if that counts as only once - since we didn't stop other than to eat some peeled grapes - or 31 times, which is how many orgasms I had. I didn't count how many she had, but it was at least once, I think.

On my last full day in Rome, on this trip, I took a very long and roundabout walk, and ended up in the Vatican. Looking up at the ceiling of the Cistine Chapel, I thought about Apolline and which pill to give her. My new Superman-y status was, I have to admit, very enticing, but I didn't want to be selfish. Should I give the antidote or the anti-Agent to her. Either way she'd survive and prosper, wouldn't she?

By the way I think I forgot to mention that Juliette had taken her again to London and Baltimore, and the Doctors had pronounced her cure as a miracle. I'd asked Juliette not to mention anything about the pill, just to say that she'd gone to Lourdes and prayed and that her prayers had obviously been answered.

When Juliette had asked me about the pill, I'd simply said it was a magical substance, and that she should read "Arabian Nights". She said she would never be able to thank me sufficiently, and I said that as long as she didn't lose any of my socks while washing, and kept the fish tank clean, that would be thanks enough. I was going to have dinner with her when I got back to Paris, and intended to ask if I could kiss her.

When I got back to my hotel after the walk the Italy job offer was already in my inbox. My main residence would be a palace south of Rome, and I would have villas or apartments in Venice, Florence, Milan, Aosta, Siena and Sorrento. In addition, I would have a vineyard in Tuscany and an olive farm in Sicily. My salary - as always tax free - would be €7.1 million a year, I would have a staff of 31, a black custom built Lamborghini, a private jet, and 70 days holiday a year. It didn't seem too bad.

I found a little pizza place just around the corner from the hotel, and sat quietly in a corner with a carafe of the house red and a calzone stuffed with vegetables and pecorino cheese. Delicious.

Another thing about sex by the way - I don't know how this happened, as I didn't look any different, but I found women (and men) almost throwing themselves at me, all the time, everywhere I went. I don't know if I was exuding some kind of scent or pheromone or something - obviously something to do with Agent XY - but whatever it was I was constantly asked for sex, sometimes quite unsubtly. Given my condition, this was of course perfect, and without the slightest hint of promiscuity I had sex several times a day usually with several different people. I mention that because the waitress in the restaurant literally dragged me off to the toilet while I was waiting for my vanilla ice cream.

My flight back wasn't until late afternoon, so on my last morning there I walked down the Spanish Steps and visited the place where the poet John Keats had died, which is now a small museum. I bought a book of his letters and a tote bag. Then I went over the road into the Armani shop and bought some shirts for me and a scarf for Apolline.

On the flight back I had sex with two of the air stewardesses, one after the other. When I landed I had three voicemails:

1. Alice, telling me she'd told Sam
2. Sam, telling me Alice had told him and asking me to call him urgently
3. Vladimir Putin, referencing the nerve gas attack in Salisbury, England, also asking me to call him urgently

Philippe picked me up. I'd miss him, he's a top man. I hoped I'd get someone equivalent in Rome. I texted Sophia and asked her to be ready for me in about an hour, I said it would be a quickie. Philippe waited with the engine running while we had sex in a doorway. By now, and I'm still not exactly sure how, I could control how long sex would take. It could last for thirty seconds or several hours, but the intensity of the orgasm was exactly the same. That's Agent XY for you.

While on the subject, I'd noticed significant changes in my cognition. I seemed to be able to understand and explain everything I put my mind to. I'd solved P versus NP and the Riemann Hypothesis, and over breakfast one morning proved the Twin Primes Conjecture. It all seemed so obvious. I'll put all the proofs in an Appendix as I don't want to interrupt my flow. For all my increased intelligence, though, I still couldn't work out what the fuck James Joyce's 'Ulysses' was all about; I don't think I'm alone in that …

I still couldn't make up my mind what pill to give Apolline. I kept changing my mind. I still had plenty of time to decide. I called Sam back.

'Hi' I said. 'You called?' I very deliberately played it cool.

'Yes, I fucking did. Alice told me what you did together.'

'What *we* did together, Sam. It takes two to tango, as you know.'

'We've been seeing one another.'

'I know.'

'And you still slept with her.'

'We didn't sleep much, if I'm candid.'

'She's having my baby. How could you do that to me?'

'You really think I need to answer that? Anyway, it might not be your baby.'

I heard my other phone go. It was Juliette.

'Listen, I must go. Let's chat again soon.' I hung up.

I answered Juliette's call, and we agreed to have our dinner the following evening. She said she couldn't organise a babysitter, so I told her it was no problem we could eat at mine and she and Apolline could stay over. I'm a pretty good cook, I have to say, but I wanted to make it special, so I called in a favour and got three of the best chefs in Paris to agree to come round the next day and cook a banquet for us. That organised, I rang Putin back. What a cunt.

The Press Release went out about my Italy role, and the congratulatory calls and messages began to flood in. I was particularly touched by what my Paris team said about me. We agreed to have a big leaving do, and I had the idea of having it in French Polynesia, which I had to visit again soon anyway. I said I'd pay for everyone.

That evening I went to the opera again – "The Marriage of Figaro" - and afterwards sat in a bar and had several Bloody Mary's. Then, somewhat foolishly, I rang Alice while I was a bit drunk.

'It's over between me and Sam' she said. She sounded a bit tearful.

'I'm genuinely sorry to hear that' I said.

'Things are such a mess' she said, and then she started crying properly.

I couldn't calm her down, in the end she just ran out of tears.

'What does this mean about us?' she asked. 'Are we going to try again?'

I said I wasn't sure, but that I would look after her financially and in any other way I could. I invited her over to Paris, anyway, for a weekend.

'Why would I be coming over?' she asked.

'To visit the most wonderful city in the world. To be cheered up. To get away from it all.'

She said she'd let me know.

I took out Madame Gironde's box and looked inside. I hadn't done that for a while. I still couldn't believe what was inside. I decided to put the antidote and the anti-Agent pills in there. I locked the box and put it back in its usual safe place, and then had a bath in the dark listening to Bach's solo cello suites.

I slept soundly, and had another of those odd and faintly disturbing dreams where I'm a fictional character.

The following morning, I had to get into the office early, as I had back to back meetings and calls nearly all day, and had to be home by 3:30pm to let the chefs in to prepare dinner. I got in at 7am, and Mark Zuckerberg (Facebook) and Alexander Nix (Cambridge Analytica) were already waiting for me. Their appointment wasn't until 9:00 and I told them they'd have to wait. They were pretty pissed off about this - they gave me the impression they weren't used to being kept waiting, but frankly, I didn't give a shit. They wanted to see me, I didn't particularly want to see them, I'd only agreed to the meeting out of curiosity.

I had a call with my counterpart in Hong Kong, which took about half an hour, and then dealt with my email backlog until 8:00 when I had a breakfast meeting with Anne Hidalgo (Mayor of Paris). A very charming lady. Then it was the turn of Zuckerberg and Nix. First, they asked me to sign an NDA, which I refused. They said the meeting couldn't continue without one, so I said, 'Fine you've given me back an hour.' They conferred briefly before saying they would continue but only if the meeting could be recorded. Although I had no real objection, I just didn't like the pair of them, I didn't like what their companies did and how they did it, and I felt mischievous, so I declined that as well. After another brief conflab, they agreed to carry on anyway. They were just getting started when I received an alert on my desk display that an ambient recording device had been detected in the room.

'Excuse me' I said, 'Didn't we just agree this meeting wasn't to be recorded, just a few minutes ago?'

They squirmed a bit. Scumbags.

'The meeting is over' I said. 'I believe you know the way out.'

'Do you know the lengths we've gone to to get here this morning?'

one of them said, can't be bothered mentioning who.

'No, and I don't give a shit' I said. 'You should have thought of that when you tried to deceive me. Please leave.' and I turned back to my emails. I'm not a forgiving person, a trait which helps me eliminate twats from my life.

They left in a bit of a huff. My uninterest outweighed my curiosity.

I'd had an hour scheduled with them, so I'd got three quarters of an hour back, which was great. I did some more emails, and had a chance to check with the chefs that everything was looking good for that evening. Everything was looking great, they said. I also asked them if they'd be sorting out the wine, and they said they would, which saved me another job.

At 10H I had a call with SPC in Estonia, and at 10H30 a call with the Italian Prime Minister. At 11H the French Finance Minister arrived. That meeting took longer than expected, so I had to reschedule my call with the King of Spain. I had a working lunch with the First Speaker for France, and we discussed the handover.

At 14H, I had a call with the El Dorado team, which again overran, leaving me just 15 minutes to chat to Angela Merkel. I did manage to make it back home by 15H30, just.

The chefs were prompt, and took over the kitchen, and were happy for me to leave them alone. This gave me the opportunity to invite Sophia round, which only took ten minutes (three orgasms), before settling down in my study and doing some more planning work on El Dorado. Juliette and Apolline were due at 19H.

Around 18H, while I was on the phone to the Pope, I received a voicemail from SPC's IT function. Here is a transcript which I include just for fun:

'Hello xxxxx. SPC IT here. We've set up a thin warm stack on your base level system, with rapid and continuous two-way feed via the triple N node. X.100 integrity maintained at super-optimal. Outline client DIS functions cross-bleed through 333-AMY protocols. M subset is handed over to M.1415 triple zero lightning function. Any questions give us a call.'

What the fuck?

I just had time for a shave and a shower before Juliette and Apolline arrived promptly at 19H. Juliette brought me a little bunch of flowers and Apolline had made me a rocket. After Juliette had put Apolline's bag in the spare room, the three of us sat down in my attic room while we were waiting for the food. Apolline did some drawing while Juliette and I talked about my move to Rome.

What can I say about the meal? It surpassed my expectations, which were very high, by a factor of about twenty million. I didn't realise that food could taste that good. And as for the wine ... wow!

Apolline went to bed around 21H, the chefs served us pudding and then left, leaving Juliette and me drinking more wine back in the attic room. I looked at her longingly all evening as we drank more and more, but was strangely shy. It's odd. I was having loads of sex - as recently as that afternoon - but I was shy with Juliette. I'm still not sure why. I'm not sure anything would have happened if she hadn't asked me where she was sleeping.

'That depends.' I said with a grin.

'On what?'

'On how much sleep you want.'

She looked at me - despite all my observational training I had absolutely no idea what she was thinking - and for an agonising few moments, I thought I'd offended her in some way - and I was already thinking about calling Sophia again - and then she learned over and kissed me. Gently, but passionately. It was the best kiss I'd ever had, since my first kiss, or so it seemed at the time. That kiss lasted for ages, during which we managed to undress one another and she climbed on top of me.

"All this to love and rapture's due;
Must we not pay a debt to pleasure too?"

When we finally climbed into bed we held one another close, clinging to each other as if we were drowning and clutching desperately at our last chance of rescue, and we both wept. We were both crying when we made love the second time, which lasted nearly all night. Utterly spent we finally both went to sleep around 5 or 6 in the morning. It was getting light.

I heard Juliette's alarm go off at 7H. She kissed me and got straight up, and left me in bed. I could hear Apolline's music playing on her Kindle. I was in a state of bliss.

As I lay there, I started thinking more seriously than I had for a while about eligibility for the SPC. It's really an important point. Indeed, it's the central point of this whole narrative, although I may not have made it that obvious, apart from the title I suppose. I guess I'll never know.

Juliette brought me in a cup of black coffee and sat on the bed and sipped hers.

'Thank you for a lovely evening. And night.' she smiled.

It was a Saturday so she was in no rush.

'How's Apolline?' I asked.

'She's fine. Don't change the subject.' she said.

'I'm not sure what the subject is. What is the subject I'm supposed to be changing?'

'Last night. Was. Incredible. You. Are. Incredible. I want to know if it was just sex, just a one off, or is there something more.'

I had spent years observing people - men, that is - in minute detail, and was intimately familiar with the physical and behavioural characteristics that define someone eligible for the SPC ... and so, by definition, someone ineligible for the SPC. As previously discussed I'm not at liberty to reveal what these characteristics are, how I spot them, or what the SPC is. What I can say however, is that only if you're eligible for the SPC will you understand what went through my mind when she asked me that question, and indeed every time I looked at someone ineligible. Of course, I don't know who is reading this - if anybody - and (if you're a man) whether you're eligible or not. Statistically you won't be. We're in a small minority.

'So?' I vaguely heard Juliette say. 'I need to know. I don't want to be hurt by you. If it was just sex, just once, I can live with that. If it was just sex, and happens again, I can live with that too.'

She took another sip of coffee and all of a sudden looked unbearably sexy. It had, after all, been over three hours. 'But if it's ...'

At that moment Apolline walked in with some pictures she'd been drawing.

'Mummy.' she said. 'I've been copying one of xxxxx's pictures. Look at this.'

Juliette looked at it, and showed it to me. It was a brilliant version of one of my Picassos. (I had it laminated by the way. Apolline's version, that is, not the original). Apolline went back downstairs. Juliette asked her to shut the door and said she'd be down in a minute.

'Where were we?' she said.

'You were asking me if it's more than just sex, I think.' I hesitated and smiled at her. 'Yes it is. I don't know if it's love, as I don't know what love is any more. I ...'

'Let's not tell one another our sad stories.' she interrupted.

'Isn't that from Jerry Maguire?' I asked.

'Sure is.' She pulled back the sheets. I was, of course, still naked. Not to put too fine a point on it, she then gave me a Class 1 blow job. And I do mean Class 1.

After the girls had left I ran myself a nice hot bath and thought about love. Was I in love with her? Was there a genuine (what one might term mathematical) difference between loving someone and being in love with them? Had I loved Emily? Alice? I thought about the clod and the pebble:

"*Love seeketh not itself to please,*
Nor for itself hath any care,
But for another gives its ease,
And builds a Heaven in Hell's despair."

*So sung a little Clod of Clay
Trodden with the cattle's feet,
But a Pebble of the brook
Warbled out these metres meet:*

*"Love seeketh only self to please,
To bind another to its delight,
Joys in another's loss of ease,
And builds a Hell in Heaven's despite."*

Ultimately, I supposed, and in my enhanced intellectual state I surmised that I was getting agonisingly close to understanding the meaning of life, did it matter? It was just a word. Whatever we feel about someone or something, we should just feel it, and not analyse it. "Nothing worth knowing can be understood with the mind" said Woody Allen's character in 'Manhattan'.

I loved Saturdays with nothing much to do. Such days were increasingly rare. I stayed in the bath for ages - kept topping it up with hot water. When I eventually got out I lay down and read for a bit (Bulgakov's 'The Master and Margarita') and then watched Toulouse v La Rochelle in the Top 14. Good game. I didn't check my phone until half time, when I saw three texts from Alice and noticed that I had voicemails from the Crown Prince of Saudi Arabia, the President of China, and Boris Johnson. I deleted all the voicemails without listening to them and then read Alice's texts:

DO YOU STILL WANT ME TO COME TO PARIS? IF SO, WHEN? XXX
HAVE YOU HAD SEX WITH ANYONE ELSE SINCE WE SPLIT UP BTW? X

I waited until full time before replying (thankfully Toulouse won!)

HEY ALICE. IN ANSWER TO YOUR QUESTIONS: YES, SOON AND YES XXX

I didn't want to lie to her. I'd done with lying. Everything in this narrative is true by the way. As I recall things, anyway. I decided to have a siesta. Isn't it great to get under the duvet with all your clothes on and go to sleep? Not quite as much fun as getting under the duvet with all your clothes off with other people though, (especially if they've got huge tits and nipples like raspberries), but that's like comparing apples with oranges. Or something like that. I set my alarm for two hours time. I didn't really get to sleep properly, but it was nice to doze. When my alarm went off I immediately texted Sophia and asked her to come over straight away, and then carried on reading until she arrived.

T minus 63 days

El Dorado. A lost and possibly mythical city of gold, of unlimited treasure, of magic and delight. For me, and for the SPC, a very real island in the Pacific Ocean where SPC members can feel - what's the correct terminology for something so immense? - unthreatened (no that doesn't quite do it justice, although it's good) (I'm struggling to think of a better word) comfortable (not bad) relaxed (pretty good) at ease (same as relaxed, well, not quite is it?) entirely entirely entirely happy with themselves. Like I've said before, it's impossible for someone ineligible to understand. The key thing is, no-one ineligible will be allowed on the island. Think about that, fellow SPC member, if you're reading this. Can you imagine how that would feel? I thought of Hamlet: "I could be bounded in a nutshell, and count myself a king of infinite space, were it not that I have bad dreams."

I haven't talked about recognition for a while. I was by now so adept at it that I didn't even need to see someone to determine their eligibility, I could do it simply by hearing them. I'd had a few telephone conversations where I'd known I was speaking to someone eligible within a few sentences.

Some of the business books talk about "purpose". We all have a purpose (allegedly) and the key thing we have to do is find it. And then, of course, to fulfill it. On one of my First Speaker training courses I heard a wonderful concept which has stayed with me. The important thing is not to be the best in the world, but the best *for* the world.

Well, I'd found my purpose, and I was doing my best for the world. The SPC world, at least. El Dorado was the greatest achievement I could achieve in all possible universes, or all those where I was eligible for the SPC anyway. It got me thinking, are there universes where I'm not eligible? Jesus Christ!

Thinking about such universes inevitably led me to Voltaire ("Tout est pour le mieux dans le meilleur des mondes possibles") through Newton ("And since Space is divisible in infinitum, and Matter is not necessarily in all places, it may be also allow'd that God is able to create Particles of Matter of several Sizes and Figures, and in several Proportions to Space, and perhaps of different Densities and Forces, and thereby to vary the Laws of Nature, and make Worlds of several sorts in several Parts of the Universe. At least, I see nothing of Contradiction in all this") to Schrödinger who once said that when his equations seemed to describe several different histories, these were "not alternatives, but all really happen simultaneously". Meow!

So, I concluded that the multiverse is a hypothetical set of various possible universes including one or more in which I am ineligible for the SPC. Together, these universes comprise everything that exists: the entirety of space, time, matter, energy, the physical laws, and the constants that describe them.

Alice had been and gone. We'd had a nice time, but it wasn't how it used to be, pre-Sam. It never could be, I'd come to realise that. The question was, I suppose, was it as good with Alice as things could get, with anyone? I didn't know. I didn't know how things could be. I had such limited experience.

I was thinking all this on the TGV down to Marseille, on my way to my last meeting of all the regional French First Speakers. There were a few things on the agenda, El Dorado, naturally, but also Brexit, the terrorist threat, climate change, the economy, unemployment, the war in Syria, freedom of speech, and compelling new evidence suggesting that aliens had built the pyramids.

I had another beer and looked out of the window. I loved travelling by train, especially through the French countryside, fast, with a good window seat facing the direction of travel, and a bottle of Grimbergen.

63 days to go. Soon, I'd have to make a decision. Which pill to give Apolline and which to take myself. I'd changed my mind regularly, but was coming around to the opinion that I would take the antidote and remain in this new enhanced state, and give Apolline the anti-Agent so she would revert to being a normal healthy little girl but with no special powers or enhancements - as nature intended her. I'd seen quite a lot of her, recently, and she was absolutely delightful, just the way she was. I'm not sure I wanted her to be Empress of the Universe, or President of the United States of Europe, or anything like that. In fact, although this was selfish, I wanted her to stay exactly as she was, for ever. I didn't want her exposed to the horrors of the world, to experience evil, or even know of its existence, or to go out with anyone, especially someone ineligible for the SPC. Especially that.

T minus 60 days

TGV back to Paris. Tired. Hungover. Just wanted to go to bed. I'll tell you how bad it was, I didn't even text Sophia. We'd had a great meeting, culminating in an almighty piss up on the last night. I'd drank a staggering quantity of absinthe, strong Belgian beer, vodka, and tequila, washed down with rum.

About an hour into the journey I thought I was going to be sick, so I went to the toilet. I sort of retched but I wasn't sick. When I got back to my seat there was an envelope on the table with my name on it. I opened it. A piece of paper containing the following few handwritten lines:

> *We know that Madame Gironde gave you a box. We have seen what's in the box and taken what is ours. Life's business being the terrible choice.*
> *Regards.*
> *Monsieur Barrett*

If anything could have sobered me up, this was it. I immediately made contact with Helene, who had sensors in every room in the house. She informed me that no-one had been in the house while I was away apart from Juliette who had tidied up the kitchen for me and done some ironing. The journey back seemed to last forever. When I eventually arrived at the Gare de Lyon, Philippe was waiting for me with a couple of police outriders (a favour from the Deputy Chief of Police, who was in the SPC). We got back to Pigalle in record time. I ran in and went straight to where I kept Madame Gironde's box. It didn't look like it had been disturbed. In fact, who could have disturbed it? Who knew it was there and what was in it? I'd told no-one I'd put the pills in there. I opened the box. There was only one pill, a green one, the antidote. I activated Helene. I asked her if she was absolutely sure that no-one had been in the house apart from Juliette.

'Absolutely sure' came the reply. 'I have cameras and sensors in every room and I've checked them all since you called.' she told me. I couldn't remember exactly when I'd put the pills in, which was odd as my memory was now nigh on perfect. There was something about that box …

The natural reaction I think would have been to look everywhere, under the box, near the box, in other secret locations, but there was no point - I knew that I'd put both pills in. I leant back on one of my sofas and took this information and its implications in. Oh Fuck, was all I could think of. Life's business being the terrible choice, indeed.

Although it had been nearly 24 hours (I'd had sex with a stranger in the bar in Marseille the night before) I still didn't contact Sophia. Instead, I switched all the lights out and listened to Beethoven's piano sonatas until I fell asleep.

This time I had the weirdest dream yet. I wasn't a fictional character, this dream wasn't about me. In the dream, I was a man sobbing my heart out, unable to breathe properly I was crying so much. I kept looking at little pieces of paper with writing on, but I couldn't read what they said as my eyes were too full of tears. I thought my heart was going to stop beating. I was hyperventilating, breathing quicker and quicker but shallower and shallower. It was as if I was drowning in my own tears.

I awoke suddenly. It was pitch black. The music was no longer playing. Helene must have turned the lights out and switched the music off. It was quiet. The kind of silence that you only hear when you're alone. I don't know why but I felt desperately sad. Perhaps it was that dream. I remembered that in the dream some of my tears had fallen onto one of the little pieces of paper, smudging the writing. I felt wide awake. I whispered to Helene, asking her to put the lights on low and play some cheerful music quietly. She chose Rossini. A good choice. I didn't want to get up but I didn't want to stay in bed. I wanted to talk to someone but I couldn't think of anyone specific I wanted to talk to. Just someone, a stranger perhaps. Yes, that would be best, but it was 4 o'clock in the morning. I closed my eyes and tried to go back to sleep, still listening to Rossini, but faintly.

I didn't wake up until nearly 10 o'clock. Most unlike me. Once I was awake I checked Madame Gironde's box one more time, just in case I'd dreamt it, but no, there was still only the one pill in there.

Sherlock Holmes said that when you have eliminated the impossible whatever remains, however improbable, must be the truth. The thing here was, it was impossible to eliminate the impossible, since what had happened was impossible. I had put the two pills in the box, definitely. No-one knew I'd done that. No-one knew where the box was, even if they did know I'd put two pills in it, and in any event, no-one could have taken one of the pills out as no-one other than Juliette had been in the house. And Juliette hadn't done it, of that I could be sure. Or could I? Juliette doing it was improbable - highly improbable I might add - but not impossible. And there were no other possibilities that I could think of. I called her and asked her. She said of course not. She wouldn't do such a thing. And I believed her. So, what had happened? And how were Omega and the mysterious Monsieur Barrett involved? In a sense these questions were academic, only relevant if the answers led to the retrieval of the second pill. But if they didn't ...

Not really sure where I was going with that so I'll plough on.

Better to have loved and lost than never to have loved at all. I've mentioned that before. Tennyson, although if I hadn't known that it was him I would have sworn it was Shakespeare. Sometimes I get lonely. It's funny, well, not funny amusing but funny odd, how occasionally I get hit by overwhelming loneliness. And it reminds me of the guy in the dream, the one I told you about. I have good friends, lots of money, a great job (which is going to get even greater), loads of wild sex, a fantastic house in Hampstead, an Aston Martin, a purpose, I'm making a difference (and a massive one at that) to the SPC, I'm booked to travel to French Polynesia with all my lovely work colleagues, the list goes on, and yet, and yet, there's something wrong. And I'm not just talking about the missing pill. There's the E bomb, of course, that's always there, but it's something else. I keep thinking about that guy looking at the little pieces of paper, like he was the loneliest guy in the world, the loneliest guy ever in fact.

I don't know why but I had a sudden urge to read 'A Tale of Two Cities' again. A desire to have Chief Inspector Morse investigate my death. Is extreme melancholy an inevitable by-product of extreme intelligence? I was certainly more intelligent than I had been, and accordingly was more aware of and more frustrated by all that was wrong with the world. And there is so ... much ... wrong ... with ... the ... world.

I finally got up and, without much enthusiasm, had a shower while listening to more Rossini. When I was dry, I got straight back into bed again and began to cry. I must have fallen asleep because the next thing I know I heard the door buzzer being repeatedly buzzed, over and over, impatiently. I asked Helene who it was. She told me it was Juliette (who must have mislaid her key). I asked Helene to let her in. I got up and put a dressing gown on and went downstairs to meet her. We met on the stairs. She looked like she'd been crying too.

'What was in that pill?' she flew at me, hitting me. 'What have you done to Apolline?'

She kept trying to hit me but I held her wrists until she eventually calmed down and sank to her knees, sobbing.

'What have you done to her?' she pleaded.

I held her close. 'I've saved her. That's what I've done.'

We had sex. It wasn't like our first time. It wasn't love. It was angry, rough, brutal even. We bruised one another. After, we lay side by side staring at the ceiling, in silence. Then she spoke.

'What was in that pill?'

'I don't know. I honestly don't know.' I said. 'All I know is that it saved her.'

'And what else? What else has it done to her? She's, she's different. I don't know I can't explain it.'

I told her nearly everything I knew, including that I'd taken one. The one thing I didn't tell her was what happens after 151 days.

After she left I called a friend of mine, Hugo, who worked at the French data protection agency, Commission Nationale de l'Informatique et des Libertés (CNIL). I was interested in his comments that Whatsapp did not have a legal basis to share user data under French law for so-called "business intelligence" purposes. He was an interesting and likeable guy, opera lover, rugby fan (Racing 92), oenophile, chess fiend, and SPC member. I had in fact first recognised him myself while queuing for a drink at the U Arena in Nanterre. He was free for drinks that afternoon, so we arranged to meet at Shakespeare and Company first to 'buy some books and then go and quaff some fine wine' (his words).

I bought a book of poetry by Paul Verlaine, 'Beyond Good and Evil' by Nietzsche, and a book about prime number factorization.

While waiting for Hugo, I thought about Nietzsche's *Übermensch*. In recent weeks, I'd found myself able to do enormously complex mathematical calculations very quickly in my head. I could anticipate and predict virtually everything that happened. It could get quite exhausting, actually.

Hugo arrived in a splendid long olive green velvet overcoat and boots, apologised for keeping me waiting, and went off to buy his books leaving me with my coffee and cake. He returned twenty minutes later with the complete works of Edgar Allan Poe and the collected Sherlock Holmes stories.

'Toilet reading!' he exclaimed. 'By which I don't mean to denigrate them, I simply mean that as they're quite short I can complete a whole story while sitting on the toilet. How are you?'

We chatted for a bit, and then I asked him if he fancied a game of chess. He always carried a little portable set around with him.

'You're challenging me?' he laughed. 'You've never beaten me before! But if you insist, of course, who am I to deny you the pleasure of losing to me?'.

He set out the pieces and then we began. I was black. I began with the Italian Game (Giuoco Piano) but rapidly changed to a strategy I'd formulated myself. After about 10 moves each he paused for quite a long time, kept looking at me quizzically, before making his next move. After another six or seven moves each he called a time out, leaned back in his chair with his arms behind his head, and stared at me.

'You've been practising,' he said.

'I swear, I haven't. I haven't played since I last played you.'

'Hmmm. Well, let's continue.'

He took longer and longer over each of his moves, while I made mine instantly. It seemed so obvious what to do. Eventually he stopped altogether.

'I see where this is going.' he said disconsolately.

'Check mate in a maximum of twelve moves?' I said.

He shook my hand. 'If you can play like that you should be in a club. What's happened? How have you learned to play like that?'

'It's a long story. Come on let's go and get a drink and I'll tell you all about it.'

I told him all about Agent XY, but not about the 151 days. He was most interested in the story of the mouse.

'But this is incredible!' he said. 'Why haven't I heard about it on the news?' He paused. 'Ah yes, silly question. Of course, it's obvious.'

We ordered our second bottle of wine, conversation topics included the Whatsapp thing, my move to Rome, and Clermont's travails in the Top 14. When the third bottle arrived, we got around, inevitably, to sex.

'You say your, um, sex drive is continuous?'

'Yes' I said.

'But so's mine!' he said. 'I think about it all the time.'

'The difference is, I have to have it all the time. *Have to*. Several orgasms a day. Preferably with someone but otherwise self-inflicted. After about two hours I start to feel nauseous if it doesn't happen.'

'Wow!' he said. 'And are you, you know, *sore* down there?' He looked at my groin. 'All that *friction?*'

'Not at all. And there's another thing too.' I leant closer, and told him about the physical changes.

'Oh, my God!' he said. 'Really?'

I nodded. 'Christ. Well, this calls for a celebration!' He called the waiter over and ordered a bottle of champagne. I told him I was flying off to French Polynesia soon to sort out some El Dorado stuff and have my leaving do.

'Leaving do? What leaving do?' I told him it was my work one.

'Well, you'll have to have another one for your friends. And I, of course, will organise it.'

We agreed a date the Saturday after I was due to get back.

'It'll be truly memorable.' he said, and bowed.

We finished off with some brandy, and then I headed off home. En route I saw Sophia and we had sex up an alley near the Gare du Nord. Twice in fifteen minutes (five orgasms).

When I got home I felt lonely again. There wasn't anything I fancied doing, so I called Alice. She was on voicemail. I called Laetitia. She was on voicemail too. I called Tom. Voicemail. Shit, I'd forgotten the time difference, he was 12 hours behind me or something. I poured myself a beer, dug out some pretzels, got a plate of Brebis Corse cheese and tapenade and crackers, and sat down in front of my home cinema screen and watched all the 'Toy Story' movies one after the other.

Then it was just "stuff" for a few days. Admin, spreadsheets, Brexit talk, that sort of stuff. Nothing I particularly recall until the day before the El Dorado trip. I woke up in the morning - Sophia had stayed over - and was so full of energy and vitality I decided to go the local athletic club track and do some running. I don't have any proper gear or anything, I just went in my jeans and trainers. When I got there the French National Under 23 athletics squad were practising. I got chatting with one of the coaches and asked if I could race with them, just for a laugh, nothing serious. He said this was a serious practice session, there was nothing to laugh about. I asked him what harm could it do, just one race, the 100 metres, timed. He asked me if I had any running gear, spikes, on me, and I told him I didn't, I would run as I was. He looked me up and down. Ok then, just the one race, he said. He led me over to the track. There was another 100 metre sprint due in about 15 minutes, so I waited, sending a few text messages about the opera I was seeing that evening with friends ('Carmen'). Soon the other runners came over, in all the gear, and looked at me up rather disparagingly I thought. I suppose I couldn't really blame them, it was rather odd. I reminded the coach to time me, he said he would, with a bit of a snigger. Off we went. I ran it in 9.34 seconds from a standing start.

'But that's not possible!' said the coach as I sauntered up to him afterwards.

'I know. Sorry' I said. 'I had a bit of a slow start. I can do better than that. Any chance of another race, maybe a longer one, 1500 metres, or something?'

'What are you, some kind of Superman?' he asked.

'Not really. Just a regular guy.'

'You know that was a World Record, right? And since I'm an official timer, it's official. It should go in the record books. It should be all over the news.'

'I'm not bothered about all that bullshit' I said. 'I'm not Forrest Gump. I just like running.'

There was a 1500 race in about half an hour. I sat chatting to the coach, and had a beer. Quite a strong one, too. Tasted good. Quak. 8%. I had another.

'You're not going to run after two of those, surely?'

'Sure am.' I smiled. 'Makes me run faster!'

Off we went. On the second lap, I got slowed down a bit as my shoelaces came undone, and on the third lap one of my friends who I was going to the opera with rang me. I took the call, but was fairly brief with him I have to say. Still, I finished in a creditable 3 minutes 15 seconds. At the finish the coach was waiting for me, along with three of his colleagues.

'See that?' he said. 'This guy just ran 100 metres in 9.34 seconds. From a standing start. With no running gear, as you can see. And less than an hour later runs 1500 metres in 3 minutes 15 seconds. After two Quaks! If I hadn't seen it with my own eyes, and timed it myself, I wouldn't have believed it.'

The coaches were all over me, asking all sorts of questions. I suppose I couldn't blame them, but I didn't want any fuss. I let them take some photos and then headed off for lunch, I'd had a sudden urge for a cheese omelette with fries, and a glass or two, or maybe three, of cheeky red.

Our flight was quite early the following morning - we'd all agreed to meet for a champagne breakfast once through security at the airport - so

I spent the afternoon packing. I'd splashed out a bit, paying for a private jet there and back for all my Paris team and their partners, and an absolutely top notch hotel for everyone. Rooms on stilts on the water, four poster beds covered with fresh orchid petals each morning, pillows stuffed with very soft fluffy stuff, outside showers, private heated swimming pools, personal chefs, beer on tap (literally), tame giant porpoises to ferry you to the beach bar, you know the sort of thing.

I didn't have a partner, as such, so I was going on my own. It hadn't worked out with Alice, Juliette couldn't come - I had asked her - and Laetitia was busy doing stuff she apparently "couldn't discuss with civilians". I was fairly confident - certain in fact - that I'd have plenty of sex on the trip. Tom would be there, of course. I didn't - still don't in fact - consider myself bisexual, but I have had sex with Tom a few times now, occasionally just the two of us and a few times in a group of three or more. Laetitia describes me as "curious".

'Carmen' is one of my favourite operas. I'm not alone I think in enjoying the 'Habanera' from Act 1 and the 'Toreador' aria from Act 2. But it's all good. Perhaps it hasn't got the *depth* of a Mozart or the *width* of a Wagner or the *height* of a Verdi - actually I'm just joshing here - but who gives a shit, if you enjoy it? And I *loved* the performance. We all went out afterwards too, and ended up in a jazz bar until 3H. Top night.

As I had such an early start I decided not to go to bed at all - I'd sleep on the plane. When I got home I put all my bags by the front door and then ran a bath (read some Nietzsche) and after that just had enough time to watch the whole of '2001: A Space Odyssey' before Philippe called to take me to the airport. He was coming on the trip as well of course. He didn't have a partner either.

The celebrations got off to a great start with the champagne breakfast, and then we all boarded the jet. Absolute luxury.

Some times in your life are just *so* good they're impossible to describe. Indeed, language being as inadequate as it is, for most of us at least, describing such times can actually diminish them in some way. Flaubert said that "Language is a cracked kettle on which we beat out tunes for bears to dance to, while all the time we long to move the stars to pity." So, I won't describe my leaving do, I'll just say that it was one of the happiest times of my life.

I stayed on for a few days when the team flew back to Paris, to sort out a few El Dorado bits including signing the contracts to transfer ownership of the island to the SPC. It was now official - we had our island, and work could now begin in earnest. I felt very proud. That night Tom and I had a quiet meal, just the two of us, to celebrate, and when he went back to bed (he'd found himself a girlfriend) I walked along the beach in the moonlight, alone, thinking about life.

I remember feeling sort of melancholy, but that wasn't really the correct description. Sad, but also happy; bitter, but also sweet; unloved, but also loved; alone, misunderstood, largely ignored, but deliciously joyful. And the gentle twilight and the warmth added to the moment.

> *"Tender is the night*
> *And haply the Queen-Moon is on her throne*
> *Cluster'd around by all her starry Fays"*

I felt wonderfully alive, and my entire body felt as if it was tingling. It got darker and darker. I slipped off my shoes and walked back towards my hotel by the sea, loving the gentle lapping of the waves over my feet. I thought I heard a sound, singing, out at sea, and I stopped for a moment.

> *"I have heard the mermaids singing, each to each.*
> *I do not think that they will sing to me.*
> *I have seen them riding seaward on the waves*
> *Combing the white hair of the waves blown back*
> *When the wind blows the water white and black.*
> *We have lingered in the chambers of the sea*
> *By sea-girls wreathed with seaweed red and brown*
> *Till human voices wake us, and we drown."*

Now what was supposed to happen, in this mood, was that I was to go back to my room alone and read some Shelley (the only book I'd brought with me was his collected poetry) and listen to some opera, but when I got back to the hotel I thought I'd have a quick drink in the bar (it was open 24 hours) which is when I saw a woman sitting on her own reading a book and sipping a cocktail. She was the only person in there.

'Mind if I join you?' I asked. 'Unless you're deeply engrossed in the book of course.'

She looked at me, sizing me up I thought.

'Sure. I'd like some company. Take a seat.'

I sat down next to her and asked her what she was drinking.

'Piña colada.'

'Hmm. Haven't had one of those in a while. I think I'll order one. Fancy another?'

'Thank you. That would be nice.'

While the waiter was making them, I asked her what book she was reading.

'The Idiot. Dostoyevsky. Have you read it?'

'Yes, I have. I always wanted to be like Prince Myshkin.'

The drinks arrived.

'Perfectly good, then, but the question of whether or not he is truly a man is at the core of the book's tragedy, don't you think?'

'I ought to re-read it. I don't remember thinking that.'

'So, are you perfectly good?' she asked me.

'Do you mean good in the religious sense, as in the opposite of evil, or good as in good at things?'

'What would you like me to have meant?' she smiled.

I smiled back. I'm going to enjoy this conversation, I thought.

We relocated from the bar stools to a comfy leather sofa just outside, close to one of the pools and beneath a palm tree. I ordered a bottle of champagne.

'What are we celebrating?' she asked.

'Meeting!' I said.

Ok it was a bit cheesy but I meant it. We chatted for a while, about nothing in particular. She seemed impressed that I'd bought an island. I was impressed that she was a cellist. We drank a second bottle of champagne between us, another cocktail each, and then that moment arrived when we knew it was time to go to bed.

She spoke first. 'So, are you married?'

'No.' I said.

'I don't mind. I'll still sleep with you. I just want to know. I don't want to start this off with a lie.'

'I'm not lying. I'm not married. I never have been. I'm not a virgin, though' I smiled. 'I don't have a regular girlfriend either, just a few people I have sex with whenever I can. How about you?'

She finished her piña colada. 'I'm not a virgin either. I've come over here to get over splitting up from my boyfriend of six years. Do you fancy coming back to my room and checking out my cello?'

SEGMENT 1597

I remember when I was a small boy, maybe eight or nine but it might have been a different age, the excitement of Christmas Eve, and waking up in the half-light on Christmas morning to find a pillowcase full of treasures at the foot of my bed. The joy, the anticipation, when I saw that pillowcase but before I looked inside was one of the best feelings I ever had.

Years later, and I'm trying to capture these four things in chronological order, I was playing Postman's Knock at a friend's party. I was maybe thirteen or something? It was finally my turn to go outside. I went into the darkened room and kissed someone properly for the first time in my life. Her lips were soft and yielding and utterly exquisite, and it was the greatest physical experience of my life up to that point. When I close my eyes, I can still experience that moment. Every kiss I've ever had since that one has been an attempt to recreate that first kiss.

I am a little hazy on the dates, but I think it was about a year later that I had my first ever orgasm. I was a late developer, that's for sure, and very innocent and naive. I didn't even know what sex was really. I suppose my first kiss with Lorraine (that was her name by the way, the girl at the party) was what I thought sex was, where it began and where it ended. Anyway, I don't think I'd ever had an erection or anything like that, and one day someone at school put his thumb through his belt and out the front of his trousers and rubbed it, and must have mentioned something about sex. I was so innocent I didn't know what he meant, but I resolved to try it anyway. That night when I went to bed I pulled the sheet over my head and pulled my pants down and starting rubbing my cock like the boy had rubbed his thumb. Soon it got hard - I couldn't really believe it - and the sensation was wonderful ... and all the more so as I had never had it before. I kept going ... and then it happened. I don't really want to compare it with Lorraine's kiss, as clearly it was quite different, but it was a fantastic moment, of course, and strange as it may seem, and despite all the countless orgasms I've had since, I can still sort of feel the intensity of that one.

I'm clear on how old I was for the final experience I want to mention, as I remember exactly where I was. I was 15 years old and was on a school exchange trip to America, staying with my pen friend who lived in a town called Williamstown in Massachusetts. His father was a doctor, and had a big old country house with grounds and stuff. They even had a maid, and on my first morning there she brought in a jar full of fresh maple syrup collected from trees in the garden. I'd never tasted anything like it. Every taste I've ever had since that one has been an attempt to recreate that taste.

You may be wondering why I've mentioned all this? Imagine if you can combining all those experiences and feelings once more, simultaneously, and with an even greater intensity. That's what it was like with Abigail that night (her name, by the way).

When we got back to her room we calmly undressed and stood looking at one another for a minute or two. That's when I had the Christmas pillowcase experience. Her body was exquisite, her nipples the size of crab apples. Then she stepped towards me and put her arms around my neck, I put my arms around her waist, and we kissed. That's when the Lorraine kiss was recreated. Then we fell onto her bed wrapped around one another. I lost count of the number of orgasms I had that night, but it was in the region of seventy. Each one like the first one ever. And she tasted delicious, just like maple syrup. It felt as if my whole life had been leading up to this moment, no, the whole of *humanity* had been leading up to this moment, since fish first crawled out of the sea. When we finally finished, it was getting light, and as I drifted off to sleep I remember thinking that I didn't want to think anything ...

"O for a life of sensations rather than of thoughts ..."

We slept until lunchtime, and then ordered room service: a chilled bottle of Sancerre (even with air con and the huge fan above the bed it was still very hot) and some tapas dishes. Then we had sex again, which if anything was even more intense than before.

"Heard melodies are sweet, those unheard are sweeter ..."

We lay there afterwards, listening to music and staring at the ceiling. I kept losing count of the number of dots on the fan. After a while she rolled a joint, telling me that its contents were a secret combination of "special materials found only on one island in the entire world". It turns out that it was the island I'd bought for the SPC. She thought that was incredible. I did too.

'So, what brought you here?' I asked. 'To this part of the world?'

'I saw a Fortune Teller' she said, 'Who told me my life would change if I came here.' She looked at me, and exhaled some smoke which was pink.

'And has it?' I asked.

'I think it might have, don't you?' she smiled.

On a hunch, I asked her who the Fortune Teller was.

'Madame Gironde' she said.

I feasted on her crab apples.

We finally got up late afternoon, and agreed to meet for dinner. She went into town to do some shopping, I went for a swim and then sat in my room in my swimming trunks doing some emails and sending messages and stuff. I decided to listen to 'Don't Let Me Down' by the Beatles which I hadn't played in years:

> "And from the first time that she really done me
> Oh, she done me, she done me good
> I guess nobody ever really done me
> Oh, she done me, she done me good"

That was exactly what I thought about Abigail.

She looked ravishing when she arrived for dinner, in a low cut white cotton dress and white plimsolls, and a hat. She asked me what I did, and I told her I worked for an organisation called the SPC. She asked me what the organization did, and as I now had the authority to tell people if I chose to, I told her.

'But that's not even true!' she said, which made me smile.

I asked her about her cello playing. She said her father had been very musical, and had encouraged her to play an instrument from an early age. She said she could play the piano too. I asked her where she lived. She said she had a small house in the Cotswolds, but was about to rent an apartment in Rome.

'You're kidding me?' I said.

'Not at all, why?' she said.

'I've just been promoted and will be moving to Rome myself shortly.'

We then exchanged one of those looks, you know the ones, where we sort of knew we were going to hit it off big style. While we were eating she took her plimsolls off and played footsie with me, so not wishing to be outdone I slipped off my sandals and did the same to her. She grabbed my foot and forced my big toe inside her until she came, at which point she let out a scream. A waiter rushed over.

'It's ok' she said breathlessly. 'I thought I saw a spider!'

When he went off she whispered to me, 'I'm not even frightened of spiders!'

'I have to have you right now' I said rather assertively. 'Can we skip coffee?'

I was due to fly back the next day, Abigail the day after, but we both changed our flights and stayed on for another three days. She said she couldn't delay going back beyond that as she had to prepare for some concerts with the Berlin Philharmonic Orchestra. I could work anywhere there was an internet connection, really, so I was very flexible.

The next three days were perfect, is all I really want to say. The only sad thing was that they had to come to an end. On our last night, we had dinner on a floating restaurant, just off the shore. We were both unusually quiet. We hadn't discussed what was going to happen after we left. Eventually I broached the subject.

'So, would you like to meet again? I live in Paris now but have a house in Hampstead, and can easily get access to see you. Or you can come to me. And then there's Rome, of course.'

I noticed a tear in her eye. I took her hand.

'What's wrong?' I asked.

'I don't know' she said. 'This has been so special. So, so just what I needed. It's been like a dream. I don't know if it can exist back in Europe?'

'Well, we won't know unless we try, will we? I'm up for trying!'

The tears were running down her face. We went for a long walk along the beach, holding hands, saying nothing. I thought I heard the mermaids singing again, only fainter this time. We walked back to the hotel.

'Let's not make love tonight. Do you mind? I just want you to hold me.'

I thought it would be insensitive to say I did mind, so instead I squeezed her hand and said, 'Of course not.'

The fact is, we held one another so close and so tightly and got into such an intimate entangled position, our naked bodies completely entwined almost as if we were one and the same person, that it felt as if we were making love anyway. And perhaps we were, of a kind. I'd never experienced anything like it.

When I woke up in the morning she was already gone. There was a note by the side of the bed which said

> *All days are nights to see till I see thee*
> *And nights bright days when dreams do show me thee*
> *Love always,*
> *A x*

She left no phone number or address.

T minus 21 days

3 weeks to go. Christ! Doesn't time fly when you're having fun? I'd been very busy since I got back to Paris, sorting things out in readiness for my transfer to Rome and assorted El Dorado administration. I'd also popped back to Hampstead for a few days.

I hadn't heard from Abigail. I'd given her my number, even though she didn't give me hers. I was undecided about finding her. On the one hand, she hadn't given me her number and hadn't contacted me. On the other, we'd had the best of times and I really wanted them to continue. And she was moving to Rome! It felt as if it was meant to be. I decided to wait a while and see if she got in touch.

I was excited about the coming weekend as Juliette, Apolline and I were going to stay in Aix-en-Provence from Thursday through to the Monday. We had tickets on the TGV and had booked a nice little hotel on the outskirts of the town. Juliette had calmed down about Apolline now. I don't mean that to sound disparaging or patronising in any way. She had every right to be angry, even though I'd saved Apolline's life. And things were turning out just brilliantly for her (Apolline that is). She was top in her school at everything, but was also the nicest and most engaging little girl you could imagine. It was as if the Agent had worked differently on her somehow, I can't explain it. She was always lovable but now she was *super* lovable! (You know how the European Tour de France riders say they're "super happy" when interviewed in English after they've won a stage or been in a breakaway or something?) Anyway, that was a few days away, and I had plenty to occupy myself until then, not least a day with the Global First Speaker in Bratislava, which as before I can't discuss.

I remember being in a particularly reflective mood around then. I thought about all the things that had happened to me since that quiz night, which seemed so long ago. How the SPC had changed my life. What an organisation. I wish I could tell you more about it, its inner workings, its raison d'être, what the eligibility criteria are. I'm sort of happy I can't though, in a way. If you knew what the criteria were, you'd understand I think.

My predictive powers being what they were, I'd been making an absolute killing on the markets, bringing in overall returns of over 40 times investment, amounting to well over €1 million a week. It all seemed so obvious. I literally had more money than I knew what to do with. I'd bought another Picasso for the bathroom and an apartment in Greenwich Village, and a controlling stake in Leicester Tigers rugby club. Also, a cute little pink Citroën 2CV for when I wanted to tootle around Paris. My move to Rome was all set. I was going to drive the 2CV there with a few of my most precious things and breakables, while everything else was going to be transported by the SPC's logistics division.

The apartment in Pigalle belonged to the SPC not me, so I was looking around for one of my own somewhere in the Montmartre area. I planned to tell Juliette at the weekend that she could live in it rent free if she wanted.

T minus 18 days

Very excited today as we're off to Aix-en-Provence in a few hours. I've had to come into the office to sort a few things out first. I've just counted how many spreadsheets I have open and it made me smile - 17 of them, all being used constantly and updated regularly. Spreadsheet Heaven, one might say.

I had time for a quick lunch before meeting the girls at the station. Apolline was very excited. She had a cute little pull along suitcase and was carrying a pile of books. I asked her what they were. "Jennie" by Paul Gallico, "Matilda" by Roald Dahl, "A Wrinkle in Time" by Madeleine L'Engle and "The Weirdstone of Brisingamen" by Alan Garner.

'Plus, I've got all the Narnia books in my suitcase.' she said.

I was pleased she wasn't reading "Ulysses", although she probably could.

'That's a lot of books for four nights.' I said.

'I love reading.' she said.

I always like sitting in the direction of travel, by the window, but Apolline got there first and because it was her I didn't mind. She sat next to her Mum, and I sat opposite. We were going to be on the train for hours, so I got comfortable and closed my eyes. I didn't go to sleep, but dozed a bit, and sort of had a daydream. I heard Apolline talking and laughing occasionally and it filled me with joy.

About an hour into the journey I received a message on my phone. I looked at it. It was from Abigail and read simply:

HI. SORRY IT'S BEEN A WHILE. LONG STORY. HERE'S MY NUMBER. CALL ME IF YOU WANT TO DO IT ALL AGAIN.
A X

I texted her straight back. Explained I was away for the weekend but would call on Monday evening. Invited her to Paris.

It was at that moment that I had my "*Eureka* moment". It was so exciting, and affected me so suddenly and profoundly and powerfully, that I spilt my coffee. I've mentioned of course that the Agent develops insight and intelligence, and I'd certainly been getting increasingly insightful and intelligent. It was as if I sort of knew nearly everything. It remains hard to explain. Anyway, I was sitting there, watching Apolline do some colouring in, when I realised what the meaning of life was.

Can you imagine? For centuries, for ever, mankind had wondered what (if any) meaning there was, and it had always proved elusive. When we thought we were getting close, just like reaching the end of a rainbow, we couldn't grasp it. Was it even graspable? And there I was, on a TGV from Paris to

Provence, sitting opposite a 10-year-old girl, that it came to me. Complete, unequivocal, undeniable. The meaning of life. I must have had a strange expression on my face as Apolline asked me if something was wrong. I smiled and said no, far from it - things were as right as they could be.

And I'm going to reveal all later in this narrative, but not just yet. I'm delighted, of course, for the obvious reason (naturally) but also because it gives some meaning to this narrative. When you started reading it you probably didn't think you were going to receive the greatest gift of your life - its ultimate meaning - and to be fair I didn't think I was going to be in a position to reveal it. Watch this space! (Did I ever mention that a lot of this I wrote in real time, just after it happened, as opposed to all after the event? I don't think I did. In fact, as I writ this actual sentence I am completely up-to-date …).

T minus 14 days

On the TGV back to Paris now. Lovely weekend. Aix is a beautiful place. We had a family room, and it was also that time of the month, so there was no sex, but amazingly it didn't seem to matter. And here's the thing. There were no major highlights, no momentous events, no earth-shattering insights, just quiet relaxed gentle enjoyment. And it was all the more enjoyable for that, I think, but I don't want to get ahead of myself.

The weather had been glorious. We'd walked around, caught a bus into Marseille, done some shopping, skipped through a lavender field, gone in a horse and cart, had lots of laughs. I particularly enjoyed it when Apolline held both our hands and we swung her up in the air.

I told Juliette about the apartment in Paris, and my idea that they could live in it rent free. That prompted a very interesting conversation. Juliette was unsure what kind of relationship we were in. I told her I was too, but did it matter? I wanted to help them, and that was it, pure and simple. She told me she loved me but wasn't *in* love with me. I told her that was fine. We discussed what love really is.

If I'm honest, I have a problem with love. I certainly don't love *myself*, for starters. I love Sally and my Mum and my Dad. I loved Emily. I loved Alice. Did I love anyone else? Had I *ever*, really? Was I capable of it?

I gazed out of the train window at the French countryside. Juliette had closed her eyes. I saw Apolline reading "The Lion, the Witch, and the Wardrobe" and smiled.

Philippe was waiting for us at the station in Paris. I needed to pop into the office so he dropped me off there and then took the girls home. I sat at my desk and cried. I don't know why. Perhaps knowing the meaning of life gets you like that? Apolline had made me a little paper wish box. It had got a bit battered on the journey, but I endeavoured to straighten it out a bit. She'd put a wish in it. Juliette had too. I put one in, that I'd find the other pill.

I stayed late in the office, until gone 9 o'clock. Everyone had left. I didn't want to go straight home, so I walked up past the Notre Dame cathedral, crossed the river, had a quick look in Shakespeare and Company (didn't buy anything for the first time ever), and sat in a bar. And cried again. I really didn't know why, I was just overwhelmed by everything.

When I'd calmed down a bit I called Abigail, but she was on voicemail. I left her a message asking her to call me back and enquiring whether she was going to accept my invitation to visit me in Paris. I had a couple more drinks, wished I'd bought a book to read but couldn't be bothered going back to the bookshop, and then got the Metro home. I thought about it but didn't call Sophia.

The house felt lonelier than normal. I'd found the meaning of life, but I could still get lonely. I thought again about calling Sophia, but I didn't want that. I wanted genuine affection, love, even, notwithstanding everything I've said about it. I had a bath but I still wasn't tired, so I watched an old movie called "Bicycle Thieves" directed by Vittorio De Sica back in 1948 I think. When it was over I picked up a cycling magazine that was lying around and read about Paris-Roubaix.

I don't know why I did what I did next, but I knelt down by my bed and prayed that the second pill would be in Madame Gironde's box again. I knew it wasn't there, of course, but what was the point of praying if not for a miracle. I really did pray too, by which I mean, I meant it. It wasn't some idle throwaway mark of desperation: for at least the duration of the prayer I actually believed in God, and that God could help me. And there was also Apolline's little paper wish box.

It's odd, looking back, but I remember feeling frightened to open the box and check. I kept looking at the box, for what felt like hours, until in the end I thought "Fuck it" (and promptly apologised to God) and opened the lid.

And there were the two pills. Elated doesn't do it justice. It must have been a miracle, because the second pill definitely wasn't there the last time I looked. I even took a photo this time, to prove both pills were in there, and then I put the lid back on carefully and hid the box where I knew no-one would find it, even if the house was ransacked.

I almost floated back to bed and lay there in the dark looking at the patterns the glow stars and planets made on the ceiling. To avoid any such traumas again it was time to decide which pill to give to Apolline and which I should take, and to bloody get on with it. After all, I only had 14 days left anyway.

T minus 13 days

I woke up feeling the best I'd ever felt, in every conceivable way. The sun was shining too. Thin streams of light were coming through the slits in the shutters. I loved that. It was early, before 7H. I leapt out of bed and ran down the stairs naked to the kitchen. I'd never done that, but I loved my body now.

I made pancakes, with blueberries and maple syrup (which made me think of Abigail), and a pot of coffee. Then I sat down with a pint of freshly squeezed orange juice and read the latest "Charlie Hebdo".

Then, I got all excited because I'd decided to have a party to reveal the meaning of life to all my friends and family, and combine it with a sort of "Goodbye to Paris". I'd invite all my friends and family, and pay for them all to stay in top hotels. Sally and Mum and Dad could stay at mine, of course.

I got into email straight away and sent out invitations, and followed these up with texts and Whatsapps and hangouts and kiks to everyone, and calls to a select few. Including SPC folk I wanted to invite there were nearly two hundred invitations, and that didn't include their partners. I was very excited.

I then made my way to the office by Metro (Philippe had the day off). Replies kept coming in all the time, and thankfully there were almost no rejections.

I didn't actually have a venue yet, but it's amazing what a limitless budget and a great secretary can do for you. By lunchtime I had a whole wing of the Palace of Versailles reserved, and had hired a project manager on a contract to "make it happen." Boy was I in a good mood. I even took a call from Michael Gove (although I must admit I told him to fuck right off as soon as he told me why he was calling).

Around 11H President Macron called and wondered whether I wanted to join him for a bottle of red at our usual place (which I can't reveal for security reasons). I thought it was a *damn* good idea, so I wrapped up a few more emails, noted down yet more party acceptances, and made my way there. En route Abigail called. She said she'd be delighted to come to the party, and was I planning for her to come early or stay on after or both? I said I'd like her to come as often as possible, so after a few childish giggles she agreed to arrive two days before and stay on for at least three days after, and possibly more depending on orchestral commitments. Fabulous, I said.

Lunch was excellent, as always, and we sorted a few things out too which again I need to keep confidential. It wasn't all serious, though, we talked about rugby, and he asked me about my 100 and 1500 metre world records. I laughed them off.

It had been well over twenty-four hours now, so en route back to the office I saw Sophia for about 5 minutes (four orgasms). She told me she was taking a short holiday at the weekend, so I said we'd better get some action "in the bank". She agreed to stay over at mine every night until she went away. At least I wouldn't go crazy.

Back in the office I was just about to open the usual batch of spreadsheets, when I realised I didn't need them anymore. For capturing and sharing data, sure, but not for calculations. I could do them all in my head, instantly. Averages, totals, multiplications, all of them. Even in the last couple of days my cognitive abilities seemed to have increased several fold. In fact, cognitive isn't quite the right word here. All aspects of my brain were hyper functioning, to what appeared to be their full potential. It's a myth of course - although widely believed - that we only use 10% of our brain's capacity. Whatever the true percentage, I seemed to be using all of mine. Everything had fallen into place.

Thinking of things falling into place, I haven't mentioned the date of the party. I'd decided to have it on T minus 1 day, the evening of. It seemed somehow fitting, and gave people over a week to get their shit together. I spent a great evening thinking about the party. People kept ringing, and asking about the meaning of my meaning of life announcement, and I said they'd just have to wait. It was fun.

I was also relishing seeing how the dynamic of the partygoers would pan out. Alice, Sam, Laetitia, Chloe, Sophia, Tom, Abigail, Juliette to name but a few. My plan was just to get pissed and let them all get on with it. I knew that Laetitia, Chloe and Tom would be up for an orgy, and was pretty sure that Sophia could be persuaded to join in... wasn't sure whether it was quite Abigail's cup of tea though and had doubts about Alice. She might be up for it if I could get her pissed. Juliette was the dark horse I thought.

T minus 12 days

Spent the morning taking the guy who was taking over my role through what I thought he needed to know, and introduced him to the team. Spent the afternoon looking at apartments with Juliette, who had agreed to live wherever I bought, so she had a vested interest. She wasn't entirely happy with the rent-free concept, so we'd come to a deal where her "salary" for house sitting, "unspecified ad hoc Paris related activity" and looking after Felix and Hermione exactly equalled what I would have charged for rent. She would pay rates and bills and stuff like that. We saw some nice places up near the Sacré-Cœur, one in particular was five stories with a basement (which would make a great wine cellar) and a roof garden with brilliant views. I fell in love with it at once, and as a cash buyer I knew I could get it. Spent the evening at the opera, 'Tosca'. Spent the night on top of Sophia.

T minus 11 days

I'm no capitalist. I hate capitalism. I hate the concept of "free markets" - it sounds nice in theory but it perpetuates inequality and poverty and permits odious self-serving right wing wankers to do all the things that odious self-serving right wing wankers want to do. So, what I do is *exploit* the capitalist system - in particular the money markets and the banking network - for a good cause. And that good cause is me. It's the Bible where it's written that the love of money is the root of all evil (not, as is commonly misquoted, money *a priori*):

Timothy 6:10 "For the love of money is the root of all evil: which while some coveted after, they have erred from the faith, and pierced themselves through with many sorrows"

I'm not so sure. It depends what you want to do with it, surely? Anyway, what I want to do with it is fuck over the entire capitalist system, help people (especially the poor and needy), spread my largesse (so to speak!) and bring a smile to the faces of those people who I like to see smile.

I mention this because after Sophia and I finished with one another this morning - we were unusually rough with one another - I checked my trading account and was delighted (although not surprised) to learn that my big gamble had paid off. Of course, it wasn't a *real* gamble as I could predict with stunning accuracy currency fluctuations, global stock movements, futures, derivatives, all that financial crap. I'd hedged several million on an incredibly complex transaction involving numerous parameters, and overnight it had come in. Yesterday morning my trading account had €13,457,200 in it. This morning it had €127,889,702 in it. I saw that as progress.

I had the account details for several of my best friends, and also of course Sally and my Mum and Dad. I transferred €1 million into the accounts of all of those friends and €5 million into Sally's and my parent's. The accompanying message was "Beauty will save the world". Dostoyevsky wrote that.

I then donated several million to various charities (SHELTER, Médecins Sans Frontières, the cat rescue home in Sheen, etc.) and bought the five storey place Juliette and I had seen yesterday. I still had over €70 million left in that account, so I set in motion a much more ambitious and complex "gamble" with €50 million of it. Working on a ratio of roughly 40:1, from my predictions, I expected to be a billionaire within a month.

Happy days. I'd probably buy another Picasso.

When I got into the office later Emmie said there were three guys waiting for me. I'm never comfortable with unannounced visits like this - I like to be in complete control of who I see and when - so I was a bit put out. They better not be Tories, I thought to myself.

I sat at my desk, checked for new emails (something in from Amélie Derbaudrenghien, the wife of the Belgian Prime Minister), got myself a coffee, and invited them in. It was a blast from the past, the guys from the Metropolitan Police Counter Terrorism Unit and MI5 who visited me in Hampstead ages ago, together with another guy who they said was from DARPA.

'We said we'd be back.'

'You did indeed. Took your time, but here you are!' I said. 'So how can I help?'

The guy from DARPA spoke first. 'We're aware of the SPC's recognition capabilities, and yours in particular. What we don't know, of course, is what it is that you're recognising and how you're doing it.'

He stopped talking and stared at me. I wasn't sure whether he expected me to respond.

After a period of silence - I get bored with these sort of mind games - to hasten their departure I said 'Noted. And your point?'

He looked at the others and back at me. 'You're aware, of course, of the increased terrorist threat?'

'Of course.'

'And it has occurred to us that if we could somehow *automate* your recognition capabilities we might significantly reduce the threat and potential for the terrorists to do harm.'

'Automate? How would you propose to do that?'

'Well, we've been developing an intelligent mechanism for identifying threat, based on a combination of factors including pre-emptive behavioural analysis, pheromone classification, physiological cataloguing, brain wave activity monitoring and neuro linguistic programming, as well as some additional characteristics that I'm not at liberty to discuss.'

'And what is this mechanism?' I asked.

He reached inside a black bag he was carrying and pulled out what looked like a cross between a smartphone and a ray gun.

'This is the prototype, which we call TIT, Terrorist Identification Technology. You simply point it at someone and it will reveal on the screen how likely they are to commit an act of terrorism, on a scale of 0 to 10. We're already working on the next iteration, which will *automatically* disable (temporarily paralyse or, if you prefer, kill) the suspected hostile if the result exceeds a pre-determined level, without any need for human intervention. Ultimately, we could deploy a TIT "shield" or "lattice" in, say, airport terminals, railway stations, public buildings and so on, so that they would be completely protected from a certain category of terrorist behaviour such as someone walking in with a bomb.'

'Sounds brilliant.' I said. 'But I'm not sure where I fit into this?'

'Because you clearly have some kind of gift or intuition, call it what you will, enabling you to recognise something about some group of people, and we're keen to leave no stone unturned. Can we somehow harness your intuition with our technology? Are we missing something? Can we improve the technology, perhaps by synchronising it - using something like Bluetooth - with the localized set of structures in the precuneus and inferior parietal lobes and the medial frontal cortex?'

I understood exactly what he meant.

'I understand exactly what you mean.' I said. 'So, what do you want me to do?'

This is all I can reveal about the conversation - they said it was classified - beyond saying that of course I was willing to help.

Later in the afternoon I went over to the Versailles office, after which I took the opportunity of visiting the Palace and meeting my project manager to check out the venue for the party. Things were all coming together very nicely.

I stayed in again that evening, as I had an early flight to Rome the next morning and wanted to start thinking about packing up my stuff for the big house move. Plus of course Sophia was coming around and I was, frankly, desperate.

T minus 10 days

Rome and back in a day. Met all the Italian Regional FS's in the morning. Lunch with the Italian Prime Minister. Spent the afternoon with my staff, guided by my new Personal Assistant Francesca. Francesca was a 29-year-old graduate in Philosophy and Mathematics from Bologna University and a former Italian skiing champion. Fluent in thirty-five languages. Consultant to the Agenzia Informazioni e Sicurezza Interna, with "scientia rerum rei publicae salus" (knowledge of issues is the salvation of the Republic) tattooed across her lower back (she showed me). Unmarried.

T minus 9 days

Sophia and I went at it all night, and couldn't stop. It was *frenzied*. We lost track of time, and also of space. My need for sex had reached a primitive, visceral, almost *invertebrate* level. It was as if my entire being was completely *lost* in the *infinite* delights of her body, completely *abandoned* to her breasts. I had crossed over into an inaccessible sexual dimension with her, incapable of returning until the heat death of the universe.

T minus 5 days

We stopped having sex, and realised that it had lasted for four days and nights, nonstop. She had to leave to get ready for her holiday. That's when I clocked that she wouldn't be at the party. Oh well, shit happens.

I had numerous voicemails and emails to deal with, which took me most of the day. I finished around 19H. It was a nice warm evening so I thought I'd stroll up to the Place du Tertre and sit outside one of the bars with a bottle of not so cheeky red and people-watch for a while. While I was there my party project manager called me - I'd asked him to update me each day now that the party was so close.

Everything was still looking good. The hall where the main event would be was now decorated. Various rooms were being prepared which people could move in and out of during the party - which was due to last for three days and nights. One room would have a string quartet, another a trampoline, another a psychedelic light show with early Pink Floyd being played and the floor covered with paint and jelly for people to writhe naked in, another with a giant screen showing 'Eraserhead' on a loop, that sort of thing. Every guest would receive a present - the ladies a diamond Tiffany necklace and the guys a Rolex. I planned to head on out there the evening before it started for one final check, and to rehearse my speech about the meaning of life.

It was pleasant to sit there. I finished my wine and then left, on my way back buying a crêpe and eating it walking down the hill.

When I got back I stripped off and climbed into the sensory deprivation tank I'd had installed in the basement. I set the timer to open the lid again in three hours, and lay back and closed the lid. It was all done by voice control, and at any time I could have the lid opened by a single command. It was also linked to Helene, so if I got bored or wanted to try something different I could ask her for example to play music or illuminate the tank and stuff like that.

Being fully conscious and alert but unable to see, hear, smell, taste or feel anything is a strange experience, not unlike the impact Theresa May makes when she appears on television. Actually, I could still taste the crêpe. I had no idea of the passage of time while I was in there. I thought about a wide variety of things. The party, naturally enough, the move to Rome, seeing Abigail again soon, Sophia's breasts, the imminent end of the Tories, what to have for breakfast, what book to read next, what movie to watch next, whether the Devil exists, which pill to take and which to give to Apolline, macaroni cheese, the Beatles, eligibility for the SPC, and

Emily and our child who was never born.

Suddenly a very gentle red glow came on in the tank accompanied by Helene's voice apologising for disturbing me but saying that some SPC personnel were at the front door. That was odd. I instructed Helene to buzz them in and tell them I'd be with them in about 15 minutes, and to open the lid. I'd been in there about two hours.

I had a quick shower, put on a track suit, and went to meet them. They were both standing, one of them staring at the Picasso on the wall and the other looking at my book shelves. They introduced themselves as Martin (Picasso) and Richard (book shelves) from SPC's Branch Zero. I noticed that neither of them were eligible.

'Branch Zero?' I said, 'I didn't know there *was* a Branch Zero.'

'You wouldn't' Martin said. 'Only First Speakers at the National Level have the necessary clearance to know about us.'

'I see. So, what is it that you do? And I ought to add, isn't it a bit late to make a house call?' (It was nearly 2am).

'It's time to tell you.' said Richard. 'We can't allow any further delay.'

'Tell me what?'

They looked at one another.

'Let's sit down. Any chance of a drink though?'

Martin wanted a Scotch, Richard a cup of tea, I got myself a beer. We all sat down in my lounge.

'Cheers!' I said. 'Now, you were saying.'

'First a few words about Branch Zero' said Martin. 'You're familiar with the fact that we borrowed the First Speaker concept from Asimov's Foundation series?'

'Of course.'

'Good. Then, along the same sort of lines, you should view us as the Second Foundation of the SPC. Its custodians, if you will, tasked with keeping it on plan by making any adjustments that are deemed necessary.'

'Adjustments? Plan?'

'Quite. There's no Seldon Plan equivalent of course, no overarching final destination. But there is, as you know, a common purpose. And sometimes we find it necessary to, shall we say, influence events in order to maximise the positive impact on our members of that common purpose.'

'I see. I think I see.' I said. 'A bit like MI5 might influence events in the interests of national security.'

'A bit.'

'So why are you visiting me in the middle of the night?'

Richard spoke next.

'We've had our eye on you from the very beginning. Extremely high potential. And you're fulfilling that potential, so far. First Speaker for Paris.

Italy up next. After that, who knows?'

He shifted in his seat and took a sip of tea.

'And it was important that you weren't overly distracted along the way, at key stages in your development.'

'Distracted?'

'Yes. By getting married for example.'

He took another sip of tea and looked at me calmly. He looked like the kind of guy that wasn't easily rattled, that could take care of himself in a knife fight, and like I mentioned he wasn't eligible. Makes a difference, you know.

I looked across at Martin who seemed equally impassive. I let it sink in.

'So, you didn't want me to get married?'

'Correct.'

'And you, er, influenced events to see that I didn't?'

'We did.'

They both remained calm.

My pulse had quickened and I was feeling not calm at all. I thought about the implications of what they'd said. For several minutes. And then I spoke.

'You had Emily killed. You murdered her, and several others besides, for the good of SPC members? You killed my unborn child? What about *me*? What about what was good for *me*? And them, for Christ's sake? What about *them*?'

'Let's not forget Alice.' said Richard.

'Alice? Alice and Sam? You arranged that too? How could you? OK ... *time out* ... I need to compute this somehow.'

Dazed, I stood up and paced around the room shaking my head. The room was spinning around me.

'I can't believe, I just can't fucking *believe* this. I... I don't know what to say.'

I looked at them. They both still sat there, looking at me, calm, impassive.

'You fucking *murdered* people you fuckers. People I love. And ... and ... you somehow engineered my fiancée to shag my best friend! And he's not even SPC! What did you do, slip them aphrodisiacs or something?'

I was on the point of losing it.

'Jesus Christ this is like some kind of fucking *nightmare*!'

Martin put his empty glass of Scotch down.

'Alice never had sex with Sam. She's Branch Zero. The whole story was fake. Sam, as your best friend, agreed to play along.'

He paused.

'And Emily is waiting outside in the car.'

SEGMENT 2584

'I can't think of anything to say.' was all I could think of to say (in so doing immortalising in my own mind the famous line spoken at the end of 'Brain Damage'). I sat down in a sort of swoon, my legs feeling like jelly.

'We'll need to debrief you' Martin said. 'We'll be back at 9 o'clock.' They both moved towards the door. 'In the meantime, we'll send Emily up so that you can get reacquainted.'

Five minutes later she was standing in the doorway. I got up slowly, and walked towards her. We stood about a foot apart looking into one another's eyes, tears streaming down our faces.

She mouthed the words 'I'm sorry'.

'It's ok' I said. My eyes were stinging. We carried on looking at one another.

'We have a son' she said.

I let out a gasp. I felt my throat tightening. I could hardly breathe.

'Is he here?'

'He's with my parents. He'll be here in a few days. I wanted to see you on my own first.'

There are moments in life aren't there? Very few, I think, that are miraculously special, or specially miraculous, or both. Ian Botham's Innings in the Headingley Test in 1981 being one of them, but outside the sporting domain they are few and far between. Some people never have them. Some people get *glimpses*, perhaps, of something out of the ordinary, but they can't explain it and neither can they see at it for as soon as they look at it, it disappears. It can only be seen out of the corner of one's eye. Even with my immense knowledge and foresight and intuition, and understanding of the meaning of life, it's beyond description. It's not simply that language is inadequate - and music too - it's that whatever "it" is, the miraculously special or the specially miraculous, transcends human experience. It's as if we've kissed an angel, or had discourse with a star. I'll tell you what springs to mind, the odd chapter out in 'The Wind in the Willows' called "The Piper at the Gates of Dawn" (which was also the title of Pink Floyd's first album of course). Dwell on that image for a while, the image of the Piper at the Gates of Dawn.

So, it was such a moment when I saw Emily again, and learned that we had a son. I don't have the vocabulary to express my feelings so I'll stick to the facts.

Although it was the middle of the night we were both wide awake, so I ran us a bath and we sat in it face to face with the lights off but with candles lit and we talked and we talked. And we talked.

She didn't go into *how* they'd faked it, she said that Branch Zero would cover all that off. She did go into *why* - because they'd told her the future prosperity of the SPC would depend on it - and what she'd done in the meantime. She'd lived in Australia, which explained the very slight Aussie twang I thought I'd imagined.

'It was terrible knowing how sad you'd be, but they assured me it was for the best, and that in the fullness of time you'd see that it's what you would have wanted.'

'Surely there were easier, better, happier ways of doing it though?'

'Apparently not. You'll have to ask them about that.'

We kept talking. It was getting light. We kept topping the bath up with hot water but we were getting tired.

'If they're coming back at 9am I guess I'd better try and get some sleep.' I said.

'Dare I ask, are we sleeping together?'

'We can sleep together yes. Sleep being the operative word.' I said.

'Is there someone else? Someone, um, *special*?' she hesitated.

'Yes, there is. I, I don't know what the future holds but I'm not ready for you just yet. I may never be. I hope you understand.'

'And all this for the SPC' I said as we climbed into bed. 'The wonderful S ... P ... C'.

Tired as I was I couldn't get to sleep. We hadn't even talked about our son, she'd said that conversation should wait until the morning. I didn't even know his name.

When I finally slept, I had disturbing dreams. Again, I was a fictional character, but this time it was as if I was inside the head of the writer who was creating me, almost as if I *was* him, in the dream. He was lying in bed, alone, sobbing uncontrollably, and shaking, and struggling to breathe, and uncomfortable. He seemed to have a problem with his arm. He kept looking at a little folded up piece of paper on which was written "Don't open until Bday" and inside "Happy B'day" and "To infinity and beyond!" The dream then changed, I can't remember into what.

T minus 4 days

The alarm went off at 8am. I was full of energy, despite only getting a few hours sleep. As usual I was desperate for sex, and thought about waking Emily up by sticking a finger up her bum, but decided against it. She looked so tired, and angelic, in her sleep. Virginal, in fact.

I left her in bed, had a shower, ate my breakfast, and sat reading yesterday's 'Le Monde' while waiting for Branch Zero to arrive. The buzzer sounded at exactly 9 o'clock. That struck me as very Branch Zero: military precision.

They sat at the breakfast table with me, and drank my special coffee and ate my special croissants while debriefing me. Unsurprisingly, and somewhat regrettably, once again I can't reveal too much of what they said. What I can say, though, is that they used technology and methods I couldn't previously even have *imagined* to pull it off. Hallucinogenic drugs, CGI, advanced robotics, memory implants, cloaking devices, enhanced prosthetics, controlled telepathy, time travel, replicants, not to mention an elaborate web of deception that took in numerous people including Emily's parents. They explained that some people knew along that it was all a hoax, and were in on it, and some people needed to believe it, including, of course, me. They also covered off Alice and Sam.

'But why bother going to all that effort?' I asked them. 'Why not just get her to leave me, or something?' To confess to shagging my best friend the night before we were due to get engaged seemed ... overkill!

'Remember the role of the Second Foundation.' they said. 'Very subtle emotional responses predicted by advanced mathematics, pushing you in the required direction.'

'Subtle? Christ! I'd like to see what you do you do when you're *not* being subtle!'

I made some more coffee.

'So, tell me. Was it all worth it, in the end? I mean, am I on track?'

'That depends on what pill you take.'

In timing that the very best writers of farce would have been proud of, Juliette (who had found her key) walked in with Apolline at that very moment, and simultaneously Emily walked in wearing my Spiderman dressing gown while Alice was leaving a message on my answering machine (low tech but I liked it) which everyone could hear.

'So now you know' Alice was saying 'That I never fucked Sam at all.'

'Go and play in the other room, dear' Juliette said to Apolline.

'Good morning!' said Emily to Juliette, kissing her on both cheeks, 'I'm xxxxx's dead fiancée'

'So can we get married now?' said Alice into the answering machine, 'And of course, the baby *is* yours!'

'Another fiancée?' smiled Juliette. 'How many do you have?'

'Well. I thought I had none.' I said.

'To lose one fiancée may be regarded as a misfortune; to lose both looks like carelessness!' she replied. 'I'll go and check on Apolline and start on the ironing.'

'So, who's she?' said Emily.

'My cleaner' I replied. 'With benefits. And a lovely daughter. Not mine, as you probably guessed seeing how old she was.'

'Oh, I don't know, you seem to be having children all over the place. Can I have a coffee?'

I've mentioned my extraordinary predictive abilities: the money markets, the weather, election results, the next Mersenne prime, the timing and intensity of earthquakes and solar flares, football results, pandemics, Tory lies, they were all easy. The dynamic of Emily, Juliette and Alice, however, beat me, without even factoring in Abigail (who was due to arrive tomorrow) and Laetitia (who knowing her could turn up any time). Thank fuck Sophia had gone on holiday.

There was one call I had to make urgently. I left Emily in the kitchen and went into the lounge to get some privacy. I dialled Sam.

'Hello, my good friend' he said cheerfully. 'Long time no hear. How are you?'

'You cunt!' I said.

'Ah. So, you've spoken to Alice then? Sorry about that old chap, but I was under instruction. Apparently, it was all for the best.'

'I really can't believe you went along with it.'

'Neither can I. Damn clever, though, the way they pulled it off. And that Alice, what a babe! I mean, I never fucked her, but I would have, if she hadn't been your girlfriend.'

'Girlfriend? I was going to marry her, for Christ's sake!'

'Well, be my guest. Any reason why you can't marry her now?'

Was there a reason? I wasn't sure. Things were certainly a little bit complicated. We agreed to find time to have a proper catch up on day 3 of the party if not before.

Just as I finished the call Apolline came over and asked me if she could watch TV.

'You don't have to ask.' I said. 'You can do anything you want here, you know.'

'Have you got some paper and a pen I can borrow?' she asked.

I found her some, and she put the TV on and then lay down on the floor doing some drawing.

'You can use the table if you like?' I said.

'I like it on the floor.' she said without looking up.

I went to find Juliette. 'You haven't forgotten you said you'd babysit for me the night before the party, have you?' she said.

'Of course not.'

'It's just that the place will be full of your fiancées and party guests. I know she's self-sufficient but she still needs looking after. You'll need to make sure she cleans her teeth, and read her a story.'

'Full of fiancées, ha ha. Believe me when I tell you that I love Apolline more than anybody in the world.'

I meant it too, I really did. I know I haven't revealed that before, and I know I struggle with love, but I do know how much I love Apolline. Of course, it's a different kind of love to, say, the love I had/have for Emily, or Alice, for example, but actually it's much more intense and completely unconditional. I worried that I wouldn't feel the same about my own children.

Branch Zero completed the debrief and left. Emily said she had to leave but could come to the first day of the party, and that she'd bring our son. She still hadn't told me his name.

'There's something very powerful in a name, you know. Remember the story of R Dragon?'

I did remember.

'But he's my son' I said.

'*Our* son' she corrected me.

'Yes, well, the point is, don't you think I deserve to know his name?'

'It's Harry.' she said. Harry, hmmm. 'That's a good name. I like that.'

'Well I'm glad because if you didn't I wouldn't change it'.

She sounded a bit miffed.

'Listen, Emily is there something wrong? Have I done something wrong? I mean, I deserve a little understanding here, I think, after what you've done, don't you think?'

'But I did it for *you*. For the ... silly SPC that you care so much about.' (It's *massively* ironic, I think, how women belittle the SPC when the whole point is, well, I'd better leave it there before I forget myself.)

We hugged. She started crying.

'What's wrong?' I asked.

'It's these other women. I never released your access codes.'

That reminded me of a conversation we'd had way back when we'd discussed whether we'd ever have sex with anyone else. We'd agreed that we would have to release the other's access codes formally first.

'But I thought you were *dead*!' I said. 'So, you'd *never* be able to release *my* access codes. Anyway, you said ...'

'I lied. There's never been anyone since you. Of course there hasn't. How could there be? *I love you.*'

Oh dear, I thought.

She had to leave, so I got Philippe to take her to the Gare du Nord as she had a Eurostar to catch. Juliette and Apolline left shortly afterwards, and I was on my own again. I threw myself onto a sofa and asked Helene to play something soothing I'd never heard before. She played a song called 'Yes I'm changing' by Tame Impala. I liked it.

My party project manager called. Did I want to listen to the bands rehearsing, which they'd be doing that evening? Evening 1 was going to be Muse. Evening 2 Arcade Fire. Evening 3 Pink Floyd. No I didn't want to listen to the rehearsals, I was sure they'd be fine. Boy, it was going to be one helluva party.

T minus 3 days

I don't want to sound promiscuous or anything, but I didn't think I was attached to any one single person in the fidelity sense - I mean, I wasn't in a stable relationship was I? I hadn't made any promises. (I don't know why I'm asking you!). Emily seemed to think I was, but until recently I thought she was dead, and Alice seemed to think I might be, but until recently I thought she'd betrayed me and was in a relationship with my former best friend (I supposed I'd better drop the "former" now). I mention this because Abigail arrived today.

I met her at the Gare du Nord and naturally gave her a big tight hug.

'Good to see you.' she said.

'Good to see you too.' I said. My hands strayed down her back to her bum, and I gave it a squeeze.

'Ow!' she said. 'That hurt!'

'Oh, sorry. What have you done?'

'Sliced my arse open while lying on a mirror. It's still sore.'

Fair enough, I thought. I made a mental note not to be too rough with her.

Before heading back to mine we popped over the road and got ourselves a couple of beers. Then she said she was hungry, so we both ordered an omelette with chips. I dipped my chips in mustard, I love doing that. We ordered a couple more beers.

'So how are the party arrangements coming on?' she asked.

'Great. It's going to be fab.'

'It starts the day after tomorrow, doesn't it?'

'That's right. It's three days long. Most people can make it for the whole three days, but some for only part of it.'

'And where are they all staying?'

'Most of them out at Versailles. Some didn't want to so they've booked into hotels. My Mum, Dad and sister arrive tomorrow and we'll all stay at mine tomorrow night and then head on out to Versailles the following morning and stay there. I'm also babysitting for a friend, so we'll have a 10-year-old staying with us tomorrow night. She's great, no trouble at all.'

'Sounds full on!'

'It will be. I'm really looking forward to it!'

'And you've found the meaning of life, and you'll be announcing it at the party?'

'Sure have, and sure will!'

'Cool. Can't wait.' She sipped her beer. 'So, we've got the house to ourselves?'

'Until tomorrow lunchtime, yes.'

'So what are we waiting for? I want some more of *that*!' and she squeezed my cock. Quite hard, actually. (For the avoidance of doubt, I mean she *squeezed* it hard, not that it *was* hard, at least, not until after she squeezed it).

We got a cab. She reached into her bag and took out some biscuits. 'Try one of these' she said.

I took a bite. 'Jesus! What sort of biscuit is that?'

'Remember those "special materials" from your island? These biscuits are made from a highly-concentrated blend, plus one or two other exceptional and extraordinary ingredients. Guaranteed to give you a very nice aftertaste!'

I took another bite. 'Hmmm. Yummy. How many have you got?'

'Enough!' she smiled.

One thing about Abigail - she wasn't shy. When I told her about the sensory deprivation tank she actually whooped!

'Now that's something I *haven't* tried!' she said. 'So let's eat loads of biscuits, get naked, and jump in it together. Only be careful of my arse!'

The taxi driver gave me a funny look when he caught my eye in his mirror.

Years ago, I read a book called 'Altered States' by Paddy Chayefsky, and I also watched the movie starring William Hurt. As Abigail and I climbed into the tank - in a super enhanced psychedelic state (she had wings, her body was made of warm liquid silver, and words came out of her mouth in the colours of the rainbow) - I had visions of us emerging later that day as giant lizards or something. As luck would have it, we didn't. Having sex while high on drugs with a sex goddess in a sensory deprivation tank takes some beating though, even if you don't turn into a lizard. My orgasm (I only had the one) lasted for three hours, during which I actually turned into a giant penis and Abigail into a breast. It may have been the drugs, of course.

Afterwards we had a coffee in a little place I know around the corner, and planned what we were going to do until the guests arrived. She wanted to go late night shopping, which was fine as I had lots of party business to attend to, and a conference call with President Enrique Peña Nieto of Mexico. We agreed to meet in a particular bar at 10pm for a late-night drink and to listen to the one and only Agathe Bissap performing *"Chants démoniaques".*

I got all my stuff done early, and went to the bar around 9.

I sat by the window and glanced up at the sky and saw a single star. I wondered how far away it was, and how long the light had taken to reach Earth, and all of a sudden I knew those things. It was 153,011 light years away. I just knew, by looking at it. And it was a brighter star than bright.

By now I had every book and poem I'd ever read in my memory, complete. So, I didn't have to read them anymore, I just experienced or "did" the whole book or poem, in an instant, but lost nothing that way. It's hard to explain, clearly. So, I *did* 'Les Miserables' and 'Don Quixote', and followed them up with 'The Grapes of Wrath' and, for light relief, 'King Lear'.

'Dance like no-one's watching'. That's what people say, and they're so right. The music in this place was brilliant. I didn't know what it was, though, so I vowed to ask at the bar when I got my next drink. I was somewhat disappointed to realise that I hadn't also acquired a genetic Shazam capability. The thought made me smile.

I'm trying to describe the night in that bar, in the hour before Abigail arrived. The bright star. The brilliant music. The dim red lighting. The laughing couples. You know the movie 'Source Code'? If not, you should watch it (Directed by Duncan Jones and starring Jake Gyllenhaal). There's a very moving moment right near the end (this won't spoil it) when time seems to freeze, and everyone's laughing. This bar felt like that. I closed my eyes and saw Apolline holding up a sparkler in the dark and writing her name with it in the air. *Christ!* What a wonderful world! And I knew its meaning. I'm so tempted to reveal it now but I don't want to spoil the party.

The music was getting better and better. I wanted to dance like no-one was watching, and couldn't resist any longer. Two or three other couples had started to dance too. I caught the eye of a woman who I could tell also wanted to dance. We walked towards one another, in time to the brilliant music, and then swayed left and right and backwards and forwards in perfect harmony, sort of like we were mirror images of one another. Whatever I did, she did, instantaneously. But how did she know what I was going to do? And then whatever she did I did, instantaneously. We were enveloped in the music, never taking our eyes off one another. We were bright stars. And suddenly it ended, and we were back in the bar, with all the chatter and the laughter. I asked her if she wanted a drink, but she said no. Somehow that was fitting. I said it was nice to have danced with her, and she said it was nice to have danced with me too.

'Would you like to know what that music was?' I asked. 'I know I do.'

'I already know.' she smiled. 'Amaya Laucirica. The one you liked best was called 'Let It Happen'. Goodbye.'

She gave me a little wave and turned to leave.

'I don't even know your name.' I said. 'And that was the best dance I ever had.'

'Sian.' she said, with a perfect frown. She pressed a piece of paper into my hand, and left without looking back.

Forlorn! the very word is like a bell
To toll me back from thee to my sole self!
Adieu! the fancy cannot cheat so well
As she is fam'd to do, deceiving elf.
Adieu! adieu! thy plaintive anthem fades
Past the near meadows, over the still stream,
Up the hill-side; and now 'tis buried deep
In the next valley-glades:
Was it a vision, or a waking dream?
Fled is that music: Do I wake or sleep?

Just after I *did* 'The Water Babies' and just before I was going to *do* 'The Waste Land', and while ignoring a call from the United Nations Secretary General, Abigail walked in laden with shopping bags. She'd also virtually shaved her head.

'You look great.' I said.

'Really? I wasn't sure you'd like it.'

'You know I like short hair. Although this is, um, very short.' I ran my fingers over it. 'Nice.' I said.

She smiled. 'I'm glad. So, you still want to fuck me?'

'Like nothing on earth.' I said.

'I've bought some sex toys too.'

'Really? What?'

'I'll show you later. Want another drink?'

She went to the bar, and I looked outside and up at the star again. I could no longer see it. Must have been cloudy. She came back with a bottle of wine and four large beers. 'Saves us going to the bar again for half an hour.' she smiled.

The brilliant music was still playing. She showed me what she'd bought, but not the sex toys. Then the brilliant music stopped and after a brief pause Agathe started her set (for want of a better word). Weird in the extreme, but somehow just what the occasion demanded. She was only on for about forty minutes, by which time I'd persuaded Abigail to show me one of the toys, and explain what you did with it.

'Really?' I said. 'People do that sort of thing?'

'You just wait!' she said. It turns out we couldn't wait long, though, so as soon as we'd finished the wine we literally ran up the hill to my place, and I can now confirm that people do really do that sort of thing.

T minus 2 days

What a day? I had a very nice lie in, don't remember my dreams any more. It always surprises me how quickly they fade, not to mention how weird they can be.

Abigail had got up, and I could hear her singing downstairs in the kitchen. Thin strips of bright sunlight shone through gaps in the shutters, and I could see the dust floating around the room. I loved that. I could tell it was very warm too.

I stretched out. If I could have designed the perfect day this would be close. Waking up after a night of wild sex. Knowing I was going to have more wild sex very soon. Hot sunny day. Didn't have to get up in a hurry. My family and all my best friends arriving over the course of the day and tomorrow, in preparation for a three day party at Versailles at which I would reveal the meaning of life. The fact that I'd learned the meaning of life. Hundreds of millions of Euros in the bank and growing daily. Soon starting a fabulous new job in Rome.

I asked Helene to play some of that fantastic music from the bar last night - Amaya Laucirica - and I closed my eyes and just lay there feeling wonderful. Emotionally, physically, spiritually, intellectually, philosophically, all the "-allys" in fact. *Perfect*. Had I reached the pinnacle? Was this what they called "self actualization"? And the thing was, it was going to get even better. I was going to meet my son for the first time. And Apolline was staying over too.

The future cannot fail me.

That reminded me, not that I really needed reminding but there you go, that it was time to decide which pill to take and which to give to her (Apolline) - and then for each of us to take them. I'd dig them out tomorrow morning and we could have them over breakfast.

Abigail walked in with a coffee and a delicious looking pastry.

'I went out and bought it.' she said.

'Looks yummy. And so do you. I think you should come back to bed!'

She pulled the duvet down and looked at me. 'Hmmm. Someone's ready!' and with a huge smile she slipped out of her dress and climbed on top of me.

We finished three hours and twenty five orgasms later when my phone rang. 'Shit! People are going to start arriving, and calling, and stuff. We'd better get up.'

'But I haven't finished with you yet!' she said. We stayed in bed for another hour, then it really was time to get up. I checked who the missed call was from: President Assad of Syria. A fuck-face; I didn't call him back.

In the shower, I *did* 'A Midsummer Night's Dream' and 'Great Expectations'. I was really starting to enjoy being able to do that: *experiencing* an entire book in a few seconds.

Although only Abigail, Sally, my Mum and Dad, and Apolline were staying in the house tonight, several party guests were coming round later for drinks before heading off to wherever they were staying, so I wanted to get ready for them. A truly *vast* amount of drink had arrived - fine wines, champagne, gin, rum, brandy, you name it - and a chef was due in at 5pm to prepare some tapas and various yummy dishes.

I was so excited I actually giggled. It was such a nice day, and everything was so well organised, that Abigail and I had time for a nice walk up to the Sacré-Cœur. We spent some time admiring the view over Paris, and then headed back via a few shops. I'd had a sudden urge to buy a plain white cotton shirt at least one size too big for me, which I was able to fulfill although the buttons were a sort of lemony yellow colour. Abigail said she liked the buttons.

When we were about five minutes from home my sister called - they were queuing for a cab at the Gare du Nord so should be with me in half an hour or so. I giggled again.

'Time for a quickie?' asked Abigail.

'You bet!' I said.

I've talked about love as if I don't really know what it is, and to a degree, that's true, but I know what I feel. The thing is, there are many different kinds of love, as there are Inuit words for snow (at least 53) or Sami words for reindeer (around 1,000, incredibly). The term used by linguists is "polysynthesis" - which allows speakers to encode a huge amount of information in one word by plugging various suffixes onto a base word.

This kind of linguistic exuberance should come as no surprise, experts say, since languages evolve to suit the ideas and needs that are most crucial to the lives of their speakers. 'These people need to know whether ice is fit to walk on or whether you will sink through it,' said linguist Willem de Reuse at the University of North Texas. 'It's a matter of life or death.'

'All languages find a way to say what they need to say,' said Matthew Sturm, a geophysicist with the Army Corps of Engineers in Alaska.

Hmmm. So why do we have only one word for love? Surely all these different loves of mine (not in any particular order just as I think of them, with the exception of the last two which I think about constantly) merit a different word?

For my sister
For my parents
For my unseen son
For Sam
For Tom
For Abigail
For Alice

For Emily
For beer (pilsner)
For wine (red)
For wine (white)
For gin
For opera
For El Dorado
For the Beatles
For Charles Dickens
For John Keats
For 'The Catcher in the Rye'
For prime numbers
For Paris
For sunny days
For kissing
For breasts
For nipples
For orgasms
For Rude Health Almond Milk
For Greek Salad
For Leicester Tigers winning
For Northampton Saints losing
For short hair
For long hair
For curly hair
For straight hair
For long eyelashes
For hot buttered toast with Marmite
For log fires
For women dancing
For Vincent van Gogh's paintings
For Picasso's paintings
For 'Blade Runner'
For '2001: A Space Odyssey'
For Bill Hicks
For Jonathan Pie
For Socialism
For the Search for Extra Terrestrial Intelligence
For the Tour de France
For cheese
For that brilliant music in the bar last night
For the Overture to Rossini's 'Semiramide'
For the opening line of 'The Go Between'

For the 'To be or not to be' soliloquy in 'Hamlet'
For the SPC
For Apolline

There are 53 loves right there. (I've missed loads out, I'm just trying to make an important point). The same word describes my love for each of them in English, but you get my point that they're all different, I'm sure?

I was due a *surfeit* of these particular loves over the coming days. From the list of 53 above I was *guaranteed* at least 33 of them imminently. (Note to self: star them later for posterity *). How wonderful is that? I was about to be absolutely *gorged* on happiness. What a great term!

That afternoon was so busy and so brilliant that I didn't capture everything straight away, so I'm writing this at my desk around 4am the following morning. Everyone's asleep now. I hope I don't forget anything, not that you'd know of course.

My favourite people in the world just kept arriving all afternoon and into the evening. Hugs, laughter, music, drinks, great conversations. Life at its very best. I floated around between everyone blissfully.

It was a gloriously hot day too. Several people quaffed champagne in the rooftop garden while others just lounged around on sofas and bean bags and even on the floor.

I felt very emotional indeed, and kept welling up with joy.

I had a very long and intense chat with Sam, interrupted only when Juliette arrived with Apolline. She - Juliette that is - could only stay for a few hours and then had to leave. She said she'd put Apolline to bed before she went.

'Where are you going, by the way?' I asked. 'You never told me.'

'I have to keep that a secret.' she said, with an enigmatic Mona Lisa-esque smile. 'You'll like it though, when you find out.'

'And when will that be?'

'When it's no longer a secret!'

She could be so exasperating, but this wasn't the day to get impatient, as the future could not fail me.

'Come and meet everyone.' I said.

There weren't many children there - certainly no young ones - but there were a few other 10-12 year olds. I set them all up with Apolline in what I called the cinema room, with popcorn and ice cream and various goodies, and they all started to watch 'Descendants'. I popped back in a bit later to check they were all ok. Apolline was leading a chorus of

Don't you wanna be evil like me?
Don't you wanna be mean?
Don't you wanna make mischief your daily routine?

People started leaving around 10. I said there was no rush, but they all said they wanted to get to their beds and have a relatively early night to prepare for the three-day party. A few got pissed and just crashed where they were lying, which was fine. I rather liked it.

Juliette left without fuss and made me promise to look in on Apolline before I went to bed, and to make her breakfast.

'I'll be back to collect her by 10 in the morning.' she said.

I checked my phone which had been on charge. Emily and Harry would arrive tomorrow lunchtime, Alice would go straight to the party, and the big announcement about the end of the Tory party was confirmed for the following afternoon. Happy days.

My Mum and Dad went off to their room around midnight, leaving a hard core of those who were still awake. Me, Sally, Abigail, Laetitia, Camille, Sam, Tom and a mysterious Belgian woman who no-one knew. We started on the drinking games. Sam was the first to fall asleep, then Sally went to bed, then Tom crashed, leaving Abigail, Laetitia, Camille and the mysterious Belgian woman who no-one knew. And me. If I could have specced it out, that would have been my ideal configuration at this stage of proceedings. It was Laetitia who then suggested we each remove an item of clothing every five minutes. No-one demurred, and within half an hour all five of us were naked on the floor. I'm not sure that we (or anybody else) could ever recreate the position all five of us then managed to get straight into with a lot of giggling - it was a topological *tour de force*, a veritable *pièce de résistance* - but we made it somehow, and then embarked on an "orgasmanova". That's my new word for it, anyway. At various times over the next two hours I had sex with all of them, which obviously includes the mysterious Belgian woman who no-one knew.

After we finished Laetitia and Camille called a cab, and the mysterious Belgian woman who no-one knew crawled off to sleep in the bath. There's a Beatles lyric there! Abigail went off to my bed, and insisted that I wake her up when I joined her.

As promised I did peek in on Apolline. She looked very sweet. Her duvet had fallen off her a bit, and her teddy bear (which was actually an elephant, but I don't think it'd be called a teddy elephant) was on the floor, so I picked it up, tucked it in her arms, tucked her under the duvet, kissed her on the cheek, and went to sit at my desk.

And here I am. The narrative has caught up with me. I'm live, so to speak. It's getting on for half four now and I'm completely *wired*. Not sleepy at all. I think I might check in on the Belgian woman in the bath before getting into bed with Abigail, as I'm feeling pretty desperate. It's been ages.

So, tomorrow, the party begins. The meaning of life. I meet my son. I'd sort the tablets for me and Apolline out first thing, over breakfast, as it'll be T minus 1 day and clearly I can't wait any longer. Also, thinking about it, I wasn't sure of the exact *time* of death after 151 days, if indeed there *was* an exact time. Better to be safe than sorry.

I'm looking out of the window. It's starting to get light. I'm still very emotional. It's been a fantastic day, and it'll be even more fantastic tomorrow. In fact, *every* day is going to be fantastic. The future cannot fail me.

I'm writing this an hour later. I did check in on the Belgian woman. She was very pleased to see me. Now I'm just about to climb into bed and wake up Abigail. Christ I'm absolutely desperate.

T minus 1 day

'Are you ok?' It was Abigail's voice. I woke up with a start. 'You looked like you were having a nightmare!'

I was momentarily disoriented, but quickly realised I was awake and the sunlight was streaming through the slits in the shutters and Abigail's nipples were tantalisingly close to my mouth.

'It was horrible. It was so *real*! You know these dreams I've been having, where I'm a fictional character and I sort of see the person who created me? It was one of those, but different. I was him, and me, at the same time. I was standing at a bar waiting to get served. Next to me was a policeman. Taller than me. More muscular. Ineligible ...'

'Ineligible for what?'

'For the SPC.'

'Oh, you even *dream* about that? You shouldn't you know, it's not real.'

'What do you mean it's not real? It's what this is all about. It's what *everything's* about. It's like the Glass Bead Game in the Hermann Hesse book. *Everything* is about the SPC. Everything about me, anyway. It completely defines me.'

'So, what happened in the dream?'

'Nothing. That was what was so disturbing. I just stood there, next to this policeman, not getting served. In the dream, I was never going to get served as long as I was standing next to him.'

'So, why didn't you move?'

I sat up. 'Because it was a dream. You can't control your actions in a dream, can you? I felt I was suffocating.'

She pushed my head back onto the pillow. 'Talking about suffocating.' she said with a smile as she lowered herself onto my face.

I went down to make breakfast. No-one was around apart from Apolline, who was sitting at the kitchen table colouring in.

'Did you sleep well?' I asked her.

'Yes, thank you' she said, without looking up.

'Want some breakfast?' I asked her.

'Not yet thank you.'

'A drink?'

'Yes please.'

I poured her a juice and opened the fridge to see what I fancied for breakfast. I asked Helene to play the 'Can Can' as Apolline always danced to it, kicking her little legs up in the air. This time I captured her on video on my phone.

'I need you to take a tablet in a minute.' I said when she'd finished dancing.

'Ok' she said, decidedly uninquisitively. How very like her.

I sat down opposite her drinking some Almond Milk and watching her colouring in. Two eggs were on the boil, and I was going to make some mouillettes. I felt so happy and optimistic that I welled up again, and then sneezed.

'Bless you.' she said, still without looking up.

I went upstairs to get the pills out of Madame Gironde's box. I could hear Abigail singing in the shower. No-one else seemed to be stirring at all. I went into the room where I had hidden Madame Gironde's box. It was undisturbed, exactly where I had hidden it. I'd made my decision. It was a really tough one though as there were pros and cons both ways. It came down not to me but to Apolline. I didn't want her to be any more special than she already was. That sounds odd, it's hard to explain. The Agent makes you - had made me - *artificially* better. Faster, stronger, cleverer, all those things, but I sometimes felt I'd lost something along the way, for all I'd gained. I felt that Apolline was perfect as she was, as she had been.

So, I decided to take the green pill - the antidote - myself, and give her the red pill - the anti-Agent. I would carry on as I was - who knows where it would take me - and she would be the special little girl she always had been, only healthy and cured of her illness. I opened the box.

Time seemed to slow down. And there was the green pill. And there was no red pill. Knowing it was in there somewhere, probably nestling in the corner, I tilted the box, but nothing happened. I turned it upside down - no red pill. I closed the lid, counted to ten, and opened it again. No red pill.

I sat down against the wall and sighed. This couldn't be happening again, surely? I shook the box violently. Still no red pill. I threw the box against the wall and it smashed to pieces. I sat there for a while, thinking that the future had failed me after all.

I heard Apolline shout up the stairs that the eggs had boiled dry. It was time. I went down into the kitchen and asked Helene to play the Barcarolle from 'The Tales of Hoffman', my all-time favourite piece of music.

'Have you got any juice left? I've got this tablet for you.' I said.

She indicated that she had.

I *did* the end of 'A Tale of Two Cities':

It is a far, far better thing that I do, than I have ever done;
it is a far, far better rest that I go to than I have ever known.

She took the tablet from me, *still* without looking up. Bless her.

'What's in it?' she asked.

'Something to make you better.' I said.

'OK.' she said, and swallowed it with her juice, and carried on colouring.

I looked at her one last time, and smiled at the memory of her doing the 'Can Can'. I asked Helene to play Edith Piaf's 'Non, Je Ne Regrette Rien', and then to let Apolline choose what music to listen to next. She chose, without looking at me.

'Your mother will be here soon' I said. 'I am just going outside and may be some time.'